Human Intelligence

Wednesday, 10:13 am ET

ARLINGTON, Va. — The young man waited for the Metrobus to turn onto Crystal Drive and begin to build up speed. Then he removed his earphones.

He did this in a practiced, casually irritated way. It was the way all American kids his age did it: wrapping the cord around his iPod hurriedly, quick elegant flicks of the wrist, as if the whole process was an annoyance he wanted over with as quickly as possible. The earphones were top of the line, a sharp contrast to his old iPod, which the young man had no use for anymore after storing all his music on his phone a couple years ago. But phones can be tracked. So he destroyed his before he left his parents' home in the morning.

The young man shoved the iPod into the breast pocket of his dress-shirt.

Hassan al-Zaid looked at his reflection in the window to his left; this struck him as a distinctly American custom: only pretending to look out the window, *through* it, but really considering one's own reflection. What he saw was a young, slender man whose dark features betrayed his Middle Eastern ancestry. Otherwise, he looked appropriately incognito. A recent UCLA grad, he could have passed as a high school senior. He didn't visit bars, but had he done so, any bouncer worth his salt would have carefully scrutinized Hassan's license.

Outside the bus's windows Crystal Drive zipped by in a blur, all manicured lawns and office buildings.

It was time.

Hassan closed his eyes and offered a quick, silent prayer to Allah, trusting that his God would understand. He let out a deep breath — only then did he realize he'd been holding it this whole time — and pressed the red STOP button on the pole next to his seat, triggering a buzzing sound.

"Sorry, I think I'm on the wrong bus," he said, to no one in particular, and a little too loudly. He stood up. His eyes darted to the surveillance camera above the front door. The driver reacted in kind, slowing the bus and coming to a stop near the curb. Hassan al-Zaid was heading for the rear door.

Patrons of the Washington Metropolitan Area Transit Authority are bombarded daily with reminders to look out for any unattended bags or packages — but none of the passengers seemed to have noticed that the young man had entered with a large black backpack and was leaving without one. The pack remained wedged below a row of seats.

The door opened with a hiss. Before stepping into the morning sun, Hassan al-Zaid's eyes swept across his fellow passengers. He knew that if everything went according to plan, they would all be dead in a few minutes.

He felt no remorse.

Hassan stepped onto the sidewalk and hurried in the direction from which the bus had come.

There was no turning back now.

**

The train had been holding for over a minute now just outside the Crystal City Metro station.

Stacey Harper rolled her eyes and exhaled, blowing some stray hairs from her face. She closed the textbook sitting in her lap, shutting it with a loud dull thud that echoed throughout the Metrorail train. Stacey sighed. It looked like she would be late again, this time because of a stupid hairdryer that wouldn't work and, of course, the goddamned Washington Metropolitan Area Transit Authority, known and cursed by those living in the nation's capital as "the Metro."

The loudspeaker crackled. Stacey leaned forward but couldn't make out any of the words. Not that any of it mattered. The train lurched forward a few feet and stopped again.

She bit her lip and leaned back in the seat. Stacey never planned to be late, but it seemed she always was. Being more than a little scatterbrained, Stacey suffered from a short attention span and an apparent inability to remember when and where to be at any given moment. All of it had caused Amy, her best friend back in high school, to come up with the term Stacey Time. It translated, loosely, to "Eastern Time plus however long it takes to be late."

Still, the force of Stacey's personality had gotten her off the hook many times with family, friends and high school teachers. The only thing was — as she'd come to find out, painfully — college professors were less forgiving.

It was one of the reasons she was now headed for an economics class at Georgetown instead of starting a career, like most of her friends. A few missed deadlines and a semester abroad in Barcelona, during which Stacey had focused more on partying than studying, kept her from graduating. She had promised her parents, who were none too thrilled about an extra semester of Georgetown tuition, that she would try harder to be organized.

This morning she was failing.

Stacey had taken a later Blue Line train from Virginia into the District after a morning workout, thinking she'd still make it to class on time. No such luck. Not with this decrepit old thing stuck in the black underground between stops.

The loudspeaker crackled again. This time she heard a voice, tinny though it was. The train operator informed the passengers there was some sort of malfunction at the Pentagon station and that they would have to get off the train in Crystal City. There would be shuttle buses to take them across the Potomac into D.C. or to Rosslyn, the Northern Virginia suburb on the other side of Arlington Cemetery that connected the Commonwealth to Georgetown.

The mid-morning crowd grumbled at the news. The train was not overly crowded and the passengers, apart from those going to work, consisted largely of students heading from Virginia to Georgetown and George Washington, along with the usual smattering of tourists. Stacey could always spot a tourist: the fanny-packs, the poorly folded maps of the District with the sightseeing spots circled in red. She smiled in spite of herself at her own abilities at detection.

Stacey hoped she would get a spot on a shuttle quickly and make it to school on time, or at least not miss too much of the dreaded economics class. She didn't want to make a bad impression this early in the semester, even though it was shaping up to be a gorgeous day and she'd rather be anywhere, anywhere in the world that wasn't a poorly air-conditioned classroom where she'd be forced to sit and listen to a lecture on John

Maynard Keynes.

***

Marine One landed gracefully on the White House lawn, returning President Jack Sweeney to his home after a ten-day trip to the Middle East. The tall commander-in-chief ducked through the helicopter door, which he'd learned to do as a result of rather embarrassingly banging his head during his first trip after being elected. The president saluted the Marines welcoming him home and stopped briefly to smile for the photographers awaiting his return. Sweeney's expression did not betray his grim mood or his frustration with how poorly the trip had gone. Right after bumping his head on the Marine One door, which had been a few years back now, he had also learned that photographers would be waiting for him wherever he went. Regardless of what was going on, Sweeney just smiled for the cameras and kept his thoughts and feelings hidden from view. He clenched his teeth as he walked toward the White House.

At least the visit to Baghdad, the last stop on his itinerary, had been encouraging. The economy was picking up there and, as jobs and money became available, fewer Iraqis were susceptible to efforts to get them to fight each other and the allied forces that remained in the country.

The rest of the trip had been less successful, much to Sweeney's dismay. There was no resolution in sight to the crisis between Israel and the Palestinians. The endless conflict fueled the problems of the entire Middle East like warm water powered a hurricane.

Sweeney had appealed again to all sides to at least resume negotiations, offering Washington as a broker for such talks. As expected, he was rebuffed. Neither the Israelis nor Palestinians seemed eager to sit down and try to solve the problems that had plagued them for so long and had cost so many lives on both sides. Sweeney's formal smile brightened when he saw the first lady, in a new white summer dress, coming toward him with the presidential Labradors. She greeted him with a chaste kiss on the cheek while the dogs wagged their tails and waited to be doted on. Normally, that would distract the president for a couple minutes; today, there was too much on his mind.

While the visit to Israel had been frustrating, it paled in comparison to the problems developing for the United States in Afghanistan and Pakistan. Order in Afghanistan was quickly deteriorating as warlords and poppy-growers took over the country. The Taliban had reemerged and, according to an internal National Intelligence Estimate, the movement was stronger now than at any point since the invasion of 2001.

There were simply not enough troops to restore order in all parts of the country. The border region between Afghanistan and Pakistan had always been particularly difficult to control. That problem was now compounded by the recent change in leadership in Islamabad. Salman Khan, the new Pakistani president, was unwilling to allow American troops to conduct operations in his country.

Pakistan had been the first stop of the trip — the thinking being that this would highlight the country's importance to the U.S. — but to no avail. Khan recently won a close election with the promise of not catering to the United States anymore, and he'd followed through with a hard line. Notwithstanding the billions of dollars in military assistance Pakistan gladly continued to pocket, the Khan regime only allowed American soldiers to serve as advisers and in a logistical capacity. The new Pakistani president had vowed on the campaign trail that only his government would decide when and how U.S. combat troops were allowed inside the country's borders. Khan was true to his word and reiterated the policy forcefully in direct talks with Sweeney during the trip.

Mussing one happy Labrador behind the ear and intoning, "Good boy, good boy" softly as the mutt puffed and panted and kicked up a hind leg, Sweeney couldn't help his thoughts turning to all those daily intelligence briefings, all those uniformed officers looking ill-at-ease on the comfy White House couches as they informed their commander-in-chief, in clear but respectful language, of the Big Problem, as they saw it. They largely agreed on this point: that the Taliban and the fighters of as-Sirat, the preeminent terrorist group in the world, had used the developments in Pakistan to expand their bases there. As-Sirat leader Omar Bashir had long been suspected to be hiding somewhere in the mountainous border region on Pakistan's northwest flank, and many of his followers now set up their camps in that area as well. They knew that American troops were not allowed to follow them there and that the new government had no intention of hassling them. If not exactly friendly toward them, this Salman Khan was at least condoning their being in, and operating from, his country. Effectively, he was providing them quarter.

Sweeney found himself briefly considering that term — *quarter* — and its history with respect to his own country. His mind wandered to Redcoats and bayonets and drums of tea. Then his eyes alit on the military aide schlepping the bulky suitcase known as The Football. The nation's nuclear launch codes were never more than a few feet away from him. This, like Marine One's overhead clearance and the ubiquitous clicking and whirring and flashing of photographers' cameras, had taken some getting used to. The power to decimate, disfigure, destroy utterly; indeed, to alter forever the course of human history — all of it contained in that briefcase named after a pigskin. Still, all of America's military might had done little to stem the growing threat of terrorism. The changed political situation in Islamabad and the United States' inability to bring as-Sirat leaders to justice had led to a surge of the terrorist group's influence in Afghanistan and Pakistan in recent months. If they'd even heard of The Football, it seemed to be doing little to dissuade new recruits from signing up.

"You have all of these America-hating young men in my country and in Pakistan," the pro-Western Afghan president had said in a frank conversation with Sweeney. "They see that we've been unable to get to as-Sirat's leaders, and they know Pakistan is a safe haven now. So they think they can join the Taliban or as-Sirat and act on their hatred toward America with impunity."

The Afghan president also warned that, unless something drastic happened, he would likely not win reelection and would be succeeded by someone who didn't view America as benevolently. The ambivalence in Islamabad was bad enough; losing an ally in Kabul would create new headaches for the West.

Standing up out of his crouch, still muttering, "That's a good boy" at the happier of the Labradors, Sweeney remembered how, on his way back to Washington, the national security adviser had vocalized what many members of the administration were feeling but didn't want to say aloud.

"We're losing the fight against terrorism. Badly. And it's getting worse."

Nobody on Air Force One had disagreed.

***

Stacey grabbed her stuff and, along with everybody else, got off the train at Crystal City, an area of Arlington undeserving of its name. There was nothing pretty about the bland office buildings overlooking the Pentagon and Ronald Reagan National Airport. Crystal City was built on a network of tunnels leading to food courts, stores and the Metro station. The tunnels also made it unnecessary for office workers to see the sun or breathe fresh air during the day. This was certainly not much of a loss for anybody other than connoisseurs of drab, 1970s-style concrete office buildings.

Stacey was lucky that the door of her car lined up with the escalator going up. She was one of the first to exit the station. She knew the area a little from an internship a couple years ago, and turned toward a back entrance leading to the bus station. Stacey dashed up the stairs, hoping this shortcut would give her the best shot at quickly securing a spot on a shuttle.

When she stepped out into the morning sun, she saw a bus designated ROSSLYN pull out of a side street near the station.

"Stop!" she shouted, chasing after the bus. After a short sprint, Stacey managed to catch up with it. She banged on one of its rear windows just as it was picking up speed. To her frustration, the bus did not stop.

Stacey gave up, put her hands on her sides and sucked in air. She was incredulous that the driver had not seen or heard her; at the very least, some of the passengers must have been aware of her attempt to board. But instead of telling the driver to stop, as Stacey thought would be common courtesy, they didn't move to help her get on. One passenger, an older man, just stared at her with an odd look: not unkind, but far away.

Stacey cursed tourists unfamiliar with Metrobus etiquette and was aggrieved to see her last chance to get to class on time drive off. She made a mental note of the four-digit number displayed on the back of the bus, vowing to call Metro to complain about the driver. As she pondered what else could go wrong this morning, a military vehicle raced past her. This made Stacey jump. Ever since the Pentagon had been attacked on 9/11, armored vehicles around the Defense Department headquarters, located right across I-395 from Crystal City, had become a common occurrence for those in the area every day. For infrequent visitors, however, they provided an unusual sight.

As if to taunt Stacey, the bus came to a stop ahead, though too far for her to try to catch up again. A young man got off and began walking quickly toward her, in the direction of the Metro station. Stacey, still a little out of breath, turned and slowly made her way back to the Metro stop. Just before she got back to the station, the young man from the bus caught up with her. She glanced over. Then she did a double-take, the recognition of a familiar face slowly dawning on her. "Hassan?" Stacey said in a tone that was half-statement, half-question, not entirely certain the young man was indeed a former high school classmate.

His head jerked in response to hearing his name, but he looked as though he regretted the reaction immediately.

"Oh, hi," he replied, making eye contact for a split second before looking down at the pavement. He paused before stammering: "I got on the wrong bus."

"I would've traded places with you," Stacey frowned. She overlooked the fact that her old classmate appeared flustered, assuming that he had simply forgotten who she was. "I'm gonna be so late for class."

The young man paused again, his eyes still not meeting hers. After a long beat, his body language changed. He straightened up, looked Stacey in the eyes and flashed her a smile, his white teeth contrasting with his dark, deep-olive skin.

Ah, Stacey thought to herself, he finally recognizes me. She'd been a little taken aback that he hadn't remembered her. After all, they'd once made out at a party junior year.

"Trust me, it could be worse," he said. He looked at the pavement again, then back at her. "Listen, Stacey, I wish we could catch up, but I really gotta run. Maybe I'll bump into you again sometime."

He waved her a quick goodbye, forced another smile and headed for the escalators back into the Crystal City underground. Stacey's eyes followed him for a second. Checking the time on her cellphone, she reminded herself that she really shouldn't be too late for class. She scrapped the plan of catching a shuttle and turned toward the taxi stand instead.

***

Alan Hausman banged his palms on the steering wheel. He did this to the rhythm, or at least the rhythm as he heard it, of the Grateful Dead's "Ripple," which blared in- and outside his car. The windows were open, but he had the stereo up so loud he still couldn't make out the sounds of the traffic surrounding him. He didn't care. Alan believed there were only a handful of perfect days in Washington each year. Beautifully warm with a light breeze — the kind of weather that lets ordinary people dream of extraordinary things. This day was shaping up to be one of them.

Alan certainly was an ordinary guy and, right now, as he was making his way up 395 in a somewhat beat-up Jetta, he was daydreaming. It was indeed one of those perfect days, and he enjoyed the sunshine and wind on his face. Life was just too good.

Most of the nation's capital was busy at work again. Congress had just returned from its annual monthlong August recess, and the summer lull that hung over the city had dissipated. Alan was among the fortunate few employed citizens who were not yet locked away in an office. His schedule had allowed him to sleep in a little. On this morning, that was a very good thing; he had come home late the previous evening after going out for drinks with his Ultimate Frisbee team. He had treated himself to a breakfast outdoors on the front lawn of the house he rented with a couple of friends. To him, there was nothing better to cure a hangover than banana pancakes with chocolate sprinkles, fresh coffee and lots and lots of fresh air.

Alan worked as a copy editor for *The Washington Post* but viewed his employment there as temporary. He felt that his true calling was to become a published author of fiction. In fact, over the weekend Alan had finished his latest manuscript — a 300-page thriller involving a government conspiracy to conceal an alien landing in Alaska. He thought about pitching it to publishers as a Grisham-meets-*Star Wars* page-turner. Even Alan himself wasn't quite sure what that meant, exactly, but he thought it sounded good.

As a conspiracy-theory hobbyist, which there seemed to be more of per capita in Washington than anywhere else in the world (with the possible exception of Roswell and maybe some hippie communities on the West Coast), most of Alan's ideas revolved around government cover-ups. His previous attempts to transfer ideas from his head to paper had not been met with enthusiasm from publishing houses. That had not deterred Alan, and he was confident his latest manuscript would make him rich and famous.

Deep in thought and caught up in his own dreams, he exited onto Washington Boulevard, which would take him by the Pentagon and Arlington Cemetery toward the Memorial Bridge. From there, he would cross from Virginia into the District of Columbia. It was his favorite part of the drive, heading across the bridge right for the Lincoln Memorial. Or, more properly put, it was his favorite part of the drive when there was no traffic. With the nine-to-five crowd already in their offices, this would likely be the case today. There were only a few cars on Washington Boulevard.

Alan, who had been speeding a little, was forced to ease off the gas when he caught up to a pair of Humvees. They were driving slowly alongside each other on the two-lane road. Though he was not in any particular hurry, Alan still honked at the military vehicles. It was not so much that he wanted to speed past them — more a sign of disdain for what the Humvees symbolized.

An avowed, avid pacifist, Alan carried his views not only on his sleeve but also on his bumper, where a sticker loudly proclaimed that he objected to using American lives, or any lives, for that matter, to procure the oil that these two behemoths, and to a lesser extent his Jetta, were using right now. "No Blood for Oil" wasn't just a slogan for Alan, but a way of life. He was a frequent participant in rallies protesting wars, many of his government's decisions, the World Bank, the International Monetary Fund and various corporations. Though he worked in an industry known for its liberal bent, Alan was way left of center even among the *Post*'s staff. His distrust of the Washington power elites was matched only by his disdain for big business.

In this case, honking was his way of saying, "*Get the fuck out of Afghanistan.*"

He was just about to lay on his horn again, as neither of the Humvees showed any inclination to switch lanes or speed up, when the Metrobus about 250 feet ahead of him erupted in a massive fireball.

Alan felt for a brief moment as though what he was watching was fundamentally unreal; it was like a dream; or no, it was like he was watching the latest John Woo movie. But the shock wave that shook his Jetta and the booming noise of the detonation were very real. The tremendous explosive concussion pierced his eardrums, the brightness of the inferno left Alan dizzy. He managed to slam on his brakes and just avoided sliding into the Humvees, which had stopped ahead of him with their occupants already jumping out. Alan felt the heat emanating from the blast site. An invisible force was pushing him back. There was nothing but a deep crater and a ball of fire where there had been a Metrobus just moments ago.

Pieces of debris began raining down from the sky, from a sky that had been so clear just moments before. "Holy shit," Alan thought. Or screamed — it was hard to tell. "Holy fucking shit."

His hands were shaking even though they were clamped to the steering wheel. His knuckles weren't the only thing turning white as the initial shock set in.

"Sir, are you okay?" The voice ripped him from his daze. A man in fatigues stood next to his car, a look of concern plastered across his face. As a pacifist, Alan had no idea that he was being addressed by a man whose uniform identified him as a captain of the U.S. Army. The insignia displaying the man's rank was as foreign to him as Cantonese.

"Sir, are you injured?" the soldier asked with greater urgency, now almost leaning into the car and speaking more loudly.

"I'm okay," Alan mumbled, thankful for the attention and suddenly more appreciative of the military. He stumbled out of his car, his vision still blurred, his ears still ringing, barely able to stand the heat blaring from where the bus had been.

Another soldier approached the Jetta and handed him some water. He pulled a candy bar from his pocket and gave it to Alan.

"The sugar will help with the shock, sir," he said. "And you should probably move back a bit. I'll be happy to assist you if you need help."

The other occupants of the Humvees had moved as close to the scene of the explosion as the heat allowed, likely to see if they could assist any survivors. To Alan, this seemed like a pointless endeavor. It was apparent that nobody could have survived the blast.

Even after moving farther away from the site of the explosion, the heat was unbearable. Despite the fiery inferno unfolding not far from him, Alan began to feel a chill.

"Oh my God," he muttered, when it sank in how close he had been to death. Alan turned pale and a feeling of nausea began to creep up from his stomach. His senses rapidly became overwhelmed with what had happened as his mind began computing the events of the past few seconds. He swallowed, tasting vomit.

Then Alan's gaze fell upon the remains of a human arm that had fallen to the roadway not far from his car. He fainted.

Wednesday, 10:42 a.m. ET

It took less than eight minutes from the first "breaking news" report, which itself had come within minutes of the bombing, until half of all Americans heard something of the attack. It would have been faster had it not still been so early on the West Coast. The major networks interrupted their regular programming and the various cellphone networks were stretched to their limits by the number of calls and text messages flying across the country, all of them saying something to the effect of *"Turn on the TV right now!"* News websites crashed, their servers unable to keep up with the sudden demand for information.

While any plane crash, building collapse or other disaster since 2001 has been presented by broadcasters with phrases like *"At this point, there is no indication that there is terrorist involvement"* well until after it had become clear no foul play was involved, the explosion of the Metrobus left little doubt that it was an attack. The detonation did not appear to have left survivors, and there was now a massive crater on Washington Boulevard that simply could not have been caused by a gas tank igniting accidentally.

The scene outside the Pentagon was eerily similar to the sites of car bombings in the Middle East. The significant difference was that this attack had taken place in the United States, a few hundred feet away from the headquarters of the most powerful military in history.

Stacey Harper learned of the explosion when she, along with all of her classmates, began receiving a slew of calls, texts and e-mails from loved ones asking if they were safe.

"I think something happened at the Pentagon," one student said, holding up his BlackBerry. Within a minute, he had received a fifth text from someone asking if he was all right. Others checked their cellphones and other mobile devices and realized that they were also being asked for signs of life by people who knew they were in the vicinity of the attack. Though classes were quickly canceled when it became clear that the first major terrorist strike on U.S. soil since 9/11 was unfolding only a couple miles from campus, Georgetown officials locked down the university. They didn't want students to leave until it was clear whether the bus explosion was part of a larger, coordinated attack. Stacey and her classmates, many of them clutched together in frightened embraces or united in prayer, huddled around television screens in classrooms and common areas. Most of the students and their professors were in shock, and all of them were on the phone to assure their families and friends that they were okay.

After more than five minutes of trying to get through to her mom, Stacey finally reached Amanda Harper, and only managed to stop her mom from crying when she assured her repeatedly that there wasn't a scratch on her and that she would spend the night at the family's home in Woodbridge.

A plan was devised quickly. Stacey would catch a ride home with her father, with whom Amanda Harper had already spoken briefly.

"Mom, I'm sure traffic is going to be crazy," she said. "Dad and I will figure out the quickest way to get home, but please don't freak out if it takes us awhile or if you can't reach us."

"Just hurry," her mother urged.

"I love you," she added after a moment but her daughter had already hung up.

***

The situation in Georgetown played itself out all across the nation. Classes in many high schools and universities were canceled and students assembled in gyms and cafeterias to get the latest information. Productivity in any workplace with a television set or computer screen slowed to a crawl. The attack quickly became the only topic of conversation on factory floors, in diners and barbershops. Of course, it was also the sole subject on talk radio, which for a brief while even eschewed the normal liberal-conservative battle lines. Immediately after the attack, there was no left and no right. There also was no racial divide. It didn't matter to the millionaire stock broker that the man next to him, who was also glued to the window of the electronics store in Manhattan to catch the latest news, was pushing a shopping cart bearing all his belongings. There were only Americans consoling one another — and anxiously wondering if there would be another strike.

The bombing halted many of the transit networks in the major cities. Instead of using mass transportation, people throughout the country either chose to stay home or used cars or cabs to reach their destinations. Nobody wanted to leave the vicinity of a television screen or computer.

The bomb had done more than destroy a bus full of people. It was also a blow to the American psyche. Just like the Pearl Harbor attack had shown decades earlier, and 9/11 had confirmed, the United States was not invincible. Its enemies could still reach the country's shores and kill its citizens.

Since that day in 2001, however, the U.S. had again been lulled into a false sense of security. Endless warnings that a new strike from as-Sirat was imminent or that Omar Bashir's recorded messages carried secret attack orders had all turned out to be false alarms. This slowly gave the country the belief that the combination of "taking the fight to the enemy" and the expenditure of hundreds of billions of dollars for homeland security was enough to completely protect the United States.

Many workplaces gave their employees the option of taking the day off and leaving for home to be with their families, leading to a mass exodus and traffic jams up and down the East Coast and in Chicago. In Los Angeles, many of the morning commuters already stuck on the freeways turned around to get back home when the news of the terrorist strike reached them. Trading was suspended on Wall Street when stocks began to plummet right after the attack.

In Washington, the White House and Congress were evacuated and the president and senior lawmakers were rushed to secure locations. Lesser members of Congress hurried to their office buildings on Capitol Hill, which were otherwise sealed off. Non-essential federal government personnel were allowed to go home, but congressional and White House staff were asked to stick around. There would be a lot to do once the extent of the attack became clear. The nation needed visible leaders and an operating government in time of crisis, not news of its elected officials cowering in safety in what would appear an attempt to save their own hides first. The American leadership would not give the terrorists, whoever they might be, the satisfaction of having shut down the government. For the first time ever, the Department of Homeland Security raised the threat level for the entire country to red. Across the Potomac at the Pentagon, the military was placed on DEFCON 3, a state of heightened readiness that had only been reached a few times in history. America was girding for war, if the need should arise.

***

Within an hour of the explosion, most of Europe also had learned that the United States was hit by the largest terrorist strike on its soil since 9/11, and the evening newscasts on the continent were scrambling to get more information. The site of the explosion was now flooded with local, state and federal law enforcement officials. Because of the proximity to the Pentagon, a group of Department of Defense forensic experts had been the first on the scene, and took command of the site, relegating most of the local officials to crowd and traffic control.

The firefighters had controlled the flames and were packing up their gear. Some EMTs lingered near the blast site, but there had been little to do for them except collect body parts. Every person on the bus was dead but, miraculously, nobody else had sustained significant harm from the attack. Alan Hausman, the closest civilian to the blast, had been treated for shock; two cyclists riding on the bike path near Arlington Cemetery had been hit by glass and received minor cuts. On the opposite lanes of Washington Boulevard, a three-car pileup followed the explosion.

In addition to scores of law enforcement personnel and first responders, crews from every major news outlet had flocked to the scene, hoping they could get there in time, before roads were closed. A swarm of photographers and cameramen accompanied them, looking for the ideal shot. The television cameras that made it to the blast area were set up near the Air Force Memorial, located on a hill just above the Pentagon. It gave the best view of the site for anchor stand-ups and was also far enough out of the way of investigators that they wouldn't be hassled by authorities.

"At this point, nobody has taken responsibility for the attack," an NBC anchor said into the camera overlooking the scene. His tie was a little crooked, but the producers were too busy to notice.

The entire area was overcrowded with law enforcement vehicles and the news networks' large satellite broadcasting trucks. Generators and cables were everywhere, and the on-air talents and technicians had to be careful not to trip over each other.

Regrettably, for producers looking for aerial coverage, the airspace above the Pentagon was off-limits for helicopters, even though air traffic from Reagan National Airport had been stopped. It didn't really matter, since the images displayed across the world were sufficiently dramatic to glue a global audience to its screen. The bombing had turned a perfectly beautiful day into a national nightmare.

While the news networks in this case quickly had access to images of the site of the attack, they lacked concrete information about what had happened. Nobody had claimed responsibility for the bombing yet, and investigators were still trying to put together pieces of the puzzle before going public for the first time. With little actual news to report, the networks kept showing the site of the attack and looped those images together with file footage of Metrobuses and the Pentagon. To the viewers, though, it didn't matter that they kept seeing the same thing over and over. They were drawn to the magnitude of the event and would have to be pried away from their sets or monitors before they received some answers about the attack, namely, "Who?" "Why?" and "Will there be more?"

Anchors, who knew next to nothing about what, exactly, had happened and had no answers to such questions, were forced to work without a script, filling the time by drawing comparisons to the 9/11 attacks and to terrorist strikes elsewhere in the world. They noted the obvious — that this was the largest strike in the U.S. since then — and ventured guesses as to who was likely responsible for the carnage. The Big Four networks as well as the 24-hour news channels all rushed to pull together experts to comment on what they saw, also with no actual information and merely relying on the video that was now being transmitted throughout the world and seen by hundreds of millions.

Wednesday, 11:57 a.m. ET

The woman at the Delta counter handed back the Canadian passport Hassan al-Zaid had given her. "Thank you, Mr. Afsani," she said with a customary smile. "How many bags will you be checking today?" "Just this one," he said, forcing a smile himself. He set down a bag on the conveyor belt next to her counter. Then Hassan al-Zaid's expression turned serious.

"I just saw the news. It's terrible what happened at the Pentagon. You think they're gonna close Dulles, or will my flight leave as scheduled?" Hassan al-Zaid asked, pocketing his forged travel documents. When he got to the airport, he had stopped at the first available television screen to make sure the explosion had gone off without a hitch. He huddled with a group of travelers who flocked around a TV monitor, standing by silently as they condemned the attack.

"I actually just checked with my supervisor," the Delta employee replied. "It looks like National is closed but Dulles and BWI are going to stay open. Frankly, I'm a little bit surprised, but it's certainly good news for you. Looks like your flight to Nassau is only a little behind schedule."

Hassan al-Zaid couldn't manage to conceal a brief smile before returning to his somber look.

"Well, at least that is some good news on this awful day," he said. "This is my first vacation in a long time. I'm flying down there for a bachelor party and all of my buddies are already in the Bahamas. I was stuck with some work in Toronto and had to take a later flight."

"I hope you have a good time despite this tragedy, Mr. Afsani," the woman said, reading the name from the boarding pass before handing it to Hassan. "You're all set to go. Your gate is B-19 and boarding should begin any minute now. Thank you for flying Delta."

After getting off the bus, Hassan al-Zaid had quickly made his way to Dulles International. On this morning, the airport did not only feature its normal activity, with travelers racing to make their planes, families waiting for loved ones, cab drivers trying to pick up fares. The terminal was also abuzz with news of the attack and speculation of what it would mean to those who had to fly. Rumors were swirling around Dulles that planes were being diverted or flights had been canceled. The fact that none of them were true didn't slow down the speed with which they circulated, and anybody wearing a uniform showing that they worked at Dulles or for one of the airlines was inundated with questions from anxious passengers.

Hassan wanted to leave the country as quickly as possible, but had left himself a little time to spare, and now used it to observe the atmosphere. It was an odd experience to know that he was responsible for the chaos in the airport — indeed, around the country. He pushed his way toward the departure gate and went over his escape again. He was on time and everything was going according to plan, apart from running into Stacey. Since the encounter had apparently not led to a speedier identification, no harm was done. He would be airborne within the hour and in Nassau by early afternoon. He anticipated that the entire world would start looking for Hassan al-Zaid while he was en route to Nassau, but it would take much longer for anybody to make the connection between himself and Canadian citizen Ibrahim Afsani. With any luck, by the time that happened, he would have ditched that identity already and left the Bahamas en route to Colombia.

Hassan glanced around. Everybody was either rushing to make their planes or huddled around the television screens, trying to get the latest news of the bombing. There was no indication he had been identified yet. With great satisfaction, he handed his boarding pass to the flight attendant at the gate. Within a few minutes, he would be airborne.

***

Before noon, all the news networks had managed to get their hands on retired generals, admirals, colonels and various national security experts, both from previous administrations and the private sector, to weigh in on the situation.

To visually enhance their coverage and to give viewers the assurance that the networks felt America's pain, all of them had taken less than an hour to come up with somber titles, such as "Terror at the Pentagon," and even more solemn melodies and video montages that were used to connect different coverage segments in lieu of commercials.

The ever-present news tickers at the bottom of the feeds compiled the few known facts about the attack, such as when and where it happened, that nobody on the bus had survived and that early estimates put the death toll at "dozens." And, of course, even the networks that normally did not show an American flag flying somewhere on the screen quickly changed that.

This was a time for the country to come together, and the news channels would try to outdo each other in terms of patriotic display.

All the analysts agreed that the strike was likely the work of Islamic radicals and resembled other attacks carried out by as-Sirat. Since the group was the predominant global terrorist network, it was a pretty safe bet to begin looking for blame there. As-Sirat, or "The Path," had been responsible for strikes across the globe. In recent years, the group had staged some high-profile attacks in England and mainland Europe, but had primarily focused its activities on Muslim countries, especially those in turmoil, such as Afghanistan and Pakistan. In addition, an offshoot of the group, as-Sirat in Iraq, had wreaked havoc in the war-torn country, claiming many military and civilian lives there.

The analysts also agreed that, if as-Sirat were discovered to be responsible for the strike, it could be the start of a new phase in the fight between Islamic terrorists and the Western world.

"For years, our aim has been to take the fight to them, to battle in their backyard in order to keep our own homes safe," remarked one of the analysts CBS had brought in, a retired Special Forces colonel and counterterrorism expert. "If this is an as-Sirat attack, it shows that they are trying to do the same. In some ways, I almost hope that this is the work of some domestic wacko instead of Islamic terrorists. If it turns out to be as-Sirat, America can probably expect more of the same soon."

Other security experts expressed similar views, forecasting an escalation of the fight between the United States and the terrorists.

With CNN and Fox News carried in most countries around the world, people on all continents watched the events unfold in real time, some with worries about loved ones in Washington, most with sympathy for the United States and the victims, and others with glee that the only remaining global superpower had been struck. There was an outpouring of support at most U.S. embassies around the world, with people placing candles or flowers at the fences, along with cards wishing the country well in the midst of its freshest tragedy. Terror had become a part of life in many places around the globe, and people there understood what those in Washington and elsewhere in the United States were going through.

Of course, there were other parts of the world where people were dancing in the streets after hearing of the attack. There, people burned the Stars and Stripes as well as pictures of President Sweeney and shouted slogans like "Death to America!" In those countries, the only thing placed at the embassy was additional Marines — a show of force meant to keep anti-American attitudes from morphing into all-out violence.

***

After passing out, Alan had been taken to the emergency room at George Washington University Hospital and treated for shock. He was then brought to a private room to recover. A couple FBI agents were already waiting for him and took down his statement. Unfortunately for them, it appeared as though Alan hadn't seen much that would be relevant to an investigation. After the FBI agents left, a nurse turned on the TV. Alan now saw through the lens of the televised coverage what he had experienced firsthand. Being so closely brushed by history was overwhelming. As a copy editor, Alan proofread countless articles about war, death and terrorist attacks elsewhere in the world. But this was different, having come so close, personally, to being a footnote in one of those stories.

What eventually helped to calm Alan down was the realization he was in a unique position. He had flipped through the news channels and listened to experts talk about homemade explosives, as-Sirat and the history of terrorist attacks in the U.S. Alan realized that the media were lacking real information and that he was one of the few people who could provide an account of what happened. It also dawned on him that, if he played his cards right, he would likely get his 15 minutes of fame as a survivor. Being somewhat familiar with how the media worked, Alan could already see himself appearing on the morning talk shows or sitting next to Oprah to discuss what it was like to be so close to an exploding bus. He pushed those thoughts aside for now and instead called his employer.

***

As the paper of record in Washington, the *Post* had a particular obligation to cover the attacks better than its competitors. With so much confusion in the immediate aftermath of the strike and so little information available, this was a tough task for the editors. They mobilized all available reporters to cover the story from every angle. Local reporters were mining their sources with Washington Metro as well as first responders; political reporters captured the reaction to the attack from Capitol Hill and the White House. In addition, the international desk was covering how the news of the strike had been received around the world, and even sports reporters were working on the terrorism angle, writing about game cancellations and prepared memorials at events yet to take place. For the *Post*, as well as for most of the other news outlets in the U.S. and in Europe, there was no other news that mattered.

So far, the paper's coverage had not been distinguishably different from that of its rivals, but Alan's phone call changed that quickly. Now the *Post* had something nobody else could present — an exclusive eyewitness who was on the scene, who'd had a front-row seat for the blast.

Alan's call was quickly routed to Emily Strauss, the paper's new managing editor, who told him that one of the guys from the national desk would write up his story. Within seconds, Alan was speaking to Arthur Kempner, a Pulitzer Prize winner and arguably the *Post*'s top reporter, who asked him about what he had witnessed. Alan told him everything he could recall. It wasn't much, but more than the competitors had at the time. He told Kempner how near he had been to the bus and how fortunate he considered himself to be.

Kempner asked whether Alan had been delayed in his morning routine, explaining that people would probably like to hear it if Alan had forgotten something in his house and went back, or had chosen not to push it through a yellow light during his commute, either of which decisions could have saved his life. Much to Kempner's regret, Alan could not provide an anecdote, but the reporter said he was happy with what he learned and that the story would be up on the paper's website shortly.

"Better get ready for Oprah," the veteran reporter told Alan.

"You know, I was just thinking the same thing," Alan said, straightening up. "You really think that's gonna happen?"

"Lemme put it this way," Kempner replied. "You may turn out to be lucky in different ways. First, you're alive, and I doubt that there were a whole lot of eyewitnesses, and you and those military guys might just have been the closest to the scene."

"Yeah, but they didn't faint," Alan said. "So maybe they got a better story to tell."

"Don't forget that those guys were military," Kempner responded. "I don't know what the rules are for them with regard to talking to the media, but I imagine they won't be allowed to. That makes you the person closest to the attack who is alive to tell about it. I see no reason why you shouldn't capitalize on that. I'm sure a bunch of TV people will try to get ahold of you through me when they see your name in my story. Do you want me to pass along your information?"

"I suppose," Alan said, smiling to himself when he thought of the possibilities. "You seem to have more experience with this, you got any advice?"

"Sure," the veteran reporter said. "Milk it for all it's worth.

"Oh, and whatever you do, don't speak to the *Times*," Kempner added with a chuckle. Then he gave Alan his cell number in case he remembered anything else from the attack.

***

"My fellow Americans. As you know, our country was struck this morning by a cowardly attack. I am sorry to confirm that there were no survivors on the bus. My prayers are with those who died, as well as with their families."

President Jack Sweeney paused and looked into the camera that was set up in the Oval Office. Though the address to the nation had been put together quickly, protocols were in place for such events that also dictated how a commander-in-chief had to look in situations like this. The president's wardrobe was meant to portray strength; he was also supposed to display a somber and serious demeanor without showing any fear. He didn't understand why a simple blue tie and a certain white shirt were deemed more suitable for the occasion than a striped blue tie and a slightly different white shirt, but he didn't question the choices. He had more important things on his mind. The president's job was to assure the public that everything would be okay and that the government, which many citizens cursed on a daily basis, was on the case.

"Investigators are hard at work, looking for clues as to who is responsible for this reprehensible attack on civilian American lives."

The president, who despised using a teleprompter, again looked up from his notes and straight into the camera.

"Here and now, I want to assure all Americans that my administration and I will not rest until the perpetrator of this heinous crime has been brought to justice. Attacks such as this are meant to terrorize this proud nation and are aimed at assaulting the liberty that we enjoy and others detest. But whoever is behind this will soon find out that a strike within our borders does nothing to deter us from doing the right thing and only strengthens America's resolve to stamp out terrorism and stand as a beacon for all those seeking freedom. God bless you all, and may God continue to bless the United States of America."

As the lights and camera shut off, President Sweeney turned to his chief of staff, Jared Watkins, who was hovering in the background as always.

"When's the FBI briefing?" Sweeney asked.

"Director Stevenson should be briefing reporters right now," Watkins replied. "He just wanted to wait for your remarks and begin right afterward."

Fiddling with a pen, Watkins looked at his boss. Not for the first time, the president's chief of staff thought about how tough it must be to lead the United States. There were so many problems — and whenever you finished addressing one, a whole crop of new ones were certain to be waiting. Watkins had seen Jack Sweeney steer the country through a recession, avert a major crisis with Russia and command American troops in Iraq and Afghanistan. He admired his boss for many reasons, but possibly most of all because he was a calm and steady leader in a storm. Now, with the country under attack, President Sweeney again did not seem rattled, especially in his address to the country. But when the lights were off, the chief of staff detected an unusual weariness in his boss. Watkins knew Sweeney's name would forever be linked to the attack, even if the president couldn't have done anything to prevent the bombing. Today, American lives were lost under his watch, and the commander-in-chief would have to shoulder at least part of the blame. On the other hand, the public would never know some of the things the Sweeney administration had done to protect the country, or at least not until documents would be declassified in a couple of generations.

In the chief of staff's book, being president of the United States was a lousy job.

"Are you okay, Mr. President?" he asked.

The question seemed to reel the commander-in-chief back from somewhere deep in his thoughts.

"Yeah, Jared, I'm fine," the president said, wiping a bead of sweat from his temple. "Let's get to work."

The answer did as little to give Watkins reassurance as the weak smile that Sweeney offered his chief of staff.

***

Following the presidential address, the networks switched over to a live feed from the J. Edgar Hoover Building, an ugly slab of concrete not far from the White House, where FBI Director Chris Stevenson was beginning his press conference. As with all high-profile cases, his job was to inform the public without revealing everything the FBI had already learned, in order not to corrupt the investigation.

While briefing rooms often look spacious and nice to the television audience, which only sees podiums with fancy seals flanked by American flags, they are often miserable and small. Away from the cameras, there were no nice drapes in the Hoover building. Instead, journalists who were lucky enough to find a seat sat crammed together, juggling recording devices, their notebooks and coffee mugs. The many lights necessary for the television cameras, along with the large number of people — enough to give any fire marshal fits — inevitably led to the temperature in the briefing room rising to an uncomfortable level. Director Stevenson felt sweat run down his back within seconds of beginning his statement.

"As you are all aware, terrorists struck our country at approximately 10:25 a.m. EST. A powerful device was detonated on Washington Metropolitan Area Transit Authority Bus 1202," started Stevenson, standing behind a podium bearing the FBI logo. He glanced at the notes he had hastily scribbled on a legal pad, wanting to make sure he had the details right. "I understand that the bus was used this morning as a shuttle to take passengers from Crystal City Metro station to Rosslyn. The attack took place on Washington Boulevard near the Pentagon. Sadly, no one on the bus survived the attack. In one piece of good news, it appears that nobody else was seriously injured, though at least one eyewitness is being treated for shock. The explosion was quite powerful, and it may take a while to determine the exact number of victims. In any case, we will not release their names until the next of kin have been notified.

"Nobody has claimed responsibility for the attack as of yet. We also don't know if the attacker or attackers were on board when the device detonated. As I'm talking to you, the tapes of the onboard cameras are being reviewed. As you may know, Washington Metro has outfitted all of its buses with three cameras each. We believe they will give us a good idea about who is responsible for this attack, as well as the number of victims.

"I wanted to get out here as quickly as possible and let you guys know where we stand, but I won't be taking questions at this time," Stevenson said. "I hope to be back within the hour to let you know anything I can about what we have found on the tapes. Thank you all."

With that, the FBI director disappeared into a hallway behind the podium of the briefing room, ignoring the questions reporters shouted after him.

***

The one witness who could have already shed some light on the attack had missed the president's address to the nation and the first FBI press conference. Stacey Harper had been on the way home with her father, who had picked her up from Georgetown after confirming that I-395 remained open to traffic. With many commuters leaving Washington early, the highway was packed and it took three times longer than usual to get to Woodbridge. When they finally pulled into their driveway, Amanda Harper was outside waiting for her husband and daughter and she put Stacey in a bear hug when she got out of the car.

"I was so worried about you," she said, trying to fight back another flood of tears as she rehashed the agony of the morning. Stacey knew better than to interrupt her mom as she went on about how she had felt when she heard about the attack and could not reach her daughter. Instead, she simply held on to her mother.

"I love you, mom," Stacey said when she could finally get a word in.

The Harpers went inside. While Stacey headed for the kitchen to get something to drink, her parents planted themselves in front of the TV to get the latest news on the attack. CNN was just showing FBI Director Stevenson's second press conference.

"... and have evaluated the surveillance tapes from the bus and the bus station. Two of the three cameras on the bus were operational, the one showing the front and rear doors, and we also got some data from closed circuit cameras at Crystal City station," Stevenson said.

"As you can see from this shot, a young man with a large backpack got on the bus along with the other passengers," Stevenson said in the background.

"Shortly after leaving the bus station, it looks as though he got up and it seems as though he asked the driver to let him off the bus. As you can see, he left the backpack under his seat.

"In this video, taken from a bank surveillance camera from across the street, you can see him getting off the bus and walking back toward the Metro station. As you see him disappear from view, he seems to be talking to another person ..."

Glass shattered and both of Stacey's parents looked at their daughter. She stood in the living room, all blood having left her face. Amid a broken glass, a pool of soda expanded on the hardwood floor.

"We are not prepared to declare this young man a suspect, but he's certainly someone we would like to be talking to as soon as possible," Stevenson continued on the television. "This is the best shot we got of him from the front camera of Metro Bus 2405." Most of the screen was filled with a somewhat grainy picture that clearly showed Stacey's former classmate Hassan al-Zaid.

"What's wrong, honey?" Stacey's father asked, rushing to his daughter's side.

"Oh my God. I'm the person in the video. I tried to get on that bus," she burst out. "And I know who they're looking for. It's Hassan, who went to Woodbridge with me. I talked to him this morning."

"If you have any information about this man, please contact law enforcement authorities immediately," Stevenson's voice could be heard in the background. "A hotline has been established and hopefully the number will be on your screen now."

Stacey had staggered to the couch and plunged down next to her mother, clutching Amanda Harper's arms with clammy fingers.

"Oh mom, I was so close to getting on that bus," she stammered.

Both of Stacey's parents shuddered when they thought of how close they had come to losing their only child. Bruce Harper also took a seat on the couch. He wanted to be as close to his daughter and wife as possible as they all went through the "what ifs" in their heads. The entire family just sat there for a few moments, holding on to each other and occasionally muttering words of comfort. Tears of shock mixed with tears of relief were streaking down their faces.

Stacey's father was the first to speak again.

"You have to call them, pumpkin."

"I know," Stacey replied, curling her hair around her index finger the way she did when she was supposed to do something she didn't want to. "But Hassan couldn't possibly have anything to do with this. I bet he's already getting in touch with them."

"You should still call the hotline, just in case," her dad said.

Stacey pulled out her cellphone and dialed the number that was still on the screen.

Wednesday, 2:42 pm ET

Director of National Intelligence Robert McClintock arrived at the Hoover building in a black SUV. Apart from beat-up cabs, the government suburbans often seemed to be the most used vehicles in Washington. In the 19th century, Congress had mandated that no new building could be taller than the Capitol itself, preventing Washington from being home to the kind of high rises that made up the skyline of other major U.S. cities. Still, even the 10-story office buildings in downtown DC did the job of blocking the breeze that was coming from the Potomac. With the sun having burned down on the concrete all day, it was brutally hot and McClintock began sweating as soon as he left the car.

This area of the city had nothing of the beauty of Capitol Hill, where the Congress and Supreme Court and their antique-inspired architecture attracted countless visitors. The only tourists who showed up at the Hoover Building were lost. Its job was not to look pretty but rather to house the premier U.S. law enforcement agency.

With a couple of assistants in his wake, both of them struggling to keep up with the 60-year-old DNI, McClintock was taken straight to Director Stevenson's office. The nation's "top spy" had been asked to brief senior FBI personnel on whether there had been increased activity among terrorist groups. While the Bureau kept taps on domestic threats, the various spy agencies under McClintock had a global reach.

The DNI was an ordinary guy, the kind of man who, before he assumed his current position and rose to "Inside the Beltway" prominence, was always mistaken for other people. This had served him well at the beginning of his career, when he had joined the CIA out of college and being non-descriptive was an asset in his clandestine work. Since then, he had gotten to know the different aspects of U.S. intelligence gathering inside and out. First as an operative abroad, then behind a desk, as a staffer on Capitol Hill and the White House and later in increasingly high positions in the various spying organizations. It was that career path that made him revered by the intelligence community. He wasn't an academic who was picked by the president to lead them. Robert McClintock was one of them. In turn, he commonly referred to other members of the intelligence community as "my guys," or, when women were present, as "my people."

When he received his Senate confirmation hearing for the current job, McClintock was widely hailed by Democrats and Republicans alike as the perfect choice for the position. One senator had referred to him as a "throwback kinda spy," stressing that he meant that "in a good way."

At the same hearing, when McClintock was quizzed about a particular issue, another senator said that "it's tough to argue with a guy who knows more about this business than just about anyone and who put his life on the line every day while working in the Soviet Union."

The DNI not only talked the talk but he had walked the walk behind the Iron Curtain and in other hot spots during his illustrious career in the clandestine services.

After some high-profile failures in recent years, most notably the fiasco of the pre-Iraq War intelligence, and concerns that the intelligence community was increasingly being politicized, McClintock was viewed as the man who would right the ship. In his third year on the job, he hadn't disappointed.

At the Hoover Building, the DNI again displayed his trademark bluntness.

"So, you got video of a suspect," McClintock said, foregoing the use of the phrase "person of interest." As all of the people in the room knew, that term was mainly created to shield law enforcers from lawsuits. None of the senior FBI officials in the room regarded the man in the picture as anything but their prime suspect.

"Indeed, and we actually got a name that goes with the picture," Stevenson said. He touched a button on the remote he held and a photo appeared on a flat screen across the room. "The suspect is Hassan al-Zaid, second-generation American. He's 21 years old. Muslim. We don't have a file on him but are working on pulling together everything we can find. Right now, agents should be searching his parent's house in Virginia and his last known residence in California." Stevenson got up from behind his desk and walked toward McClintock, who stood by the screen and looked at the photograph. He waited for the DNI to make eye contact.

"There is no doubt that he is the guy on the tape," Stevenson said. "We've had at least three dozen phone calls all identifying him, including that girl he spoke to after getting off the bus. Apparently she went to high school with him not far from here and ran into him by chance this morning."

"Any chance this isn't our guy?" McClintock asked.
"Sure there's a chance," the FBI director responded.
"But it would have to be a huge coincidence. In theory, an unaffiliated suicide bomber could have been on the bus and Hassan al-Zaid just happened to be the luckiest guy in the world because he was on the wrong bus at the right time. It would also mean that he left his backpack accidentally."
Stevenson tapped the face on the screen before adding, "And, if all of this were the case, why hasn't he contacted us? All in all, there is a chance this isn't our guy but that chance is pretty damn remote."
"Fair enough," the DNI said. "Makes sense. So we assume we know who did it."
Though McClintock hadn't inquired about whether they had any leads on al-Zaid's whereabouts, the FBI Director gave the intelligence chief a brief rundown.
"Unfortunately, we don't yet seem to be close to arresting him," Stevenson said. "Now that we have a picture, it should really help us with the manhunt and getting the public involved. Right now, you got at least 250 million pairs of eyeballs looking everywhere for our person of interest and I hope that the searches will give us some clues about where he is. Obviously we are monitoring airports, train stations, bus terminals and we are also setting up some checkpoints along the major roadways leading away from Washington.
"This guy has a head start but he's a young kid so I'm sure he'll make a mistake soon. It's also not like he can count on sympathy from anybody in this country and nobody in their right mind would want to be associated with him right now, so I'm hopeful we'll get him soon," Stevenson concluded.

The FBI Director was nearly a polar opposite of McClintock. Whereas the DNI was of average built and plain looking, Stevenson was tall and handsome and nobody ever confused him at dinner parties with anybody else. Before being named to the position by his college buddy Jack Sweeney, he had worked as a lawyer in the private industry where he had made a fortune. His wealth showed in the expensive suits he wore and the cars he drove.

His deputy, a career agent, had joked when they began working together that "you used to have to take a whole lot of bribes to afford a car like that. At least we don't have to worry about that with you."

Stevenson had only limited relevant experience prior to being asked to lead the Bureau – he had served a brief stint as U.S. attorney early in his career. His selection had initially resulted in loud criticism from Sweeney's political opponents and some editorial pages, as well as some grumblings within the Bureau. But he had proven himself to be a capable steward of the FBI and silenced all critics, who had to begrudgingly admit that Stevenson was an excellent director.

"Well, we got a name and a face. Shouldn't be too difficult to find him," McClintock said. While Stevenson was showing some emotion about the attack, the DNI was all business. "Are you releasing the name to the press? I'm sure you've sent it to all of my agencies to see if he has any known associations."

"We haven't made a decision on releasing the name," Stevenson said. "With so many people identifying this kid, it seems that it'll only be a matter of time before someone leaks it to the press and it shows up on the

Internet, even though we asked all those who contacted us to not share that information with anybody else. With regard to passing along the name," he looked at one of his deputies who was the liaison between the Bureau and the intelligence community and nodded, "I guess that's been done."

"Good," McClintock said. He had always liked the FBI director and never had an issue when they worked together in the past. He knew that Stevenson was in an unenviable position and things would get worse the longer he could not deliver the suspect. He also was aware the he would become a target of scrutiny soon as well but McClintock wasn't worried about himself. "I'm sure my guys will shoot you over anything we have on him," he said, concluding that topic and shifting gears.

"Now, with regard to why I'm here. There is really no indication that this attack can be linked to any of the international terrorist groups we are monitoring. There certainly was no uptick in terms of chatter.

"Often, within a couple of weeks before an attack is scheduled to take place, we at least get some indication that something is about to happen, even if we can't figure out the details," McClintock explained, pacing in the FBI director's office as he spoke. "That hasn't been the case this time. We haven't seen a new as-Sirat video in more than a month and the chat rooms we monitor also haven't had an unusual amount of activity. We're always behind on monitoring phone calls because of the volume of those we are listening in on, but there also doesn't appear to be anything unusual there. So, we have little to go on with regard to international terror groups pulling the strings on this one.

"I guess the early signs point to a lone wolf," the DNI concluded.

Stopping so-called "lone wolf" terrorist attacks was a nightmare for homeland security officials and the intelligence community. While they had ways to monitor terrorist groups through electronic surveillance and, especially with regard to potentially dangerous domestic groups, through human assets that were used to infiltrate them, there was comparatively little they could do against a determined individual. There was simply no way to monitor all of the sources that allowed people to figure out how to build bombs in their basements, and, of course, anybody who was in the U.S. legally could simply buy assault weapons and ammunition, go to a mall or a school and kill as many people as possible. If lone wolves maintained operational discipline and did not trumpet their plans to the world on their Facebook pages or a tweet like "2morrow I will bomb u all," there was very little law enforcers could do to detect them until after they made their move.

Most of the men in the room nodded. Though the attack had taken place only a few hours ago, the early signs pointed to a lone wolf. Whether this had made it more difficult to prevent the strike wouldn't matter much to a public that wanted to be kept safe and believed that homeland security had not done its job whenever there was an event. In that way, those tasked with keeping the country safe got a really bum deal. Often the public would never find out about their successes, but any failure was magnified, even if there was nothing that could have been done.

"Well, let's wrap this up then, now that we have a suspect," Stevenson said, eager to get back to work and learning more about the target of the investigation. McClintock nodded and packed up his documents. "Keep me up to date and, if my guys can help in any way, just let me know."

***

Stevenson was proven right about the details of the investigation leaking out soon. Shortly after the meeting at the Hoover building concluded, about five hours after the attack, ABC News was the first to broadcast that the man in the picture was believed to be Virginia resident Hassan al-Zaid, a recent college graduate. The network supplemented its coverage with footage from a local affiliate showing FBI agents camped out at the al-Zaid residence in Woodbridge. The other networks were not far behind in bringing the news to a nation eager for any morsel of information. At the Washington Post, the newsroom was bustling with activity. All hands were on board, even those who had taken the day off had come in if they were in the vicinity of Washington or worked remotely. This was the biggest news event in years and nobody wanted to miss out on being part of it.

The news of the raids in Woodbridge and the leaking of the name of the person of interest resulted in the decision to task three staff writers and two editorial assistants to pull together all available material on Hassan al-Zaid. The Post would try to give its readers as much information as possible in the morning edition and would also update its website to get people to come back to washingtonpost.com.

At the request of managing editor Emily Strauss, Alan went to the newsroom after being discharged from the hospital. Though he was not expected to do any copy editing, he was supposed to work with Kempner on an article detailing the attack. In return for his help, Alan had been given the rest of the week off and was cleared to use his new-found fame in any way that would not be damaging to the paper.

He was just discussing the article with Kempner and Strauss when the sports editor barged in with one of his reporters.

"You gotta hear this," he said. "This is Mario Puente, one of the guys who covers local sports for us. Two years ago, he did a lengthy profile of Hassan al-Zaid and he's been covering him for years before that."

"Go ahead, tell them," he added with a wide grin and a nod to the young sports writer.

"When I was starting out here, I covered local high school athletics. That's when I first met Hassan," Puente said, fiddling with a piece of paper. "He played soccer at Woodbridge and was one of the most talented kids on the entire East coast. He was a midfielder at Woodbridge High, took them to state once and was a high school All-American as a junior and senior.

"He then accepted a full ride to play for UCLA."

"Here it comes," the sports editor interrupted, unable to contain himself.

"Hassan lost the scholarship at the end of his sophomore year," the young reporter continued, visibly pleased with the bombshell he was about to unveil. "UCLA was supposed to play Maccabi Tel Aviv, an Israeli soccer team, in an exhibition match and Hassan refused to play, citing 'the Zionist's oppression of the Palestinian people.' With him being a local boy, I did a story on it and talked to him and others on the team. They said his coach had asked him to just fake an injury so he wouldn't have to be kicked off the team but Hassan refused, saying that he had to do what is right."

Puente waved the paper he was holding. "I got a copy right here."

He paused, letting the information sink in.

"Let me get this straight," Kempner was the first to break the silence. "This kid was a freaking All-American who is now a person of interest for the FBI, which basically means he is their top suspect in the largest terrorist attack since 9/11 and he lost his scholarship at UCLA because of his anti-Israel views? That's great stuff!"

"You're sure this is the same person?" the managing editor asked. "I mean, 100 percent positive?"

"Absolutely. I've seen and talked to him many times, although the last time has been a while back. When they showed that photo of him for the first time, I thought to myself: 'That looks like the kid from Woodbridge who went to UCLA'."

"Well then," Strauss said with a nod to Kempner. "Art, let's get something on this up on our website right now before some blog beats us and then you can work on an overnight piece. Our young sports writer can pull up all his files and notes on the guy to supplement your piece. You know what to do, so let's get to it."

***

The FBI raid of the al-Zaid residence had unveiled a treasure trove of information and, within minutes of forensic experts entering the house, Jerome Wilkins, the lead agent on the scene, was on the phone with Director Stevenson.

"We can stop this 'person of interest' nonsense. We have our man," the veteran FBI agent told his boss. "There is a video of him on his computer claiming responsibility and pledging allegiance to as-Sirat and Omar Bashir. The file was open on the computer in his room, just waiting for us to find it.

"There are also some bomb-making materials in the basement," he added. "But no sign of him or his parents. We're sending the video to you right now through the secure network. You should be able to watch it any minute now."

"Good work," the FBI director said. "We already have an APB out for him and I'll authorize another for his parents. See if you can find recent pictures. We probably want to distribute a good one to the media as quickly as possible."

Stevenson hung up the phone, then picked it up again and called his chief of staff.

"I need to talk to the president in 10 minutes. Also, we need to get an APB out on this kid's parents. Make sure all our travel databases are searched for their names and future bookings cross-referenced. And then set up a secure conference call with everybody."

The FBI director let out a deep sigh and then logged into the secure network from the computer on his desk and clicked on the video link.

The screen showed the torso and head of a young man with Middle Eastern features. His black hair was long and wavy. Stevenson made a mental note to have the experts put together a bunch of pictures with how Hassan al-Zaid would look if he changed his hairstyle and color.

The suspect was wearing a simple white t-shirt that highlighted the darkness of his skin, a color that could be the result of genetics or a summer working outdoors. The background of the video seemed to be that of a normal teenager's bedroom with a bookshelf and a window. He was a fairly good looking kid, Stevenson thought, with a sympathetic face, even features and brown eyes. What was an American kid like doing blowing up a bus instead of being out and about, trying to chase girls, the FBI director wondered before pushing "play."

"With the help of Allah, blessed is his name, I will carry out a strike at the heart of the enemy," Hassan began in a voice that, to Stevenson's surprise, was completely free of an accent. Though he knew that the young man in the video had grown up in the U.S. and was believed to have spent his entire life here, he still expected the terrorist to have an accent.

"For too long, America has pushed other countries around to satisfy its own greed, killing hundreds of thousands in its wars against true believers in Afghanistan and Iraq. Though proclaiming to want peace and to promote religious tolerance, how is it that America's actions are always targeted at Muslim countries? How is it that the United States always stands with the Zionists against my brothers and sisters? You lament your own few dead without caring about all of the Muslims that have perished. Americans are ignorant of the hardships that their country has caused to millions. The United States is not bringing peace, it's bringing oppression. Since you are doing nothing to educate yourself about your country's actions, it is time that the fight will once again be brought to your doorstep."

The young man on the screen had grown more agitated. He was pointing at the camera.

"It's time for somebody to give you a taste of your own bitter medicine. I will prove that you can no longer feel safe on your buses. You also should not feel safe in your malls or believe that your children are safe in their schools. It has been too long since America was last reminded what will happen if it tries to oppress my brothers and sisters. I pray that there will be others, who, like me, grew up right here, and realize that they are the ones who have to fight back. Although I'm tempted to die a martyr's death when I strike, I believe there is much more I can do in this fight. There is no such thing as a Muslim American or American Muslims. America has made sure that these two don't go together. I call on all of my brothers and sisters to join the fight against the infidels. The time has come for us to pick up arms and throw off the chains the oppressors try to tie around the true believers.

"I pledge allegiance to Omar Bashir and as-Sirat. The Path is at war with America and I am willing to give my life to make sure the right side prevails in this struggle. All praise be to Allah."

Stevenson stared at his screen for a moment.

It was nice to know who committed the crime – a confession was rarely delivered on a silver platter like this. But it was mind boggling to see this kid, fresh out of college, turn on his country like that. This wasn't a grainy as-Sirat video with a Yemeni or Saudi national speaking Arabic with English subtitles.

He was looking at the first successful homegrown Muslim terrorist.

This wasn't a guy wearing a turban in a cave with an AK 47 in the background. Instead, the video showed a completely normal kid from suburban America who happened to be Muslim and decided that, instead of going to the mall, he should build a bomb and blow up his fellow citizens. The realization sank in that this would change everything.

Stevenson picked up the stress ball from his desk and squeezed. His knuckles turned white.

What if others like him would follow Hassan al-Zaid's battle cry? While hard data were lacking on the number of Muslims in the United States, it was believed to be between three and seven million. Stevenson shuddered at the thought of even a tiny fraction of them, armed with American passports, driver's licenses, credit cards and the ability to use these assets to easily travel or buy weapons, turning on the United States.

The phone rang, for the moment tearing Stevenson from his thoughts.

"Please hold for the president," a voice said after he picked up. Next, he heard the pleasant baritone of Jack Sweeney.

"Chris, what's the latest?" the president asked.

"Well, Mr. President, I think there can be no doubt that the young man from the photo is our terrorist." Stevenson said. Though they had been friends for decades, he always maintained formalities when addressing his boss, no matter how hard Sweeney had tried to get him to drop the "Mr. President" stuff.

"I just finished watching a video of his confession and my agents apparently have also found some bomb-making materials at his parents' home in northern Virginia. We know from an eyewitness that he was on the bus and dozens of people have identified the picture as well. So this is fairly easy. Let's hope it will be just as easy to find him."

"Well, Chris, I'm sure you'll be up to the task," the president said.

"There is something else, sir," the FBI director said. "I suggest you watch his confessional as soon as possible. I would recommend that we keep it under wraps. It is, to say the least, highly incendiary and I really don't think it would be good to give the public a look at it. It's quite stunning. In many ways, this kid is as American as you or I. I'm worried on the effect it could have."

"Sounds reasonable. We can always release it later, I guess," the president said. "Please make sure I continue to be briefed frequently. I want to be very much involved in this personally."

"Of course, Mr. President," Stevenson said. "I'll make sure you have a summary of the latest events on your desk every hour and I'll get in touch with you if there is a major development, though I hope this is wrapped up soon."

"Did you know he was a high school All-American?" the president asked. "My staff just told me about it. It's all over the news. Let's go public as soon as possible with the information that we have identified the terrorist. We want to let the country know that the FBI is doing its work and we're gonna need as many eyeballs as possible to make sure we catch him quickly. And I trust your judgment on the tape. Let's not release it yet. I'll take a look at it shortly. Anything else?"

"No, Mr. President, that's it for now." Stevenson said.

"Good, Chris, keep up the good work and keep me informed."

After hanging up, the FBI director willed himself to momentarily put his thoughts on the video aside and he turned his attention to organizing the largest manhunt in U.S. history.

***

Just as his picture and his name were beginning to be splashed on TV screens and news websites throughout the world, Hassan al-Zaid was again in line at an airport, this time in Nassau.

He eyed his fellow travelers, looking for any traces of recognition on their faces. It was hot and humid in the airport but he would have been sweating even if it had been perfectly air-conditioned. Hassan al-Zaid shifted his weight from one foot to another, hoping to finally get on the plane.

This would be one of the diciest moments of his escape, the one he had always been most worried about.

After arriving in Nassau, he walked from the plane to the terminal and cleared immigration with no trouble at all. He went to a bathroom to discard his Canadian identity, changed his clothes and gotten back in line, this time at a Continental counter.

He told himself to calm down. There was no way a Bahamian airline worker or immigration official would think that the man wanted for a terrorist attack in Washington would already be leaving the Bahamas a few short hours after the bombing. In addition his changed clothing and a rudimentary disguise should help.

Hassan al-Zaid was now using the travel documents of a French citizen who was returning to South America after a trip to the Bahamas.

Still, though his mind told him that he would not be found out in Nassau, he was relieved to see that there were no TVs at the Continental counter and, when he had cleared that, at the immigration desk.

He gave his travel documents to the immigration officer who barely glanced at them before putting the exit date in the passport.

"I hope you had a good time here, Mr. Abussi," the man said, featuring the rich Bahamian accent. He handed the documents back to Hassan and his smile revealed two bright rows of teeth.

At that point, Hassan al Zaid knew he had made it.

"I had a blast," he said, grinned and then turned to find his gate.

Once the U.S. authorities put together his escape plan and interviewed this immigration officer, Hassan hoped that he would remember the "I had a blast" comment. It would make for an excellent headline. He marched out of the terminal toward his next plane. Another hurdle had been cleared and he now truly felt that he was slipping away, out of reach of the Americans looking for him.

Wednesday, 4:22 pm ET

Stevenson again stepped to the podium in the briefing room, his every move accompanied by camera shutters. It was his fourth press conference of the day and he would rather be anywhere than in the hot briefing room. There was so much else for him to do right now. Yet, in a time of crisis, the country needed to see its leaders, not some spokesperson, so Stevenson had to keep trotting out in front of the media whenever something new happened. At least this press conference would serve a purpose.

Using his multimedia screen, the FBI director pulled up a recent picture of Hassan al-Zaid, which had been found at his parents' house. He obviously did not want to use a screen grab from the confession video because anybody with any sense would immediately ask where they had got that from.

"I want to thank all law enforcement personnel involved in the investigation of this morning's terrorist attack," he began. "It is their work that allows me to announce at this point that Hassan al-Zaid, the man you can see in the picture behind me, is the main suspect in the bombing. During searches of residences in Virginia and California, we have discovered enough evidence to issue an arrest warrant."

Another round of camera shutters filled the room, along with the sound of reporters shifting in their seats, itching to start asking questions.

Stevenson raised his hand and waited for the murmur to die down.

"Though he is not yet in custody, I'm confident that it is only a matter of time before Mr. al-Zaid is arrested.

In addition, at this point we have no evidence pointing to this morning's bombing to be part of a wider terrorist attack. As you might know, the Department of Homeland Security has therefore just announced that the threat level would be lowered to orange.

"I ask all Americans to be on the lookout for Hassan al-Zaid and to come forward with any information that they may have about his whereabouts. At the same time, I urge people to be cautious. This man is believed to be responsible for a heinous act of terror and we must anticipate that he is armed and dangerous. Do not try to capture him on your own. Instead, if you see him, contact law enforcement immediately.

"I'll gladly take a couple of questions now."

The room erupted in reporters yelling over each other to get to ask the first question, even though they realized the futility of their attempts. The first question would always go to the Associated Press or one of the major networks.

"Jessica," Stevenson said and pointed to the pretty AP reporter in the center of the front row.

"Director Stevenson, can you give us some more information on what kind of evidence you have found linking Hassan al-Zaid to the attack?"

"Sure. First of all, we have an eyewitness placing him on the scene. In addition, several people have identified him from the surveillance tape. That is what led us to Mr. al-Zaid initially. The resulting investigation, which included searches in the Washington metropolitan area and in Los Angeles, unearthed additional incriminating evidence, including documents and also materials used to build an explosive device. Rick."

The ABC News reporter in the front row rose. "Have you found any clues regarding his motives? There are news reports that al-Zaid lost a soccer scholarship because he refused to play a team from Israel. Apparently, that decision at the time earned him some accolades on websites and in chat rooms of radical Islamists. Is this attack related to the same beliefs that resulted in the lost scholarship?" Stevenson paused. He would have much rather answered questions about evidence and what was being done to capture al-Zaid than the motive. As was sometimes the case, some reporters were a step ahead of the information he had on a small aspect of the investigation. Naturally, Stevenson thought as his mind was racing to find a good answer to the question, it would always be those things that were coming up in a press conference.

"I don't want to go into too much detail, but I would say that, according to documents we have recovered, Mr. al-Zaid had some misgivings about policies that the United States pursues," he said carefully.

An NBC reporter jumped in.

"According to our information, this man was born in the U.S. and raised here. He was an All-American high school athlete and some would argue he is as American as you or I. Do you classify this morning's attack as an act of domestic terrorism or as an attack of Islamic radicals?"

"Well, listen," Stevenson began, using a time-tested delaying tactic to buy himself a couple of moments to think. "I'm the director of the FBI. I don't concern myself with labeling attacks. My job is to put criminals behind bars and that is what everybody here is trying to do. You may want to ask that question to others. Okay, I have to get back to work. Thank you all."

Stevenson escaped into the hallway behind the podium, the sound of the camera shutters slowly fading as he rushed back to his office.

***

"ALL AMERICAN TERRORIST!?!?"

The headline was splashed in all caps below a picture of Hassan al-Zaid on the Drudge Report. Complete with the trademark blinking sirens, the link led to the AP story summarizing the latest developments in the case.

"Where is al-Zaid?" another headline asked, linking to a Reuters article on the massive manhunt that was unfolding. Other links went to first reactions from acquaintances of the terrorist, with high school buddies saying the customary things such as "He was a great guy," "There is no way he did this." But there were also statements from college friends who said that, while they never thought he would become a terrorist, Hassan al-Zaid had become increasingly withdrawn and "radicalized," as one former teammate put it, while at UCLA.

Art Kempner, sitting at his desk in the Washington Post's newsroom in downtown DC, scanned all of the headlines and he was pleased to see his own story listed up high on Drudge.

The Pulitzer Prize winner looked like the old school reporter that he was, straight out of central casting for a 1940s movie in which journalists wore Fedoras with little cards on the rim that said "Press" and rushed into phone booths to speak to operators or to say things like "hold the presses." The white hair that he kept cut short was a rarity in an industry increasingly dominated by young journalists eager to make a name for themselves. His thick glasses and his clothing could be described as "retro." Art would say that he was just wearing what felt comfortable and that his style had not changed much since he was a young reporter.

At many press conferences, he was by far the oldest person in the room, apart from Members of Congress, of course. In fact, not too long ago a new Capitol Hill reporter had mistaken him for a senator.

"I'll be happy to tell you my views on our energy policy, young lady," he had said, smiling. "Sadly, that won't help you much because I am just a lowly reporter like you."

He later overheard how the novice was set straight by a member of the press corps.

"Oh my God, do you have any idea who that was? That is Art effin' Kempner. He wins the Pulitzer, like, every other year."

That, of course, had been an overstatement of his accomplishments, but he was widely regarded as one of the best in the business.

Though clearly "old school," he was one of the newsroom dinosaurs who had successfully transitioned into the new media age. Art understood the importance of the Internet for journalism and he also, though reluctantly, sometimes played the pundit on cable news. The only news program he did like and never minded appearing on was "Meet the Press."

He read a story about anti-Muslim backlash in Minnesota, where an Egyptian college student was berated by fellow female students as a terrorist and had her head scarf ripped off. Art expected that it would not be the last such story he would be seeing over the next few days.

About ten hours had passed since the attack and there was no end to his day in sight. He would grab a quick dinner before finishing up the paper's lead article. This was the kind of story that gave traditional newspapers the creeps. What if the terrorist would get caught after tomorrow's issue had gone to print? By the time people would get their Post, they would already have better and newer information from television news and the Internet. A gut feeling told the veteran reporter that this would not happen. There appeared to be no sign of al-Zaid, which Art found disconcerting, to say the least. Everybody in the country was looking for this kid. How could he just disappear?

The reporter grabbed his Blackberry, certain that the short dinner he had planned would be interrupted by breaking news of some kind or an editor who needed him for some reason or another. He headed for the exit, estimating that he would have no more than 20 minutes to eat. He would be right. Shortly after ordering his sandwich, an FBI source called to let Art know that Hassan al-Zaid's parents had been located.

Luxor, Egypt -- "You must be mistaken," Dr. Farouk al-Zaid said for at least the tenth time, shaking his head and clutching his wife Delek's hand. However, his voice lacked the conviction it had at the beginning of the interrogation. "There is an error of some sort, some kind of misunderstanding. Hassan is a good kid. He was just at the wrong place and somehow you now think he was involved in this."

Hassan al-Zaid's parents were sitting side-by-side in uncomfortable metal chairs in a community room of a Nile River cruise ship. The interview was being securely broadcast to the FBI via a camera sitting atop the table that separated the couple from several U.S. officials. The al-Zaids were groggy, frightened and unguarded, the perfect circumstances to get honest answers. An hour into the interrogation it appeared to those on the scene and those watching from Washington that the couple did not know anything about the plot or had any idea where their son might have escaped to after carrying it out.

Farouk, usually a tall and proud man, sat slouched over, sweat pouring down his face and he repeatedly put his head in his hands. He had worked hard to give his wife and only child the best life possible after moving to the United States to attend medical school and becoming a doctor. Now, he had a feeling that his life's work was for naught, not wanting it to be true. He had some of the same dark features that Stevenson had observed in Hassan, but his complexion was ashen now, with only his thick, black mustache giving his face some color.

His wife Delek, normally a beautiful woman, had fallen apart even more. She had been crying almost nonstop for the past 45 minutes, at times sobbing uncontrollably. Her eyes were red and broken, her face covered by long strands of black hair. The sobs kept shaking her body and she was holding on to her husband as everything else in her life appeared to be slipping away.

A check of Hassan's credit card purchases earlier in the day revealed that he had booked a cruise up the Nile for his parents. The discovery had unleashed a flurry of activity. During the interview, the al-Zaids said the trip had been a present from their son – telling the questioners that it was his way of thanking them for putting him through college after he lost his soccer scholarship. The two had left for the cruise a week ago and were scheduled to be out of the country for four more days.

Stevenson had been informed of their discovery when it was 5:00 pm in Washington and 11:00 pm in Cairo. At about the same time, several U.S. officials were also alerted and a plan of action was formed. The Egyptian government was notified and asked to cooperate and assist the Americans in their mission to find Hassan al-Zaid's parents. They eagerly agreed, not wanting to appear in any was as though they were standing in the way of a terrorism investigation. The government in Cairo dispatched two military helicopters with Egyptian security forces to the embassy. The aircraft were met by U.S. officials, who boarded and took off toward Luxor, where the cruise ship was docked. The captain had been notified of the helicopter's arrival and also provided background information about his ship. There was no television on board and passengers also did not have Internet access, making it entirely reasonable, especially in light of the time difference, that the al-Zaid's had not yet heard about the attack.

Shortly after 3:00 am, the helicopters had landed and the entire delegation boarded the ship and was taken to the cabin. With the Egyptian security forces standing by with drawn weapons, Farouk and Delek al-Zaid had been woken up and taken to the community room. They were frightened and confused.

At first, the U.S. military attaché to Egypt, who led the interview, had tried to ascertain whether the al-Zaids were aware of the Washington attack and asked question about why they were in Egypt to probe for inconsistencies. When Hassan's father became belligerent and threatened legal action, the attaché pulled out some pictures showing the remains of the bus, the picture taken of Hassan and news stories describing him as the lead suspect.

The al-Zaids reacted with shock and disbelief, claiming repeatedly that there must have been a mistake.

"Do you really think I would fly out here as a representative of the United States of America at this hour unless I was certain that this was not a mistake?" the military attaché asked.

Though both of Hassan's parents steadfastly maintained that a completely logical explanation would be found, it was clear that their confidence was shaken. Still, the enormity of the accusation did not allow them to admit to anybody, other than possibly themselves, that their son could have been involved, though they became visibly scared and confused.

The al-Zaids agreed to fly back to Cairo for another interview and then be taken to the United States. Though the consensus was that they had not been aware of the attack, or that they were the greatest pair of actors the seasoned interrogators had ever encountered, it had also been decided that they would be taken to Cairo – even without their agreement. Fortunately, their decision to cooperate in any way possible eliminated the potential headaches that could have resulted from forcefully removing two American citizens from another country.

At 5:00 am Egyptian time and 11:00 pm in Washington, the helicopters were on their way back to Cairo with Hassan's parents on board.

***

Bogotá, Colombia -- Far away from Cairo and Washington, Hassan al-Zaid allowed his mind to truly rest for the first time since waking up. For now he could stop running. The past twelve hours of his escape had gone just about exactly as planned. He again went over everything, trying to figure out if mistakes had been made but was unable to come up with any.

His trip to the Bahamas as Canadian citizen Ibrahim Afsani, one of the three fake identities he had obtained, was his second to the island in a week. His escape had been meticulously planned and quite costly.

Six days ago, he had flown from Washington to Toronto, using his actual passport. From there, he had traveled to Bogotá, Colombia, using a French passport and the name Mohammad Abussi, and then on to

Nassau. He used that identity to check into a hotel not far from the airport at the beach.

Hassan had then flown to Freeport, the closest Bahamian city to Florida, and left the island via a fishing boat, giving the captain $5,000 in cash to smuggle him back into the United States. The Bahamian fisherman, thinking he was dealing with an illegal immigrant, had not asked too many questions and just pocketed the cash. It was a low-risk maneuver for Hassan al-Zaid, because he could at any time produce his real American passport and claim he was just out on a fishing trip.

Back in the U.S., he returned to Woodbridge, having his parent's house to himself after sending them off to the Nile cruise. He needed the house empty as he was finishing up his preparations and made sure that all parts of the plan were in place.

After he reached the relative safety of Nassau and discarded his Canadian identity, he flew to Bogotá, using his French passport. There was nothing suspicious about Mohammad Abussi, especially since the computerized log showed that he had arrived in the Bahamas six days ago from Colombia. He seemed just like any of the hundreds of thousands of people who came through Nassau's airport each year looking for a good time in the Bahamas.

The countries he used for his escape had been carefully chosen for their traditionally lax immigration and customs policies. In addition, cash ruled everything there and Hassan had brought plenty, just in case there was any trouble. Coming from a wealthy family, he had a sizable savings account, which he emptied a week ago. In addition, he had accumulated as many credit cards as possible over the past two years and, after the last monthly billing cycle, he had begun maxing out all of them. He knew that, one way or another, he would never pay another bill but had to wait until the last moment before accumulating debt in order not to be flagged. The "convenience checks" that credit card companies routinely sent to their customers had, in fact, been very useful for him. He had cashed many of them and, all in all, still had $35,000 after all of his expenses.

In total, making it safely to Bogotá had cost him another $30,000 and two of his identities. It was not safe anymore to use Mohammad Abussi. His last passport was the one that would have to get him to his final destination. It identified him as an Algerian national by the name of Yusuf Ramza. He was raised speaking both English and Arabic and had learned French in high school and college. His language skills were good enough to allow him to pass as a French citizen to a non-native speaker or as a French Canadian. Hassan felt most comfortable using the passport of a country in which Arabic was spoken, along with French. He was confident that his identity as an Algerian student would hold up.

As he made his way to a hotel in downtown Bogotá, nobody had given him as much as a second look, even though a recent picture of him was shown every few minutes on televisions showing CNN. A hat and dark sunglasses was the entire disguise he needed here. Besides, nobody expected him to be in Colombia. All eyes were turned to the United States.

He had reached his hotel shortly before 10:00 pm local time after making one stop, and now he was stretched out on his bed with his adrenalin pumping. He was excited about having made it this far without complications. A backup plan had been in place but it was better to not have to resort to it.

His next flight would not leave for a few hours, so he hoped to get some rest. He would need all of his physical and mental abilities over the next few days. Still, before going to bed he turned on CNN to get the most recent information on the status of the investigation. He watched a recap of the day's events, including the video of him getting off the bus. It was fascinating to him to watch something play out on television screens around the globe that he had been planning for so long.

For the past four years, he had dedicated his life to the cause. He had given up friends and teammates, lost his scholarship and spent all of his free time plotting, training and preparing. School really had only been an afterthought in his life, especially in his senior year when all of the pieces of the plan had come together. Hassan al-Zaid knew that the law enforcement apparatus of the most powerful government in the world was sparing no expense to hunt him down. He also knew that just about everybody in his home country, including people he cared about, hated him. That didn't matter to him now. Instead, he felt a great sense of relief that everything had worked out just as planned. A million things could have gone wrong but they did not.

After half an hour of watching the news and learning how much his pursuers knew, he turned off the TV. Just before he willed himself to sleep, he thought of the people he had seen on the bus before he deposited the backpack and got off. He felt no regret.

***

Andan, Pakistan – Just as Hassan al-Zaid fell asleep in Colombia, half a world away, as-Sirat leader Omar Bashir got his first look at the man who had joined him as the most wanted person on earth. He was sitting in his favorite chair, sipping on ginger tea and enjoying some dried fruit.

It was morning already in the mountainous region between Afghanistan and Pakistan. The two countries shared a border of more than 1,300 miles and, despite all of its might, the U.S.'s powerful arm had not been able to extend its reach to Waziristan. As-Sirat had its headquarters here, in the Federally Administered Tribal Areas of Pakistan.

Though Omar Bashir had learned of the Washington attack shortly after it happened, he was just now looking at news footage. In order to not elicit suspicion, no satellite dishes were allowed in Andan. The small town was basically a front operation for as-Sirat. With American drones and other means of electronic surveillance presenting many challenges, numerous precautions had to be taken in order not to arouse suspicion. Andan was not a big town but it was built on top and near several coal mines that had long been exploited and abandoned. Now, the system of caves and tunnels housed not only Omar Bashir and several of his deputies and bodyguards but also dozens of as-Sirat fighters at a time. The town, which consisted of about 50 buildings, was now known for its dyeing operation and it provided a front that allowed the terrorist group to receive supplies and to move its fighters to other parts of Pakistan or across the border into Afghanistan.

As-Sirat members and their supporters had gone to great lengths to not draw attention to Andan. The town had no landlines and cellphones were prohibited so that the group would not be vulnerable to electronic spying. The tunnels received most of their power from generators to not alert anybody looking at whether the town's energy consumption matched its assumed population. There were a couple of satellite phones but those were only to be used in emergencies.

The measures put into place had kept the as-Sirat leaders safe for years now. There was little worry about the locals giving up the headquarters' location. They were fiercely loyal to as-Sirat and deeply anti-American. In addition, they knew that anybody in Andan not killed during a U.S. attack would certainly be murdered by as-Sirat supporters later. Though many people knew about Andan's role and Omar Bashir's whereabouts, none of them would sell the as-Sirat leaders to the despised enemy, not for a buck, or a $25 million reward or for the entire wealth of America.

As an additional layer of protection, Pakistani security forces were saturated with as-Sirat sympathizers who would get in touch with the group if a raid was planned. Knowing all of this, Omar Bashir believed that there would always be time to disappear into the nearby mountain ranges if the Americans would ever figure out where he was. The group had numerous hideouts in the area that would be nearly impossible to find for the Americans.

All things considered, life was not so bad for the as-Sirat members in Andan. A major downside to the security precautions was that the group was largely cut off from direct communication, such as phones, Internet and TV. For the most part, messengers were used to relay information. Every morning, a courier brought video tapes of the previous day's newscasts along with copies of several international newspapers and magazines to Andan.

Before becoming the most wanted terrorist in the world, Omar Bashir, the offspring of a rich family from the United Arab Emirates, had been an executive at his father's media conglomerate. It was during that time that he not only learned to promote himself but also how the media could be manipulated to do one's bidding. He was a tall, telegenic man who took great care of his appearance, even in his hideout below Andan. Omar Bashir also had the kind of voice that spoke with the passion and urgency to make people listen. He used it to try to ensnare impressionable young men into the swelling ranks of "The Path." When he had begun to fight the United States and its allies, he had used his knowledge of the communications business to find recruits, raise money and to fight the message machine of his enemies. He accomplished his goals with a fairly sophisticated public relations operation. While he was under no illusion that he could change the minds of his enemies, his efforts were aimed at poor and disenchanted young Muslim men.

As-Sirat sought to capitalize on poor economic conditions in Middle Eastern countries and Omar Bashir each day was on the lookout for the kind of news he could use for his propaganda. That included United States air strikes that caused civilian deaths, just about any action Israel took against the Palestinian people, efforts to give women more rights in Muslim countries and anything else he could spin into showing that the western world was oppressing the true followers of the Quran.

The generators below Andan also powered an array of media equipment, such as cameras, a video editing booth and a makeshift sound studio in which the numerous messages of Omar Bashir and his deputies were recorded. In order to not steal his own thunder, the as-Sirat leader relied mostly on written and audio messages and only sent out videos on special occasions.

After studying the CNN footage from the previous day and printouts from news stories on the attack for more than two hours, Omar Bashir sat quietly in his private quarters. He was delighted that America had been struck, even though this might delay his own plans to attack the United States within its own borders. As-Sirat had been largely laying low in Europe and America, opting to go for a major attack instead of smaller ones like car bombs or simply acquiring assault weapons and killing as many people as possible in shopping malls or kindergartens, which had been considered as alternatives.

The group was in the final stages of planning and carrying out a large-scale attack on a U.S. nuclear power plant – a strike that would make 9/11 appear small.

A congressional investigation, made public and eagerly studied by as-Sirat, had shown that America's nuclear reactors were only poorly guarded. The group was currently putting asset into place to take over such a plant and hopefully cause it to melt down. For years, the U.S. had feared that as-Sirat would obtain nuclear weapons, such as those available for sale in some of the former Soviet Republics, and smuggle them into the country. Little did the Americans know that the terrorist group felt that such a plan was bound to fail. Instead, as-Sirat would rely on using nuclear material already in the country.

In order to be able to do their part in this one mission, several of the group's members had studied nuclear physics for years, including the faithful man who was currently waiting inside the United States to lead the operation. Others, the foot soldiers, would cross the U.S. border from Mexico over the next few weeks. He would have to quickly get word to the leader of the operation to not risk discovery. If the American threat level remained high, the attack would have to be postponed. However, that was not too much of a problem. The as-Sirat fighter whom Omar Bashir had handpicked for the mission about a decade ago had been patiently waiting in the United States for years now. A couple of months more would not matter, especially if it would lead to a greater chance of success.

Contrary to the suggestions of his enemies that he was not in charge of his group anymore, Omar Bashir was a hands-on manager of as-Sirat, and he would have known about any plans to blow up a bus in Washington. Therefore, the attack puzzled him. Obviously, the man who had carried it out was a Muslim, that much was clear from the media reports. However, it did not yet appear to be clear whether that was the reason for his action. After reading one of the articles on Hassan al-Zaid, Bashir recalled some as-Sirat members telling him some time ago about an American student who had to stop playing for his university team because he refused to appear on the same field as the Zionists.

Omar Bashir decided after some contemplation that he would be able to exploit the situation either way. If the bomber acted out of solidarity with as-Sirat, then that could be spun to show that even Americans were turning on their own country. If the attack was just a random act of violence, such as the occasional school shootings in America that gave him so much delight, Omar Bashir thought he would be able to exploit the backlash against Muslims in the United States that was sure to follow.

Thursday, 6:23 am ET

When the country began waking up to the news that the terrorist was still at large, FBI Director Stevenson had already been back in his office for hours. He had rushed home for a short rest not long after watching the interview of the al-Zaids in Egypt. He would have preferred to just work through the night, but better judgment as well as his deputy and his chief of staff prevailed. He needed to be on top of his game and for that he needed sleep, which was difficult to come by in a situation like this. After getting just three hours of rest, he was back at work.

Hassan al-Zaid's escape baffled him. Criminals make mistakes, they leave trails, but it was as though this one had just managed to disappear even though an entire country was looking for him. They knew he had traveled to Toronto a week ago, but were unable to find out what he had done there. He also never showed up as having returned to the U.S., so he must have gone back across the border undetected, which was not a major feat but puzzling. What was the point of returning to the country without using a regular border crossing?

The suspect had also spent more than $2,000 on tickets leading away from Washington. He bought train tickets going up and down the coast, three Greyhound bus tickets and plane tickets to various destinations leaving from Dulles, Reagan National Airport and Baltimore's BWI. Stevenson believed that following up on any of those would be a waste of time, but diligence demanded that some of his agents checked all of the destinations. Instead, the FBI director believed that the key to the escape was in Toronto.

The phone rang. It was Stevenson's chief of staff, informing him of a meeting with the president at the White House to discuss the situation. The FBI director frowned. Most times, he liked having the hands-on Sweeney as his boss. But most times he could also deliver good news. This time he would have to go to the White House empty-handed and admit that he did not have the first real clue as to where Hassan al-Zaid was.

***

Though some of the names of the victims had already leaked out, the FBI did not release a list with the casualties from the attack until authorities had been able to get in touch with a next of kin for each of them. The final death toll was 37, including the bus driver. Twenty-seven men had died and 10 women. Most of the passengers had apparently arrived at Reagan National Airport just shortly before the attack, making it more difficult to identify them. It also meant that the tragedy had affected all areas of the United States instead of only Northern Virginia. Fortunately, no children had been on the bus. The youngest victim was 34 and the oldest 70. Along with the list, the FBI also released to the media excerpts from the video recorded by the two operational surveillance cameras on board. The new footage, which was played over and over on all news channels, showed Hassan al-Zaid getting on the bus along with several other people. He was carrying a large backpack. Then, not long after the bus started moving, the video showed him getting up and making a gesture toward the driver, who could not be seen from either angle. The bus then stopped and

Hassan al-Zaid exited through the rear door, this time without the backpack. Stevenson had not been a fan of releasing the tapes but the White House had overruled him.

On the Today Show, the clip was played for the seventh time that morning. NBC had managed to secure Alan Hausman as an exclusive guest for the morning. With some advice from Art Kempner, he had negotiated an appearance fee of $15,000. Though such a payment was highly unusual for the network, NBC gladly paid that sum to the eyewitness who was closest to the scene of the attack and willing to talk about the experience.

"Alan, what is it like to see this footage, knowing that this is the bus you witnessed blowing up?" the host asked.

"It's a weird feeling, and I really want to express my condolences to the families of the victims," Alan, who was sitting in a studio in Washington, said. He had cleaned up considerably for his day of media appearances, having shaved his scraggly beard and exchanged his usual attire of jeans and some sort of t-shirt with a message on it for a button-down and khakis.

"I feel extraordinarily blessed to be alive," he said. "It's a scary feeling to know that I was a few seconds away from death and that I would not be sitting here had I driven faster or left home just a little earlier." Alan had been worried a little about his appearances. It was not the fear of speaking to an audience of millions that made him nervous, but rather the self-awareness that he could come off as a bit of an ass to people who did not know him well. But he didn't need to worry.

His answers were genuine and his sympathy for the victims just as heartfelt as his own relief to be alive. He had struck a couple of other deals to appear on The View and on an MSNBC evening program, pocketing a total of $40,000 in fees. In addition, Alan hoped that, in the longer interviews, he would also be able to talk about his ambitions as an author, though Art had warned him against that.

"Don't look like someone wanting to exploit the situation for personal gain. The entire country is grieving, so you'd look like an ass," the media veteran had told him. "This will get your name out there. If your books are good, then someone will publish them for you because you'll have name recognition."

On the Today Show, Alan really did not feel like talking about himself. Before they showed the clip of the terrorist, they had on the wife of one of the men who died. She was crying throughout the interview and it was heartbreaking to watch her grieve over her dead husband. Alan didn't understand what the point was of dragging her in front of a camera or her motivation to agree to appear. He was quite sure that she, unlike him, was not paid. Instead, she just wanted to tell the country that her husband had been a good man. He hoped that the appearance on national TV would help her in the process of recovering from the tragedy.

Alan would be on for another segment in the last hour of the show, so he waited in the Green Room while munching on some fruit and muesli.

"Our next guest is standing by in Columbus, Ohio. It is professional soccer player Bill Cusack. He is a midfielder for the Columbus Crew and attended UCLA with Hassan al-Zaid. Bill, how shocked were you when you learned that your former teammate is wanted for carrying out a terrorist attack?"

"Initially, it was a tremendous shock," the soccer player said, clearly more comfortable in an interview setting than Alan. "As soon as I saw the photo from the surveillance video I said to myself: 'That guy looks like Hassan.' But the more I think about it, the more sense it makes. I know people often say in these situations that they would have never expected their friends or neighbors to do something like that, but at UCLA, I definitely saw Hassan become more and more radical in his religious views. And, of course, that culminated with him leaving the team."

"Did you have anything to do with him after he lost his scholarship and his spot on the squad?" the female host asked.

"Yeah, I'd still see Hassan around campus and talked to him a few times," Cusack said. "Sometimes, he was the great guy he was when he was a freshman, but other times he would go out of his way to begin discussions about U.S. aggression against members of his faith and stuff like that. It was as though he was looking to get into arguments with me.

"It totally makes me think I should have done something, like report him to Homeland Security or something, but you never think someone would do something as crazy as what Hassan did. But again, in retrospect, I guess it kinda all makes sense."

"Thank you for your insight. Our guest was Bill Cusack who plays professional soccer for the Columbus Crew. He was a teammate of Hassan al-Zaid at UCLA and his roommate when the team was on the road."

***

At the White House, Stevenson was led to the Oval Office. Though he knew the way, he was being escorted. Even the FBI director could not simply stroll around by himself in the heart of America's power. President Sweeney and Director of National Intelligence Director McClintock were already there and engaged in conversation with some breakfast items at a nearby table. They looked up when the door opened and greeted Stevenson.

"Mr. President," the FBI director said with a nod. "Director McClintock. I hope I'm not running late."

"Not at all Chris," the president said and pointed to an empty chair. "Bob was here early. I have asked him to join us because our intelligence community believes that there are indications that Hassan al-Zaid is not in the country anymore.

"Now I want to be clear. I don't want there to be any sort of turf war over this," Sweeney looked at both of them over the rim of the reading glasses that he usually only wore away from the cameras. "I hope that you both will exchange all of your information and work together to find this guy. If he is abroad, the FBI can work with Interpol while the intelligence community can do what it does. So I want both of you to be in close contact and speak at least a couple of times each day on the progress you are making."

His guests nodded.

"Now, where do we stand, Chris?"

"Well, obviously, we haven't found him yet and the trail is remarkably cold, sir," Stevenson said with an almost apologetic tone of voice. One of the assets of this president was that he brought out the best in his staff. The people working under him wanted to impress Sweeney and therefore tried a little bit harder. In the eyes of many of the White House staff, and even Cabinet-level members of the administration, a compliment from the president was worth more than a raise. Conversely, not being able to deliver gave some people the feeling that they were letting down their commander-in-chief. That was how Stevenson now felt. He first had that sensation of thinking he personally had failed Jack Sweeney when they worked together on a group project at Harvard and only managed a B.

"His escape seems to have been well planned," the FBI director continued. "I believe that the suspect's recent trip to Toronto has something to do with his disappearance. Our records show that he traveled there but did not reenter the country. I think, and many of our top people agree, that a key to the escape may be found there. Of course, it would be great if we could get the information that the intelligence community has gathered. If we are just chasing our own tail here, our resources could be put to much better use.

"Now, I just had a briefing with our forensic experts, and they said that the explosion was quite powerful for a homemade device," Stevenson said. "He must have brought a hell of a lot of explosives in his backpack, so we are wondering if he had somehow obtained some higher grade material as well."

"How would that help us?" the president interjected.

"It could give us some clues not only about his whereabouts but also possibly about whether he was working with somebody else. Let's say that he did use military explosives instead of something homemade. That means he must have either stolen or bought it illegally somewhere. The sources for obtaining that stuff are much more limited than building explosives from household items and fertilizer that you can buy at any Wal-Mart.

"If it turns out to be military grade explosives, it would also open up the possibility that we were wrong about al-Zaid being a lone wolf," Stevenson continued. "Others could have been involved in the attack since it's not easy to get that kind of stuff, even for a young man who has shown an extraordinary knack for planning."

"Interesting," Sweeney said, pausing to digest what he had heard and running his hands through his hair. As was the case with most presidents, he had begun graying rapidly after he was elected to office the first time. It did little to diminish his still youthful appearance. In fact, his staff assured him that the gray hair helped him make inroads with voters who had always felt that Sweeney was too young and inexperienced when taking office. Since he was in his second term already, the president cared little about polling and often wondered why it was still being done. His advisers had told him it was to help him establish his legacy, an assertion at which Sweeney laughed. Sitting at his desk in the Oval Office opposite of his FBI director and the DNI, he knew that his legacy wouldn't depend on how people felt about his hair color. Instead, it was the current situation that would determine how his presidency would be judged down the road.

"I think we should keep this information to us for now, especially since this is just a theory at this point, right, and not supported by any facts?" Sweeney asked.

"Yes, Mr. President, it's just something that seemed unusual to the forensics people when they got the first glance of the site and the devastation the bombing caused," the FBI director said. "We'll know more when we have a detailed analysis."

"Well, Chris," the commander-in-chief said. "The country is rattled and I don't want to create more concern by prematurely floating a theory that more people might be involved. Also, it seems like we're currently still working under the assumption that Hassan al-Zaid acted as a lone wolf."

He looked at McClintock and Stevenson who both nodded.

"So, if there were other terrorists who helped him, it seems as though they might get a false sense of safety. I expect that this information will not leak out, Chris. But tell your forensics people from me that they are doing a good job."

Though Stevenson did not entirely agree with the decision to not spend more resources pursuing the angle that there had been accomplices, he again admired his friend's ability to quickly and calmly analyze a situation and make a decision without waffling. Most often, those decisions would turn out to be right. Maybe there was something he was disregarding here, Stevenson thought. Sweeney had always been more of a "big picture" kind of guy.

The phone on the president's heavy oak desk rang. Sweeney took the call but indicated with a wave of his hand to Stevenson and McClintock, who had risen from their seats, to remain in the Oval Office. The president listened for a couple of minutes without speaking and then only said "Thanks," before hanging up.

"Gentleman, there is another problem," he said. "Apparently, Hassan al-Zaid's confession, the one we found at his parent's house, has been sent to al-Jazeera. They aired it in its entirety a few minutes ago. My press secretary followed up right away to see why they didn't give us a heads up. Apparently, they got it FedExed this morning and decided to put it on the air. It arrived with a letter that said all our networks would get the same tape within the hour. That's pretty clever, because it forced them to put it on the air to ensure that they broadcast it first. Now that it's out, I doubt we can convince our networks to sit on it.

"Our communications people suggested that we should tackle this head on," the president added. "Chris, I think either you or I or Homeland Security should make an on-camera statement saying that this attack was carried out by a young man who obviously had some issues with our policies but that he is in no way representative of Muslim Americans and to warn anybody that we will pursue any kind of attacks on Muslims to the fullest extent of the law."

"An excellent idea, Mr. President," Stevenson said. "I think we have to stress that his statement is aimed to incite hate and violence, which are in contrast with the teachings of Islam. The last thing we need is a holy war here right now."

"I'll have my guys put something together. Actually, on second thought I'm inclined to do this statement myself," the president said.

"I think we should put the full weight behind the White House behind this," he added, hinting at the hierarchy of statements that was part of the rules in Washington. A prime time address from the president was the most serious of responses to a crisis, those from Cabinet members also weighed heavily and, if an issue was to be downplayed, some press secretary usually released a statement.

"Okay, we all have work to do," the president said, indicating that the meeting was over. "Remember to stay in close contact and keep me in the loop."

McClintock and Stevenson were shuffling out when Sweeney stopped them in their tracks.

"Chris, can you give my chief of staff the names of the people who found the stuff at Hassan's house and your forensics people. I want to get a message from the White House to them thanking them for their fine work."

Sweeney turned to his Director of National Intelligence.

"Bob, do the same with whoever found out that the terrorist is not in the country anymore. Also, stick around for a few more minutes. We should probably still go over the China matter now that you're here."

***

After the major networks had also aired their copies of the taped confession and America got a look at Hassan al-Zaid and heard his voice for the first time, the White House demanded that the president be given time to address the nation. All networks happily obliged.

"My fellow Americans," the president began, speaking this time from the Rose Garden. His advisers had thought that it would look better for Jack Sweeney to be outdoors. It would give the country the appearance that he was not hiding and that there was nothing to be scared of.

"Earlier today, many of you probably heard from Hassan al-Zaid, the man who took responsibility for yesterday's cowardly terrorist attack."

Sweeney's bright blue eyes looked straight into the camera. His good looks, according to polling, had once helped him notch a come-from-behind win in a key primary state over a dour opponent. At the time, young women had turned out overwhelmingly for him. He was still very popular among that demographic, a fact his wife frequently teased him about.

"Let me be frank, I wish that video had not been aired. It aims to divide us at a time when we need to be united. It asks some Americans to pick up arms to fight against others at a time when we have a common enemy hiding away in a cave somewhere. So, I wish this man had not been given the platform to promote his message of hate. But for us to allow his tape to be aired is exactly one of the many things that sets us apart from oppressive regimes and terrorists like Omar Bashir. They hate the idea of an America in which people are allowed to speak their mind without fear of prosecution and where people can worship freely. So maybe there is something good that will come out of Americans listening to this message of hate. It should serve all of us as a reminder that we are better than that. Now is the time for us to prove again that terrorists underestimate and do not understand America.

"In the long history of our country, this is the first time that an American Muslim has turned on the United States and engaged in an act of terrorism against their home country. Just one, out of the millions of Muslims who, every minute of every hour of every day, are doing their part to make this country great. So, while the terrorists would like nothing better than for American Muslims to take up arms against their country or for some of our citizens to take up arms against the Muslims in our midst, I call on all of you to show them that they have once again misjudged us."

Jack Sweeney shone in situations like this, even though his speechwriter had felt the remarks ran a little long. Handsome and distinguished, he was a president Americans were largely fond of, even those who disagreed with his policies. He had always been successful in rallying the country around the flag when the need arose. The president loved addressing the nation and had the ability to make it seem to people as though he was speaking only to them.

"Let's also remember that these terrorists do not represent Islam. Islam is not a religion of violence and hatred, but that is exactly what the terrorists are offering. Later today, I will attend a memorial service for the victims of yesterday's attack at a mosque here in Washington. I ask all of you to do something similar. Visit a mosque, get to know a Muslim neighbor a little bit better or simply go to the White House website where you can see what kind of accomplishments and sacrifices Muslims have made to make America the great country that it is. For example, there are currently thousands of Muslims serving in our Armed Services and many others work for the government.

"Let's show the terrorists that they have again misjudged America. Let's show them that we stand united against the threat they pose and that we will not allow anybody to divide us. May God bless all Americans and this great nation of ours."

In a classic law enforcement "good cop, bad cop" routine, the Justice Department, immediately following the president's speech, released a statement letting Americans know that any crime against members of another religious group or ethnicity would be punished to the fullest extent of the law and could also be prosecuted under recent hate crime laws, which would call for even more severe punishments.

***

At the Hoover Building, Stevenson was sitting on the couch in his office, his feet resting on a coffee table, looking at classified pictures that appeared to show Hassan al-Zaid at the immigration desk in Nassau. The photo's time stamp indicated that it was taken the previous day – just a few hours after the bombing. According to a package of documents that DNI McClintock had sent over, the terrorist had entered the Bahamas with a fake Canadian passport on a flight from Dulles airport. There was also a picture from a Dulles security camera of a young man wearing a baseball cap pulled deep into his face. There was no way to determine that it was Hassan al-Zaid, but the guy in the photo from the U.S. was wearing the same clothes as the one entering the Bahamas.

He picked up his phone and asked to be connected to DNI McClintock. It took just a few seconds until he heard the voice of the Director for National Intelligence.

"What do you think?" McClintock said. "Looks like he flew the coop right after the bombing. And your hunch on Toronto seems to be right. They have some excellent forgers and he might have picked up his passports there."

"Well, that hunch doesn't do us any good now," Stevenson grumbled. "I assume you don't think that he's on the Bahamas anymore."

"I doubt it. It's just the quickest way out of the country and planes go to all parts of the region from Nassau. My guess is that he didn't stay there longer than a couple of hours. However, nobody using that passport has left the country. We already checked that. I really don't think somebody who planned his escape so well would think that the Bahamas is the best place to hide.

"The president has seen the same information and the State Department has already contacted the Bahamas to give the FBI unlimited access," McClintock added. "There is also a possibility that he used a boat to leave the country, so the Coast Guard and the Navy are moving some resources that way."

"How does a 21-year-old plan all this?" Stevenson said, vocalizing the thought that kept haunting him. It was not so much a question directed at McClintock and more a way for the FBI director to voice his frustration that the terrorist had managed to slip out of the country. "My daughter is in college and she can barely get her passport renewed or any other part of her life in order without me helping her. Yet somehow this guy managed to get a fake passport that is good enough to allow him to leave this country hours after a terrorist attack. Heck, even I would have no idea where I would get great false documents."

Stevenson threw up his hands.

"It just all makes me think that he must have had accomplices. Also, someone who flees the country normally has a destination they are trying to reach. Where do you think he is going to go?"

"If I were him, I'd try to get as far away as possible," McClintock said. "His parents are cooperating with us. They were even more rattled after watching the video tape their son made and I think it shattered any hopes they had that their son was not involved in this. We are flying them back here as we speak or they may already have arrived back stateside. En route home they gave our guys a list of all of their relatives living abroad. We have people covering them and tapped their phones just in case he tries to contact them."

Stevenson pulled a folder from his desk.

"I have something for you, too. I just got something from our computer guys who went through al-Zaid's laptop. It looks like he had a hotmail account that he stopped using a while back. But right after he lost his scholarship and was hot stuff on some of the more radical chat rooms and message boards, it looks like he tried to contact some of the people who praised him. Back then, it appears as though he was looking for like-minded folks in the LA area. I'll make sure it has been sent to you."

"Interesting," McClintock said. "I'm sure we have some databases that we can crosscheck this against. There are a lot of fairly radical Muslims in LA that we have our eyes on. For the most part they are just talking or raising small amounts of money but maybe some of them could have pointed al-Zaid in the right direction if he was trying to contact as-Sirat.

"I'll have my guys check this out immediately and then get back to you. If we flag somebody, how do you want to proceed? Knock on their doors and rattle them or watch and listen?"

"I guess it depends on what we find. I don't want to scare them into running if we don't have any hard evidence, but if we do, I think we should take them in quickly and put as much pressure on them as possible."

"Well, we'll probably know pretty soon what kind of contacts these guys have had abroad," the DNI said. "If they are on any of our lists, I can tell you by the end of the day who they have been talking to."

Stevenson smiled to himself and shook his head.

"Must be nice," he said. The FBI director always marveled at the sweeping powers and lack of oversight that the intelligence community enjoyed. On the other hand, he would not want to have the same authorities domestically because they would completely erode civil liberties.

"I hope you come up with something. Let's say we speak again at 3:00."

"Sounds good," McClintock said and hung up.

Stevenson leaned back and rubbed his eyes.

"How does a 21-year-old do all this by himself?" he asked the empty office, thinking again of his daughter and the way she was struggling with something like a grad school application.

Maybe one of the LA contacts would turn out to be an accomplice he thought. Fighting back his fatigue, he reached for the phone and called for more coffee, wondering all the while where the terrorist was now.

Thursday, 11:09 am

Somewhere over the Atlantic, Hassan al-Zaid was trying to stretch his legs. He had left Bogotá with no trouble and was now just a couple of refueling stops away from his final destination. He had been airborne for a few hours already, but his trip to Pakistan would take many more. With a baseball cap pulled over his eyes, he tried his best to get some more sleep but he was not one to be able to rest easily on airplanes. In addition, the enormity of his endeavor was sinking in more and more. Knowing that he was finally on his way to Pakistan and the nervous excitement of hopefully connecting with as-Sirat kept him up. But taking any sleeping aids was out of the question because he could not afford drowsiness.

Countless scenarios of what would happen upon his arrival kept swirling around in his head and prevented him from dozing off. His thoughts again went to his parents, hoping that they would be okay. Hassan knew that the shock must have been hard on them and he didn't want them to suffer. But in any war there was collateral damage.

***

Because the news was so significant, one of the couriers had brought a video tape of al-Jazeera broadcasting Hassan al-Zaid's confession to Omar Bashir right away. The as-Sirat leader retreated to his private quarters deep below Andan and watched it twice, stunned by what he was seeing.

For his purposes, the tape was priceless. Though as-Sirat recruited its fighters predominantly in Muslim countries, every now and then there were Europeans who joined the cause. His group had had success with Muslim populations in the United Kingdom, and Andan also sometimes housed fighters from Chechnya and the former Yugoslavian republics.

But this was different. The United States was the great devil, the main enemy. To have a normal, young American not only wanting to join the cause but also carrying out an attack against his country on his own was truly a gift from Allah. While there had been Americans arrested for allegedly wanting to strike against their own country, none of them had been associated with as-Sirat and, much to Omar Bashir's regret, none of them had been successful. While he wanted as-Sirat to remain the largest and most dangerous group fighting the United States and prided himself on being America's enemy number one, he really did not care who struck the great Satan. As long as U.S. citizens were killed, he was happy.

Early on, after the U.S. attack on Afghanistan, there had been one young American caught with the Taliban, but he was just a dumb kid who had not known what he was getting into. Any other subsequent efforts to recruit Americans had been unsuccessful. This was different. This was a young American making an informed decision after the battle had been waging for years.

Just as the United States had been completely unable to infiltrate as-Sirat and only occasionally managed to get someone involved with the Taliban to give up relatively useless information, Bashir and his group had been largely unable to penetrate from within the fortress that was America.

It had always been much more difficult to get his men into the United States than any other country, especially after the attacks of 2001. While Europe's immigration policies had allowed a small but steady stream of his men to legally move there, the same had not been true for the U.S.

Still, there were a handful of as-Sirat sleepers in the United States, pretending to live normal lives while only waiting for a chance to give theirs in the fight against America. These men had to be extraordinarily careful and communicating with them had become very difficult because of the surveillance of phone networks and the Internet. Omar Bashir's thoughts again turned to the loyal soldier who would soon lead his group's greatest attack yet. He had just had the latest message sent to this man. In it, he had raised the possibility that the Washington attack would cause a delay of their own plans. If America was on guard, it would be more difficult to carry out the strike, so it would be better to wait until the great devil was sleeping again.

The as-Sirat leader closed his eyes and allowed his mind to envision what would happen if others were to follow Hassan's appeal to Muslims. Maybe this young man's heroic act would finally give as-Sirat a foothold in America. Instead of smuggling in fighters illegally through Mexico and risking that missions would be derailed by the immigration police or false documents, as-Sirat fighters with American passports would be able to inflict untold damage on the United States. Omar Bashir and his lieutenants had drawn up plans for several attacks, hoping to exploit vulnerabilities, such as the one they believed to have discovered at nuclear plants. Finding more people like this young man would allow the fight against the main enemy to be taken to another level. As-Sirat would be able to strike more often and at a grander scale.

It would also force the enemy to spend more resources within its own borders as opposed to now, when the entire might of the U.S. counterterrorism apparatus was focused on fighting as-Sirat abroad. If there would be a greater threat from within the United States, money and manpower would have to be spent to combat it.

The as-Sirat leader called his deputies to his chamber and together they watched the video again.

"Allahu Akbar," mumbled Khalid el-Jeffe, as-Sirat's second in command. "Allah has given us a great gift." Though it was already late at night in Andan, the five men deliberated for hours on how they could best capitalize on the latest development.

Thursday, 2:57 pm ET

East Lansing, Michigan – While most people in the United States were shocked and outraged at the bus attack, Shareef Wahed was not among them. Of course he had loudly lamented the bombing and condemned Hassan al-Zaid.

"That is not what Islam is about," he had said repeatedly over the past 24 hours when conversation inevitably turned to the attack. Several of his fellow graduate students had expressed their sympathies, telling him that it was unfair that Muslims like Wahed might feel a backlash because of the actions of one member of his faith.

"It is good of you to think of me at this time," he had responded in his accented English, "but let's all pray for the victims and their families."

On the inside, though, Shareef Wahed had first rejoiced when he had heard of the attack and then spent a sleepless night worrying about how the bombing would affect his own mission.

After his morning class, a lecture on advanced physics, he had driven the nearly 90 miles to Detroit, which had one of the largest Muslim populations in the United States. The as-Sirat sleeper was careful to obey all traffic laws and parked his car at a mall far from the city center. He then took a bus to a completely different area of the city and made his way to an Internet cafe.

There, he logged into a hotmail account. There was a new account each month to avoid being tracked. No e-mails were ever sent or received by any of them.

Instead, when he wanted to get a message out, he simply typed it up, using code language, and then saved it as a draft. The recipient would then log onto the same account, read the message and delete the draft. Every account was used just once a month, always on the second Thursday, and they rotated among several providers of free Internet e-mail accounts.

For this month, the login name was Lech_W1983@hotmail.com. The code was to use the first name and first initial of the last name of all male Nobel Peace Prize winners in order, starting in 1901, and then adding the year in which they had won the award. The password was the last name of the winner spelled backwards plus the year in which they had won minus 14. In this case Aselaw1969.

Shareef Wahed opened the saved draft.

> *"Dear Andrew, the doctors said that it may be too early to allow Uncle Bryon to travel.*
> *Maybe we should push the visit back a month or so and see how he is feeling then. I am sure the others will understand.*
> *Give my best to Emma.*
> *George"*

Wahed read the message twice. The text had been composed in Pakistan by an as-Sirat member whose native language was English and who received his instructions directly from Omar Bashir. Just in case this type of communication would find its way into America's surveillance net, they did not want to be tripped up by using poor grammar. Wahed read the message a third time, just to be sure, and then deleted the draft and emptied the trash. Then he deleted all Internet cookies, cache and browsing history. Lastly, he emptied the trash again. Confident that his presence had been erased, he left the Internet cafe.

It looked like the operation would be pushed back. He was disappointed but also understood the need to be careful. Success was more important than speed. Still, he had waited many years for a moment that was now so close and he wished that he would not have to wait any longer than he had to.

He did not have to respond. The fact that the message was deleted next time the account was checked from Pakistan would be answer enough.

Shareef Wahed made his way back to the car and drove toward the campus of Michigan State University. He had lived there for several years now, studying nuclear physics. The university had an outstanding program in that field and it was a bonus for him to be close to the large Muslim population of Detroit and the proximity to Canada was also a plus. It might allow him to flee the United States should his cover ever be blown.

He had grown up in Jordan and began his studies there before joining as-Sirat. After proving himself during his training in Afghanistan, Omar Bashir had selected him for the current mission.

Though he only stood at 5'4", Shareef Wahed was carrying the heavy burden of the hopes of as-Sirat's leaders on his slender shoulders. He was to oversee the greatest strike in history, an attack that was sure to plunge America into chaos.

Shareef Wahed entered the United States on a student visa and now, several years later, he was close to his doctorate degree in nuclear physics. He suspected there were some others like him, just waiting in the U.S. for their time to strike.

During his time in America, he had been a model citizen but, in order to avoid suspicion, a poor Muslim. To keep his cover as a moderate believer of Islam, he would occasionally have a drink and did not partake in all of the daily prayers. He was forced to curse his as-Sirat brothers when the subject of terrorism was raised and, when he became an American citizen a year ago, had to pledge allegiance to the great enemy. He could not wear the traditional clothing he liked or even grow a beard. Instead he had to attend basketball games and cheer for the Spartans. Occasionally, he had even accompanied the people who thought they were his friends to Christian church services.

"You will be forced to live the life of an infidel," Omar Bashir had told Wahed before he left Afghanistan many years ago. "It will require great strength to do things you do not want to do. But you have to become one of them to defeat the Americans. Allah willing, you will be rewarded for your sacrifices in paradise."

His leader had also joked that his life in America might turn him against his brothers.

"Maybe you will grow fat eating cheeseburgers and take a blond wife who will not wear a burka and insist on driving and working," Omar Bashir had said.

That concern, even though it was only voiced as a joke, was unnecessary. If anything, Wahed's hatred of America and the infidels only deepened. He loathed the country and its people. Fat and arrogant, they stood by as his brothers were oppressed. They pretended to believe in a God, but the country was clearly the most godless place on earth.

Throughout pretending to be someone he was not and despising all of the people he studied and socialized with, the thing that motivated Shareef Wahed was that one day, he would lead proud fighters in a mission of unrivaled magnitude, give his life for the cause and Allah would forgive him for not being able to be a dutiful Muslim all these years. That day was now close. The time until the attack was not measured anymore in years or even months. Instead it was now just weeks away and soon it would be merely days. His dark eyes sparkled when he thought of the prospect. Then he looked at the speedometer of his car. He was traveling a couple of miles above the speed limit and immediately slowed down. Though he was now a U.S. citizen, he aimed to never attract any attention. Who knows what could happen.

While most of his communication was done through the e-mail system, he had met a couple of times during conferences abroad with other as-Sirat members who would also play a role in the plot. It had felt so good to see one of his brothers and discuss the plan. Soon, the first fighters would arrive and make their way to Chicago where they would meet up before the attack on the Braidwood nuclear power plant. At least two other men with knowledge of nuclear power plants would join the attack though he did not know their names yet. That way, they could accomplish the task of overriding the automatic security systems and hopefully get the core to melt down. If that did not work, they would try to release as much radioactive material as possible. In any case, casualties should be enormous, with the wind carrying death to Chicago.

***

Chris Stevenson returned to his office following another press conference. The task of briefing the media had again fallen to the FBI director, but at least this time he got backup from Homeland Security Secretary Alicia DeBerg.

A man used to success, Stevenson had looked weary at the podium, a fact that was not lost on his packed audience of reporters and made its way into several of their articles.

"Stevenson appeared tired and frustrated at a press conference that saw two top officials get grilled over the security lapses that allowed Hassan al-Zaid to flee the country," the Associated Press said in its story.

The FBI director had announced that evidence suggested that the suspect managed to leave the country. It was little more than confirmation of something that had become clear when a planeload of agents had taken off from Washington to fly to Nassau.

Following the announcement, he and DeBerg had been quizzed by reporters over how a 21-year-old had been able to foil the entire U.S. law enforcement and homeland security apparatus.

With no good answers, both officials had grown somewhat frustrated with the questions, leading to an increasingly tense press conference.

DeBerg took the brunt of the criticism, having to defend the decision not to close Dulles Airport after the attack. The fact was that she had wanted all Washington area airports closed but was overruled by the president, who decided that only Reagan National would be shut down right after the explosion.

Obviously, as a Cabinet member, DeBerg deflected all blame from the commander-in-chief throughout the press conference.

"In a situation like this, we have to constantly weigh the level of the threat with the inconvenience to public life and the disruption of commerce. What terrorists want to accomplish is to interrupt our life and to scare us. We felt it was best to immediately establish a wide perimeter around Washington and placed great confidence in our airport security," DeBerg had said. "I would like to remind you that there has not been an airline incident in quite some time. While it is truly unfortunate that the suspect has eluded us so far and while it is easy to second guess our decisions after the fact, we took what we believed to be the best course of action for the country at the time."

The entire press conference led to a series of stinging headlines such as "Sweeney administration rattled" and "Homeland Security under fire."

Reporters had resorted to writing such stories because there was very little news to report, apart from that the intelligence community would play a greater role in the search for Hassan al-Zaid because he was now out of the country. While any threat to homeland security usually led to a large bump in the approval rating of a sitting president, flash polls and online surveys showed that the country was clearly unhappy with the bungled response.

***

President Sweeney's visit to the mosque on Massachusetts Avenue had been largely uneventful. A few people had protested outside the security perimeter, holding signs with disparaging comments about Islam, but all in all it had been a good event. The network coverage had been highly favorable, as his advisers thought it would be. However, Sweeney knew that this was not about polling numbers or his popularity.

During the short drive back to the White House, he reflected on what he viewed to be one of his most important tasks in the coming days. He had to do everything he could to keep the country together and prevent the rift between Muslims and other Americans from widening.

The motorcade streaked by some cheering tourists. It was important for the president to be seen out and about, not hidden away at an undisclosed location. Sweeney had to show the country that there was nothing to be afraid of.

In the few minutes it had taken to get back home, it had gotten visibly darker. That meant little to the president, who knew that he would have to keep working for hours. It would be another long night for him.

***

Alan ended the day zero for three with regard to being able to discuss his literary aspirations during his television appearances. He was on his way home after the last taping, an MSNBC show featuring top newsmakers. Alan was sitting in the back of the town car that was taking him home to Virginia, contemplating the roller coaster ride of the past 36 hours. It also began to dawn on him that his 15 minutes of fame were over. He had been a novelty right after the attack – the guy who saw the bombing happen and walked away unscathed. But, of course, he had very little else to contribute. So after recounting that split second in which he saw the explosion, there was really nothing else he could say, apart from praising the quick response of the military. On all three shows, he was asked if he had done anything differently the previous day, something that might have delayed him and therefore saved his life. But there really was nothing, making him an utterly boring talk show guest after he gave his brief eye-witness account of the attack.

Things on the set of "The View" had been crazy. After engaging him in conversation for a few minutes to get him to recount his story, the hosts had spent the rest of the time fighting, with one of them arguing that the Sweeney administration had made the country vulnerable by cutting back homeland security funds and relaxing several other policies that, according to the president, had infringed on people's civil liberties. The other hosts had reacted vocally and a shouting match erupted.

Alan had taken the advice of Art Kempner, who had warned him to stay out of any kind of political arguments while on the air. This, the reporter had cautioned, would only lead to trouble. There were already enough Washington Post reporters who frequented the airwaves and were only too happy to voice their political views, a fact Art despised. He believed that his sole responsibility was to report the facts and dig for stories that might otherwise go untold. Sadly, with reporters wanting to get their names and faces out there, Art's view was quickly becoming a minority opinion.

Alan had heeded the advice. The veteran reporter had not steered him wrong yet and was the main reason why Alan had almost doubled his yearly salary in a span of two days. So while his short time in the spotlight might be over, he had at least cashed in.

As a sign of gratitude, Alan had invited the reporter to a dinner that he had put together to celebrate "Stayin' Alive," according to the evite he sent out to some friends.

"It's just the theme of the evening," he had told Art with a wink. The hippieish copy editor and the Pulitzer Prize winner had found out that they very much enjoyed talking to each other despite all of their differences. "You don't have to show up in 70s clothing. I also invited some of my best friends. I'll have to warn you, though. Most of them are avid conspiracy theorists and they will probably have endless questions for you or suggestions of things you should cover."

To the reporter, this actually sounded like a nice break after two busy days and he had accepted, though he rejected Alan's offer to buy him "a new TV or a Playstation" for helping him get the appearance fees.

"I couldn't work a Playstation if my life depended on it," Art had said. "It was my pleasure to help and you are an enjoyable young man. I'll gladly come to dinner and I'm even looking forward to your conspiracy theorist friends, but there is no need to make a fuss about me helping you."

So the dinner was set at Alan's favorite Mexican place in the shopping area of Shirlington, just about five minutes from the Pentagon. It would be his first chance to catch up with some of his buddies after the whirlwind of excitement from the previous days. That, it appeared, would now be over.

Alan turned to the driver, who had left him alone to his thoughts after a couple of attempts to start small talk had failed.

"What do you do when your 15 minutes of fame are over?" he asked.

"Man, you should be happy about it," the driver responded. "Who wants to put up with all that hassle? Whenever I drive a celebrity, people always put cameras in their faces and don't give 'em a moment of peace and quiet. Not much of a life if you ask me."

"I suppose you have a point," Alan responded.

The car pulled up in front of his apartment building. Alan pulled out a ten and handed it to the chauffeur.

"Thanks, man," the driver said. "See, I'm happy you're not a big shot. Those assholes never tip. You have yourself a good night."

**

Though the DNI had practically lived in his office since the attack, it was necessary for McClintock to make an appearance at the cocktail party in Georgetown. It was the typical "Inside the Beltway" gathering of administration officials, ambassadors, lobbyists, lawmakers and their staffers, other "famous for DC types" and, of course, a couple of gossip reporters who had finagled their way to an invite. Washington's rich and famous always liked to get their names into the news as having hosted a party that had attracted other rich and famous Washingtonians. In this case, a DC socialite, who never even thought twice about postponing the event in light of the national tragedy that had taken place the day before, was pleased to see that her gathering had attracted one of the men of the hour and that the DNI was making an appearance despite his obvious obligations to the country.

McClintock politely declined all requests to comment on the crisis and instead withdrew to a corner of the room to talk business with a senior member of the Armed Services Committee. Between hors d'oeuvres and his customary pink lemonade, the subject of the attack came up in that conversation and the DNI, a little too loudly, offered his own commentary on the situation.

"I tell you what," the grizzled intelligence veteran confided to the Mississippi Republican. "When they find this kid, I hope they give me a few hours with him in a locked room with no cameras. I'll make Abu Ghraib look like spring break for him."

A gossip reporter for the congressional publication The Hill was well within earshot of the remark and, within the hour, thehill.com splashed across its website what McClintock had said. Minutes later, the Drudge Report linked to the article, also displaying the full quote.

It was picked up by the cable news networks and widely interpreted as yet another sign that the administration was rattled by its own failures.

Several pundits predicted that heads would soon begin to roll. It was part of politics. When things went bad, somebody had to take the fall and speculation began who it would be. In this case, the FBI Director and Homeland Security Secretary DeBerg were emerging as the early favorites.

***

Stevenson had just concluded the last of the meetings he had scheduled well into the evening and was in the process of going over the day's events with his chief of staff when his office phone rang. The display showed an internal number.

"Please give me some good news," Stevenson said in answering. He listened intently before interrupting the speaker, Deputy FBI Director Aaron Slattery.

"No, Aaron, you must have misunderstood. I said: 'Please give me some good news,' not: 'Why don't you add another headache to everything that is going on'," he said -- a feeble attempt at humor that was nevertheless rewarded with a chuckle from his deputy. "Listen, I'm still in my office, why don't you swing by so that we can discuss it. I'll see you in a bit."

He hung up the phone and immediately picked it back up and punched the speed dial number for the White House.

"This is FBI Director Stevenson," he said. "Who is still there?"

Fortunately, the White House chief of staff was also still at work.

"Farouk al-Zaid had a mild heart attack," Stevenson told her. "As you might know, he and his wife have been placed in voluntary protective custody in one of our facilities in Virginia. That is where they were when it happened.

"I don't need to tell you that this already looks pretty bad for us and it would look even worse if something serious were to happen to him. From what it sounds, though, they caught it right away and might actually have saved Mr. al-Zaid's life. But try to explain that to people who already hate us. They will believe that we tortured him to get information or something."

"Do you think I need to tell the president about this now?" the chief of staff asked.

"He's been quite insistent on wanting to be kept in the loop on any development, so I'd go ahead and tell him," Stevenson replied, just as Deputy FBI Director Aaron Slattery entered his office. "My deputy just arrived, so I should have additional information shortly, just in case the president wants to know more. I doubt it, in this case, but better to tell him too much than too little."

The FBI Director hung up the phone, looked at Slattery and took out his wallet. He removed a $20 bill and put it on his desk.

"Seriously Aaron, I'll give you $20 bucks if you give me some good news," he said with a weak smile. "God knows I could use some."

"Well, I guess the good news is that you can keep your twenty," Slattery responded and the two top FBI officials shared a brief laugh.

"Actually," Slattery added, "This could have been a lot worse. The doctors said that, because we had a medical team on site, we prevented a more serious problem. Mr. al-Zaid should be just fine in a few days. He'll have top doctors and nurses with him 24/7 and no expense will be spared to make sure he gets better."

"Poor guy," Stevenson said. "I can't imagine what he must feel like after finding out that his son is a terrorist."

The FBI, based on the initial interrogation in Egypt, all available evidence and follow-up interviews, including lie detector tests that the al-Zaids had consented to, was convinced that Hassan's parents had no idea about what their son had planned to do before leaving on their trip. It looked like he had wanted to strike when they were safely out of the way.

Slattery nodded.

"My son was caught shoplifting when he was in high school," he said. "That was 15 years ago and I still remember the feeling when they told me about it. I can't fathom what it must be like for the al-Zaids right now.

"You spend your whole life trying to raise your son the right away and then he turns out to be all kinds of fucked up, killing his own people and causing his parents unspeakable grief. He ended up almost killing his dad, too. The way I see it, Hassan is responsible for this heart attack. I hope we catch him alive so that he has to face his parents and not just justice."

"At this point, I just hope we get him … dead or alive," Stevenson said.

Omar Bashir had wasted little time after watching Hassan al-Zaid's confession to put together a message of his own. His audio tape, which messengers would take from Andan to Islamabad and from there get it into the hands of al-Jazeera, praised the attack and the attacker.

"A new phase in our fight against the oppressors has begun," the as-Sirat leader said. It was the second take of the message. Buoyed by the events of the past couple of days, Omar Bashir had been too excited when they began recording, going on for too long about the evil United States. This message needed to be relatively short and concise. The as-Sirat leader never worked off a script, relying instead on his natural oratory skills.

"America should take notice that its own people are turning on their country. First, it will be one, then it will be dozens, later it will be hundreds and soon it will be an army of those who will rise to take on the great devil from within."

Though his English was fairly good, Omar Bashir's messages were always delivered in Arabic. After all, their main target was not the United States but rather young Muslims.

"I call on the faithful to rise against the enemy, not only in America but also anywhere else where those following the true religion are oppressed. We have seen that one determined man striking from within can rattle the enemy. Imagine what thousands could do."

Omar Bashir and his top lieutenants had agreed to put out a tape quickly. The aim was to get it aired while the attacker was still at large. Sadly, they feared that Hassan al-Zaid would likely be caught soon or die a martyr's death. In fact, they believed that, if it was the Americans who caught him, they would kill him immediately instead of risking a trial during which his side would be heard.

The same messenger who was to take the tape to Islamabad had also brought news from Pakistan's capital. Apparently, Hassan al-Zaid had inquired years ago about where he should go if he wanted to make contact with as-Sirat.

Though the messenger had few details, it seemed that, following the dismissal from his university sports team, he had reached out to some of the people who had praised him on message boards that were sympathetic of as-Sirat's cause. One of the men he had contacted, the owner of a Pakistani restaurant in Anaheim, indeed had some ties to people associated with the group and Hassan al-Zaid had asked him whom he should get in touch with if he ever wanted to be more "directly of service" to as-Sirat. Not wanting to compromise himself too much, the restaurant owner was vague in his answers but, after meeting several times with Hassan al-Zaid and believing that he was serious about possibly joining as-Sirat, he gave the young man a couple of contacts who might be able to help him should he ever be in Pakistan.

After realizing that it was Hassan al-Zaid who had carried out the Washington attack and managed to flee the country, the restaurant owner drove to Tijuana, Mexico, visited an Internet cafe, and used a new skype account and a prepaid credit card, to place a call to

Islamabad. As carefully as possible, he told one of his contacts that it might be possible that Hassan al-Zaid would try to get in touch with him and provided as much background as he could without naming names. The contact in Islamabad, a teacher at a madrasah, had then passed on that information to someone else, who had told the messenger about it.

Upon learning the news, Omar Bashir and Khalid el-Jeffe debated what should be done if, against all odds, Hassan al-Zaid were to manage to escape to Pakistan and make contact with as-Sirat. Both men agreed that the young American would be a tremendous asset to the group, mainly as a public relations tool but also as someone who had spent his entire life in the United States and could help them understand the enemy better. Though they felt that the chance was very small that Hassan would make it to Pakistan safely, the two men allowed themselves to dream. It could be done and would be a tremendous victory for as-Sirat.

They decided that, should he make it to Islamabad, they would keep Hassan there for a day to be certain that there were no pursuers, have all of his belongings destroyed to make sure he could not be identified through them and then get him to Andan as quickly as possible.

They both realized that a video tape with Omar Bashir and Hassan al-Zaid, the two most wanted men on the face of the world, would not only be a powerful image but also a slap in the face of the Americans.

The U.S. government had announced the previous day that it would pay $25 million to anybody who could provide information that would lead to the arrest of Hassan al-Zaid, the same amount offered for the capture of Omar Bashir and $5 million more than for

Khalid el-Jeffe. It could be a great coup for as-Sirat to present both of them on one tape, showing that America was powerless to capture either of them.
"You have been with The Path for 20 years, Khalid," Omar Bashir told his friend and closest adviser. "This man has been with as-Sirat for less than a week and is worth more than you. I worry about you, my friend." Both men laughed, giddy with the recent developments and the upcoming attack on the nuclear plant, and then discussed how a successful escape could also show other Muslims in the U.S. who might contemplate taking action in the name of as-Sirat that it was possible to hit America and then get away.
The potential benefits of Hassan's attack were endless and the more Omar Bashir and el-Jeffe talked about it, the greater the opportunities seemed.

***

In his latest story on the manhunt, Art Kempner, citing two high-ranking but unnamed intelligence sources, wrote that Hassan al-Zaid had escaped from the Bahamas to Bogotá. According to the article, a Bahamian fisherman had also come forward, in return for immunity and a reward, testifying that he had smuggled the suspect back into the U.S. a week ago. With that piece of the puzzle in place, the FBI had been able to put together how Hassan al-Zaid had managed to flee the country with relative ease.
A lifetime in journalism had given Art some of the best sources in the business. He thought of them as more than people he contacted for stories. Some of them were friends, others were buddies and he often

supplied them with more information than he received. Above all, his sources knew they could trust him to never burn them.

It were those relationships that allowed Art to shed light on what was going on at the highest and lowest levels of government. In this case, two high-ranking intelligence officials had spilled the beans.

Art had long sought to figure out what got people to tell reporters things that they were not meant to pass on and there was a long list of reasons. Of course, sometimes leaks were authorized to get out certain information. But mostly, people were just not good at keeping secrets. Often he was approached by someone who was disgruntled or disillusioned for some reason or another and telling a story they were not supposed to tell was their way of payback. Art was very careful with those kind of sources. He did not want to be an instrument of their frustration or vengeance.

Other sources were acting out of idealism. They were a type of whistleblower, only did they not go to the proper authorities within their agency or company but rather contacted Art to report some sort of wrongdoing. Those sources often led to great scoops. What he liked best was to put together the pieces of a puzzle by talking to countless people and sifting through documents, each bringing him a step closer to finding out what was going on. Often he would take his newest piece of information or a hunch to one of his best sources and they would confirm whether he was on the right track. Sometimes it felt as though they were rewarding him for doing things the right way and working tirelessly to dig up something that somebody else had covered up.

In this case, though, things had been much easier. Both of his sources had given him a scoop because they were convinced that the information about Bogotá would come out soon enough. In addition, both of the members of the intelligence community had said that it would be good for this piece of news to get out as quickly as possible.

"We sure ain't close to finding this son of a bitch, maybe somebody in South America will," one of them had said.

The quote was off the record, but not the information, so Art was the first to break this piece of news.

***

The sophistication of the escape fueled FBI Director Stevenson's belief that the terrorist must have had outside help. With the Bureau increasingly on the sidelines, he decided to steer additional resources to a task force examining that possibility. He hoped that, if accomplices could be found, they could be used to track Hassan al-Zaid. Mindful of the president's request to keep a tight lid on things, he selected a team of senior agents that he deemed most trustworthy.

"I want no leaks and you report back only to me," he had told them repeatedly. "I just want you guys to figure out if it is even possible for this kid to pull off the attack without help."

As a starting point, Stevenson gave the team a copy of a draft report on Hassan al-Zaid that some of the Bureau's best investigators had put together and that he had just received.

Now, the FBI director sat on the couch in his office, the only place in his office with anything that could be described as having "a view," and also studied the report.

Ever since he had become the lone suspect, dozens of FBI field agents had left no stone unturned to find out everything they could about Hassan al-Zaid to better understand his motives and possibly find clues regarding his whereabouts or associates. They had talked to family members, friends, teammates, professors and neighbors. In addition, the investigators had studied any recoverable document on his computer, any correspondence they could get their hands on and even Hassan al-Zaid's college papers. They had gone through credit card and bank statements, phone and library records. They sifted through any database imaginable to see if the name Hassan al-Zaid showed up anywhere.

While this effort remained a work in progress, Stevenson had been given periodic updates and now held in his hands the first comprehensive report on what the investigation had uncovered.

After sifting through the document, the FBI director was stunned and mesmerized by its findings.

The report basically said that it appeared as though Hassan al-Zaid had been living his life over the past couple of years mainly for the purpose of training and planning for the attack and the subsequent escape.

The agents had found out that the suspect had been a popular, fun-loving and completely normal kid in high school. Hassan al-Zaid was an excellent student and, as a standout athlete, he had enjoyed great popularity, many friends and several girlfriends. His life was that of a completely ordinary American teenager, at least that of a popular standout athlete. Hassan al-Zaid loved sports and was a fan of the New York Yankees, the Green Bay Packers and the Chicago Bulls. During the soccer off-season, he would play tennis and pickup hoops. He enjoyed going to the movies, loved video games and went to parties, where he would have an occasional beer but never got drunk. By all accounts, he had never used drugs or smoked.

Unanimously, all of the people who had only known Hassan al-Zaid in high school and were not in touch with him in college, such as some of his friends, teammates and teachers, said that they did not believe that Hassan was capable of carrying out the bombing. Separately, several of them had told investigators that the idea was preposterous.

Then his life changed drastically when he moved to UCLA. People still in touch with him then said Hassan al-Zaid quickly became a different person.

Shortly after starting college, he had told his parents and some friends back home that he began attending a Los Angeles mosque, an experience he at the time described as "eye-opening" in letters and e-mails. Investigators had been unable to figure out which mosque Hassan had initially attended, one of the many areas in which the report was still incomplete.

According to his credit card bills from that time and library records, he read many books on Islam during his freshman year and also took a class on the subject in his second semester. Investigators had contacted the professor of the course and also found a couple of students who attended it. They all said that they remembered Hassan well because he was very argumentative in class to the point of being combative, lamenting that Islam was being taught from a "western perspective."

As opposed to the people who knew him before going to college, those who met him after he moved to Los Angeles did not dismiss the notion that he could have become a terrorist.

It was as though they were investigating two completely different people. One was a normal American high school kid, the other a terrorist-in-training.

The FBI field agents were unable to locate anybody at UCLA, apart from his teammates on the soccer team, who ever called Hassan al-Zaid a friend. His coach and several of the other players praised Hassan's work ethic and said he was easy to get along with in his first year and never complained about sitting on the bench as a freshman.

They did mention that he rarely went out with the team or attended parties. Also, nobody the investigators contacted ever remembered seeing Hassan drink alcohol. In a change from his life in Virginia, he now performed the five prayers that devout Muslims observe daily.

Bill Cusack, who roomed with him when the team was on the road, said the prayers or any other part of Hassan al-Zaid's religion were never an issue and that the two never had any problems during his freshman year.

However, the members of the soccer team all told the FBI that they noticed a change in Hassan in his second year at UCLA. He had become more aggressive and would often argue with teammates about religion and world affairs.

At the same time, Hassan al-Zaid's behavior also changed in other ways, according to the documents the FBI agents had examined. He had purchased some books on explosives, martial arts and weapons. In addition he had used his credit card several times to visit the Los Angeles Gun Club.

Shortly before he refused to play against the Israeli soccer team and consequently lost his spot on the team and his scholarship, those who knew him back then said that he had become even more withdrawn.

His parents had told the FBI that his dismissal from the soccer squad had led them to have several long discussions with their son. As an upper middle class family, they could afford to continue paying for Hassan's education but both parents said it was at that point that they started to get worried about the path on which he seemed to be embarking.

He assured them that there was no need to be concerned, arguing that he had just taken a principled stand and vowing that he would be fine and his grades would not suffer. From that point on, his contact with his parents grew more sparse. One FBI psychologist involved in putting together the report had said the case was a "textbook example" of how young Muslims slowly become radicalized by severing the bonds that had tied them to another life. His parents had simply chalked up to the decreasing contact to their son having established his own life in Los Angeles. However, the investigators were not able to determine that he had much of a life at all. His landlord told the FBI that he was gone almost every weekend but he had no idea what he was up to. He often left with a large backpack and the landlord had just assumed that Hassan al-Zaid simply enjoyed the outdoors.

It was at that time, about 20 months before the attack, that Hassan's behavior changed again. He purchased some books on how to "disappear" in the United States and, shortly after that, stopped using his credit cards and didn't leave much of a paper trail. He only began using the cards again to amass as much money as possible in the past few weeks.

"It must be assumed that al-Zaid has been planning this attack and his escape for more than two years," the report concluded. "We have been unable to find any close contacts and the few acquaintances he maintained do not appear to have any association to radical Islamists. It is likely that al-Zaid used a variety of tools to acquire the kind of training that as-Sirat members usually get in camps in Pakistan and Afghanistan."

The FBI director studied the report carefully. It had answered some of his questions but raised others. It certainly gave somewhat of an explanation for why Hassan al-Zaid had not been caught. He seemed incredibly disciplined, well-organized and dedicated. But the document provided no answers about what triggered his change in personality or why he decided to attack the United States.

It was difficult for Stevenson to understand how a person could live years of their life only for a single purpose. Hassan al-Zaid had been living in the United States, even if it was on the fringe of society, biding his time, preparing and waiting for the right time to strike.

The FBI director shuddered at the thought of others like him being out there.

***

As always, the chili con queso and the salsa had been fantastic and Alan and his guests were waiting for their main courses while sipping on some Coronas. There were nine of them and they were sitting in a back room to give the other patrons some peace and quiet. Large groups tended to be loud. A tenth chair was still empty. Art Kempner had gotten some new information that he had to add to his latest article. He called and said he would be a few minutes late but also expressed hope that he would likely not be called away from Alan's celebratory shindig.

The reporter arrived along with the food and Alan tapped his fork against the bottle in front of them. The chatter seized.

"Guys, I'm pleased to introduce Art Kempner. He's just some guy who works with me at the Post," Alan said, as though the Pulitzer Prize winner needed an introduction in this circle of political nerds. "He is the main reason why I'll be able to pick up the check for all of you tonight, so I invited him to our weekly conspiratorial gathering. Please take it easy on him."

"Hear, hear," the eight other men said and toasted to both Alan and Art.

"So, by 'Take it easy on him,' do you mean we shouldn't ask him about why he has never written about the black helicopter program?" a guy who looked like he was still in college and wore a George Washington University t-shirt, said. Everybody laughed.

"Something like that," Alan smiled. He pointed to the aluminum foil wrapped around the man's burrito. "At least wait to ask until you can use that to make a hat so the government can't read your thoughts. We'd hate to lose you to some secret prison in Utah."

Art, who knew from the moment he walked in that he would enjoy the evening with these guys, chimed in. "You conspiracy theorists baffle me. Nothing you guys say ever makes any sense," the reporter said with a straight face as the room fell into an uncomfortable silence. Art extended the pause for as long as he could by letting his eyes sweep across the room before continuing with a grin.

"Everybody knows that you make the anti-brain reading hats from saran wrap, not aluminum foil, and that the secret prison is in Idaho and not in Utah. Duh!"

They all erupted into laughter that wiped out the tension from a moment before. The joke also let them know that they didn't have to be in awe of the great journalist.

"You guys just ask away," Art added with a smirk. "Reporters are notoriously cheap. Normally, I have to write a fluff piece for a good meal like this, so the least I can do is answer some questions in return for fajitas."

Alan gave his colleague a sad look.

"Famous last words," he said, and then everybody started talking at once, asking the Pulitzer Prize winner about warrantless wiretapping, Guantanamo, extraordinary rendition, secret prisons and government cover-ups.

"For the record, even though this is off the record," Art said, using a good reporter's customary caution, "I do not believe that the moon landing was staged, that the CIA killed Kennedy or that we blew up the World Trade Center.

"I do think," he added, "that for every major story that we uncover, there are many cover ups that never get detected, regardless of whether it is a Democrat or a

Republican in the White House. Just look at Clinton and Lewinsky or even Nixon and Watergate. Those things were more or less discovered by accident and there is a good chance neither of those scandals would ever have been reported had it not been for some fortunate breaks. I think that is a good illustration that every government at any time is engaged in some stuff that they don't want the public to find out about. And I believe that they are successful in keeping those things hidden in many cases."

"Ha, you're totally one of us," said the oldest man in the group, a guy with a full beard who looked like a more disheveled version of Karl Marx.

"Who knows?" Art replied with a wink. "I'll tell you guys another thing, though. I do believe that the public shouldn't know everything and sometimes it's good that our government keeps things secret. So I'm all for protecting the country by not revealing everything we do. But stuff like Watergate and the Lewinsky affair should come out."

"So, has anybody ever asked you not to print something in the name of national security?" It was the kid in the GW t-shirt who asked the question.

"Twice, and both times we tweaked a story a bit, but we have never just canned a story. We try to make some of these determinations beforehand," the reporter said.

The group began debating that point as another round of drinks arrived, with some of the men taking the position that elected officials are fully accountable to the public that put them in office and the others conceding that there may be instances where it could be harmful to allow the public to know all.

Then the reporter had a question.

"I'm really interested in conspiracy theories and I would like for each of you to name one thing that you think the government is covering up," Art said.

The answers came pouring in, with many of the men expressing their beliefs that various aspects of the 9-11 attacks were not what they appeared, including that a missile had struck the Pentagon and that United Flight 93 had been shot down. Other conspiracy theories included that the government had helped flood New Orleans, that voting machines were fixed to rig elections and that the government added substances to the drinking water to make its citizens sick.

"Well, at least we can all agree that this week's attack happened," Art said. He raised his glass. "I mean, our gracious host saw it happen."

"Just because Alan sees something happen doesn't mean it really did," said the GW student, mimicking somebody drinking from a bottle. "Saturday night, he was convinced that this hot brunette was into him. Turns out 'she' was a heavy metal fan named 'Chuck.' If I hadn't seen the crater myself, I would have said he was still drunk from the night before."

They all laughed again.

"I actually don't think everything about that attack adds up," the bearded man said. "I can't put my finger on it, but something doesn't seem right."

"Come on, Rick, you say that about everything," Alan interrupted the older man with a chuckle in his voice. "Last week alone, something didn't feel right to you during the episode of 'The Apprentice,' when you got a ticket for running a red light and when you thought your AT&T bill had been opened."

That remark caused another wave of laughter. The bearded man raised his arms and added to the humor by maintaining that "the envelope was glued differently than normally."

"Thanks for making my point, Steve," Alan chuckled. Art raised his arms, pleading for silence.

"I tell you what," he said. "I think that people can find inconsistencies in most things that happen. Even with 'The Apprentice,' Steve.

"Something always seems odd or a little bit off, whether it's ahead of elections or when it comes to major events like assassinations or moon landings. So how about this: Since we all know that this attack is real because Alan was right there and witnessed it, let's all look for some things that don't appear to make sense. I don't want to discourage you from looking for conspiracies, but I do want to show you that there are oddities about everything, even events we are absolutely sure of."

"We're gonna blow your mind, Mr. Skeptical. Just wait until we show you that the attack was actually a commercial for Coca Cola," Steve said, and everybody laughed again.

"How about this, then," Art offered. "We'll all spend some time trying to find something truly inexplicable or admittedly weird about this attack. Then we'll reconvene here in a few days and that time I'll pick up the tab. I think meeting you guys has given me a story idea, but I'll have to sleep on it. Of course it means you must keep your findings to yourself at first and not immediately post them on your blogs or twitters or whatever you have. And, of course, keep those saran wrap hats on so that the government doesn't find out that you're onto something."

They all agreed that it sounded like a good deal and, after checking their schedules, decided to meet for another dinner the upcoming Sunday.

***

Shareef Wahed sat in his East Lansing apartment and once again went over the planned assault of the Braidwood nuclear power plant. He never used a computer for this, relying instead on handwritten notes that he kept hidden in his residence. The chance of anybody discovering the documents and making sense of them was practically zero. Somebody would have to tear apart his place to find them. If that happened, Shareef Wahed figured that he was under arrest or dead already.

The Government Accountability Office, back when it was still called the General Accounting Office, had put together a report for Congress on nuclear power plant security. The study had found that the reactors were generally extremely poorly guarded. While the U.S. government and power companies running the plants had done very little with that information, as-Sirat used it to build its grandest plan. Among other things, GAO had found that there were often only a dozen or fewer security staff on duty at these plants.

Seeing how many of these people were often poorly trained, the as-Sirat planners had felt that overrunning the defenses of such a plant would be the easy part of such a mission. The difficulty was in picking the right target and maximizing the damage.

While it was relatively simple to scout many buildings

in the United States because they were so easily accessible to the public, getting information about nuclear power plants was more difficult. It had taken the group a year to pick the plant in the Chicago area as a good target. While most of the foot soldiers taking part in the mission would enter the United States from Mexico, the location would allow additional troops to quickly get to Chicago from Canada if necessary. After picking a primary target, Wahed had moved into position by enrolling in Michigan State University, not too far from Chicago. He was not allowed to be part of the operation that did the surveillance of the Braidwood plant. Wahed was too valuable to arouse suspicion. His only job was to learn as much about these plants as possible to figure out how he could force a meltdown once as-Sirat had taken over the reactor. He was tasked to do this without ever coming to the attention of U.S. authorities. Wahed had followed his orders with great diligence, which was one of the reasons why the attack was just now ready to be carried out even though it had first been drawn up several years ago.

In order to find out as much about Braidwood as possible, some as-Sirat's sympathizers with citizenship in countries that allowed them to enter the United States without a visa had been tasked with firsthand surveillance of the plant. Over the past few years they had visited the Chicago area disguised as tourists, trying to gather as much information about Braidwood as possible.

In addition to those efforts, as-Sirat supporters in western countries had been asked to use the Internet to put together extensive files on hundreds of potential targets. Most of these sites were actually not being considered as targets because as-Sirat leaders felt it was important to lay as many false trails as possible in case the electronic surveillance efforts of the Americans became aware of these searches.

The files had been collected by couriers and brought to Andan on flash drives. As-Sirat did not trust e-mail and rarely used the tool to communicate. At a computer in the caves below the town, Omar Bashir and his planners had a cache of hundreds of pages of documents on Braidwood that they used to plan the assault. These included maps of the area, satellite images readily available online and highly useful for putting together an attack. The power company operating the plant had even put a document with emergency measures on the Internet, likely hoping to ease the concerns of those frightened of having a nuclear reactor in their backyard. It was just another piece that would help make the planned attack more lethal. Other documents that had been useful included the personal reports of the as-Sirat spies, promotional materials from the plant itself and many more.

Of the people who were already beginning to make their way to Mexico, three would have the information of how to carry out the assault, just in case the U.S. Border Patrol managed to arrest some of the fighters. If all three of the strike team leaders would be caught, two more stood ready to fly to Canada and cross the border to the U.S. from there. All in all, 50 men would try to enter the United States. Omar Bashir felt that half that number would be sufficient to easily take over Braidwood and defend the plant long enough to complete the task, but he anticipated that not all of the men would make it to Chicago.

If everything went wrong, even ten as-Sirat fighters might get the job done, but it was better to be on the safe side regarding the number of men needed. The as-Sirat fighters would have superior training and firepower. In addition, they would have the element of surprise on their side.

Omar Bashir had initially wanted to carry out the attack on America's Independence Day but the group was simply not ready and it had been agreed to push back the assault until the end of September.

Now, it looked as though the big day would have to be delayed even further because the United States would be on guard.

In Michigan, Wahed studied his notes. He was ready and would remain so until the mission received the green light. A feeling of nervous excitement had been building within him. Everything was coming together just right. Wahed believed there was an 80 percent chance that the mission would turn out to become a complete success. In addition, even if he didn't manage to melt down the reactor core, he should be able to bypass all security systems and release enough radioactive material into the air and the water to make the area around the plant uninhabitable for years to come. If the initial assault was successful, Wahed believed that as-Sirat would manage to kill tens of thousands of people, whether directly or slowly over years to come. Maybe they should carry out the attack on Thanksgiving, when Americans celebrated the beginning of the slaughter of an entire race and stuffed their faces. Surely, security would be at a minimum on that day as everybody would want to stay home and eat all day.

Wahed beamed. He would make Allah and Omar Bashir proud.

* * *

In the last of their daily calls, DNI McClintock briefed FBI Director Stevenson on the latest information. As reported by Art Kempner, the intelligence services had indeed unearthed evidence placing Hassan al-Zaid in Colombia not long after the attack.
He had apparently used yet another passport to leave the Bahamas to fly to Bogotá. McClintock had sent over a couple of pictures, one seemingly taken from an airport security camera and another by the camera in a hotel lobby.
It was beyond Stevenson to figure out how the intelligence services were able to get their hands on the images. He figured that there was not much point in asking McClintock because he would likely not get an answer other than "that's above your pay grade," or "you don't have the security clearance for that." It was part of the constant struggle between government agencies that were trying to protect their turf, their influence and their funding instead of being completely open with each other. Of course, Stevenson also felt a bit guilty for holding back information on establishing the task force that was supposed to look into the possibility of the terrorist having had accomplices. He justified that decision with wanting to get some preliminary results first before discussing the matter with anybody else.

Friday, 1:17 am ET

Bagram Air Base, Parvan Province, Afghanistan – The squadron of U.S. terrorist hunters from Fort Bragg returned to base from another mission. This time, the special operations forces unit had engaged some Taliban fighters on the Afghan side of the border near the Khyber Pass. It was a successful quick strike mission against a small number of fighters. Their superior fire power and tactics had prevailed and four Taliban fighters were killed in the assault. The others had scattered but would certainly be back. While it was important to keep the Taliban on their toes, the special ops soldiers were beginning to get restless. It had been a long time since they had carried out a meaningful strike against as-Sirat. With a new government in place in Pakistan that appeared to prefer alienating the U.S. rather than the radical elements within its own population, there had not been a cross border excursion in over a month, and common wisdom said that all of as-Sirat's leaders were safely somewhere in Pakistan. All the U.S. was allowed to do was to fly unmanned and unarmed drones into Pakistan, but there was no way they could distinguish terrorists from regular Pakistanis. All that could be done with the drones was to take pictures of different areas in which as-Sirat leaders could be hiding and check for irregularities. Without any clues and with little help from the Pakistani government, it was like asking Mr. Magoo to pick a single person out of a crowd at a football stadium without being given a description of whom he was looking for.

Captain Ken Gorsula, who had led the mission, told his men to return to the barracks and rest while he went to the command center to report back. He also wanted to make a point to express that the men were growing increasingly frustrated with their mission assignments. They were the best of the best and had been sent to Afghanistan specifically to find and fight terrorists. Now, they were largely grounded or participated in small skirmishes with the often poorly equipped Taliban, a task that others could complete. Sadly, political realities had, in effect, clipped the wings of the 300 special operations forces soldiers at Bagram.

For Gorsula, the fight against as-Sirat had become a personal affair with the Washington attack. His mother had e-mailed to let him know that his godfather and uncle, a former Special Forces soldier and his inspiration for joining the military, was one of the victims. Gorsula had immediately requested leave, hoping to make it home in time for the funeral. With operations restricted to the Afghan side of the border, where things had been relatively quiet since many enemies had withdrawn to Pakistan, it was not like he was much use at Bagram anyways. He never anticipated that his request to go to the U.S. for a family function would be denied, but that is what happened.

Much to his dismay, Gorsula had been told nobody from special ops was allowed to leave Afghanistan at this point – undoubtedly the bone-headed idea of some suit in Washington. As though their lives didn't already suck enough. They had signed up for the special operations to do some good for their country, not to sit on their hands in Afghanistan while the terrorists were laughing their asses off in Pakistan. The guys were itching for action, Gorsula thought, and it was tough to keep them sharp in this state of limbo. Canceling all vacation requests had lowered morale even further, especially because there was no point to it. If they could not do what they were trained to do, why not let them go home and blow off some steam there.

Gorsula wished he could talk to the Pentagon suit who thought it was a good idea that he remained in Afghanistan while his family laid his only uncle to rest back home. After he got back from the debriefing, he'd let out his aggression on the battered Golden Tee machine in the arcade, Gorsula thought as he stepped into the command center.

***

It was very early in the morning on the East Coast when the two men got out of their car. After an evening that had involved some beers and led to their decision to "show these ragheads," the duo had driven from just outside of Richmond to Woodbridge. Now, they pulled a couple of gasoline canisters from the trunk of the beat up Ford Taurus. They had driven around their target a few times but had seen nothing to deter them from carrying out their plan. A couple of beers during the drive from Richmond had ensured that they were still slightly intoxicated and not once had the thought crossed their minds to turn the car around and call it a night. The stretch of Interstate 95 from Richmond to Washington was known for being closely watched by the highway patrol, especially following enactment of a law that gave Virginia some of the toughest speeding penalties in the nation. Yet the two men had not aroused suspicion. They had stayed at the speed limit all night, resisting the urge to get to their destination more quickly.

They had found their target easily, thanks to media reports and Google Maps. The house they were looking for had been all over the news recently. They figured it would be empty at this hour and were not disappointed. The forensics experts had long left the site and the owners of the house were in protective custody.

The local police department had been asked to pay special attention to the al-Zaid residence but that order was disregarded. What was the point to guard the home of a terrorist when the FBI had seemingly already removed everything that was not bolted down from there? So the two cops who were supposed to check in on the residence periodically were instead enjoying an early breakfast at an all-night diner.

This allowed the two men with their gasoline canisters to make it to the home unimpeded. After breaking a glass panel in the back door, they examined the house. "A cryin' shame that we allow anybody into this country," the taller of the men said. They found Hassan's room, recognizing it from the videotape that they had watched repeatedly, each time with growing hatred of foreigners.

"Check it out," the other man said as he urinated in the room, which was now largely empty after the forensic experts had completed their work. After leaving his mark, both of the men went downstairs into the living room and doused it with gasoline. Then they lit a newspaper they had found and tossed it into the room as they exited the house.

In the middle of the night, it took a long time before the fire was discovered and, with no other homes in danger, the fire fighters did not exactly kill themselves to get there quickly once they learned which house they were called on to save.

When the flames were finally extinguished, not much was left of Hassan's childhood home. By that time, the two men were already back in the Richmond area and congratulated each other on a job well done.

***

A like-minded man in Cleveland was not as fortunate. When he had stopped by an all-night convenience store to purchase cigarettes and restock his fridge with a case of Bush Light, he had initiated a confrontation with the Indian man behind the counter.

"That job you got should go to an American," the man, who had been unemployed for six months but would not dream to work a night shift at a 7-Eleven, said.

"I am an American, sir. My parents came here long before I was born," the clerk responded politely, hoping that his voice would not convey his fear.

"That don't make you American, you fucking terrorist," the man said before deciding that he would teach this guy a lesson. He reached across the counter and pulled the slender man over to his side before starting to pummel him with kicks and punches. Fortunately, the clerk had managed to trigger the silent alarm and it took less than two minutes for a police cruiser to arrive on the scene and arrest the attacker.

All in all, including the arson of the al-Zaid residence and the Ohio convenience store assault, there were 35 cases of crimes committed that night by people who wanted to take action against terrorists, with the worst of them resulting in an Egyptian man having to be taken to an ER after he was attacked by a group of college students in Texas.

While all of that happened, Shareef Wahed and the other as-Sirat sleepers and sympathizers inside the United States rested peacefully in their respective homes.

Friday, 6:00 am, ET

Robert McClintock had summoned the available heads
of the various U.S. intelligence agencies to his office
for an early-morning meeting. Those who could not
make it were teleconferenced in.

With Hassan al-Zaid out of the country, the burden of
finding him was being placed more and more on the
shoulders of the intelligence community.

"We're talking about a 21-year-old kid who is
thumping his nose at us," McClintock said right after
welcoming them, setting the tone for what would
quickly become a tense meeting. "Our intelligence and
law enforcement agencies will be the laughing stock of
the world if we don't find him soon."

Most of the attendees were not only worried about the
United States looking foolish but also about their own
jobs. The same people also thought that the DNI was
being unfair. If they were dealing with a lone wolf
attacker who had been planning his escape for many
months and managed to slip out of the country, it
would have been remarkable had he been found
already.

On the other hand, the various intelligence officials
also knew that perception was reality. What it came
down to was that, if the public perceived that law
enforcers and the intelligence community had failed in
this case, securing the tens of billions of dollars in
funding that they needed each year would be much
more difficult. Some congressman in a tough
reelection fight would go on a crusade against wasteful
spending and say things like: "What are we spending
all this money on intelligence gathering when we can't

even find a college kid who killed a bus full of Americans?"

So, in addition to wanting to find Hassan al-Zaid in order to bring him to justice, there were other considerations to take into account.

Maybe it were those considerations that made McClintock unreasonably harsh, the head of the State Department's Bureau of Intelligence and Research thought to himself as he listened to the DNI rant. He also believed that McClintock's tirade was not a wise move. With so many participants at this briefing, word would leak to the press that there had been a tense meeting with the various intelligence agency heads and that the DNI had lost his cool. That prediction would prove to be correct. A first account of the meeting and McClintock's blow up, written by the New York Times intelligence beat reporter, hit the web shortly after 8:00 am.

In the end, as McClintock was catching his breath, the director of Homeland Security's Office of Intelligence and Analysis, a longtime friend of the DNI, spoke up and said what many of his colleagues were thinking. "Bob, you know quite well that it will be very tough to find him in short order after he made it to South America. Unless, of course, he makes a mistake. And so far, he has not been making many mistakes."

"I don't give a shit about the difficulties. I want you to find this little fucker no matter what it costs," McClintock yelled, slamming his left fist on the heavy desk for emphasis. "Meeting adjourned."

After his chief of staff had shuffled out the visitors, the Director of National Intelligence let out a deep breath. He had not enjoyed doing this and would apologize to all of the meeting participants in due time, once they learned the truth. He hoped that they would realize then that his tirade had served a purpose. It had to appear to the world that the United States was rattled. It was all part of the plan.

McClintock checked his watch, leaned back and closed his eyes, thinking of his last meeting with Hassan al-Zaid the previous week.

"May God protect you, Hassan," he thought and said a prayer for the young man who was supposed to help him find Omar Bashir and take down as-Sirat.

According to the schedule, Hassan should be arriving in Pakistan soon. It was the latest stop in a long, long journey that was coming to an end soon ... one way or another.

Friday, 6:15 am ET

"Hey, Hassan, you got a call," the Special Forces soldier said. On the day of the attack, he had been in one of the Humvees that were remote-controlling the Metro bus and preventing bystanders to get too close to the staged attack. Alan Hausman would likely have recognized him as the man who handed him a bottle of water right after they had set off the bomb.

Hassan had been wide awake for an hour now. He had finally found some sleep and the other members of the team had let him rest as much as possible. They all knew that Hassan needed his strength now that the mission was going into its final phase.

The Gulfstream V was less than 30 minutes away from landing at a small airfield near Islamabad.

Hassan went to the back of the plane where the secure phone line was installed, plunged into one of the comfortable leather chairs in front of the row of electronic devices, and took the headset that one of the team's communications specialists handed him.

"This is Hassan."

"Hassan, this is Jack Sweeney," the man on the other end of the line said.

"Good morning, Mr. President," Hassan replied, sitting up straight even though his commander-in-chief was not able to see him.

"I just wanted to make sure I spoke to you one more time before you landed to wish you well. I'm sure you heard about your father. I'm so sorry about that but our best medical people are there for him and I have been assured that he is on track for a full recovery," the president said.

"Thank you, sir," Hassan responded. "I know everything is being done for him."

"Normally, I would say in a situation like this that a grateful nation stands behind you," the president said. "But we know that isn't true in your case."

Hassan smiled as he thought of a play on words.

"Sir, I guess in my case it is more of a hateful nation than a grateful one."

"I wish it weren't so, son. What you are doing is an exceptional act of heroism and I wish every American, instead of condemning you, knew that you are putting your life on the line for your country."

"Sir, the fact that they all hate me only means that the first phase of our plan is working. I'm not too worried about it. After all, I'm flying above Pakistan right now and the more America hates me, the safer I'll be here."

"I guess you got a point there, still ..." Sweeney's voice trailed off before he started speaking again.

"Well, I just wanted to wish you luck again. We'll do everything here to maintain your cover for as long as possible. And when it is all over, America will be as grateful to you as I already am. Those of us in the know are wishing and praying for your safety and your success."

"Thank you, Mr. President."

"No, thank you," Sweeney said. "I hope to talk to you in the White House in a few days. God bless."

The line went dead and Hassan headed back to his seat as the pilot announced that the plane was beginning its descent. A long journey was nearing its end.

***

It had been more than five years ago when Jim Hearst, Jr., a former CIA colleague who had become a congressman for his Virginia district and the senior Democrat on the House Select Committee on Intelligence, sought a private meeting with McClintock, who at the time was the number two man in the CIA. The purpose of the lunch was, according to Hearst, "to run a crazy idea by you."

The two friends had met over all-you-can-eat Brazilian steak at Fogo de Chao, a restaurant halfway between Congress and the White House on Pennsylvania Ave. It was not exactly halfway but the food was excellent, so no Member of Congress ever minded making the trip.

After the obligatory pleasantries and cheese bread, the two had settled into their private room and Hearst began talking about one of his constituents, a high school senior who had come up with an idea that the lawmaker deemed to be so interesting that he felt compelled to present it to a senior intelligence official. The lunch, scheduled for a brief 45 minutes, took more than two hours. It could have taken 10 but the restaurant was closing and McClintock had a meeting with the vice president. During the two hours, however, he listened intently to the outline of a plan that captivated him and appeared to be ridiculous one second and brilliant the very next.

"My constituent, a kid named Hassan al-Zaid, pulled me to the side after a photo-op with some of the student athletes from my district. He said he wanted to discuss a national security matter with me," Hearst began. "I had a hole in my schedule, so I thought 'Why not?' and we started talking. He began by telling me that he was a devout Muslim and a proud American. In school, he had studied the 9-11 report and kept thinking about one of the conclusions that we were lacking human intelligence in our fight against terrorism and that electronic surveillance alone would not get the job done."

McClintock nodded. It was true that the United States had been unable to penetrate as-Sirat or any other significant group of Islamic radicals. They normally got their recruits from Muslim countries and would immediately grow suspicious of anybody appearing to have American roots. It had been much easier to infiltrate the Soviet Union than as-Sirat. At least with the Soviets, you could offer bribes. Those types of incentives didn't matter to the Islamic fundamentalists. Another major problem was as-Sirat's structure. New recruits would normally first be sent to one of the many camps in Afghanistan and Pakistan. From there, they would go on to participate in terrorist missions or to fight the Americans in Afghanistan or Iraq. They would never get close to the leaders of the group. So even if the CIA would manage to find a person to get close to as-Sirat, they would likely not be able to do much damage to the organization as a whole. At best, they could expose a few terrorist camps with new recruits and instructors. Still, if those were destroyed, new ones would be built shortly and very small damage would have been done to the group as a whole.

For many years, the intelligence community had tried to figure out a way that would allow the U.S. to get an asset deep inside as-Sirat but hadn't managed to come up with anything. Two recent attempts to place someone at the periphery of the group had ended with the death of the CIA agents, putting on ice any further efforts to try to infiltrate as-Sirat. McClintock had been very much involved in the plans and losing two men, the last of whom had been found dragged to death and beheaded in Kabul, had troubled him deeply. He had convinced the CIA director to pull the plug on any other similar efforts. It simply could not be done.

"When reading the 9-11 report, Hassan for the first time thought about joining the CIA to use his background to try to infiltrate as-Sirat. He is a patriot and told me how much he is bothered by the bad name that terrorists are giving his religion.

"While he was pondering how he could best serve his country, he watched a movie with some friends in which a bank robber is holding hostages. In the movie, the hostages are exchanged with other people and that gave Hassan an idea. What if the people who were brought in were volunteers with terminal illnesses? It would take away the bank robber's leverage because his new hostages are as good as dead anyways and are just making their last weeks count in a meaningful way.

"Hassan told me that he came up with his plan right there. What if we staged a terrorist attack with him as a suspect as a way to give him credibility with as-Sirat? Having an American 'turn' on his country would be perceived as a great story by their PR machine," Hearst had said, waving away a waiter. "With all the media coverage and to be above any suspicion, we would have to make that attack as real as possible. We can't just blow up an empty building or a remote-controlled plane. There need to be surveillance tapes and other evidence so that initially nobody will doubt that there really was an attack and that Hassan was the perpetrator. It has to be very public. The entire world has to believe that this is the act of an as-Sirat sympathizer and we have to deliver a suspect to the media on a silver platter.

"To make it look as real as possible, with real victims and real grieving families, he suggested that we find volunteers with terminal illnesses who want to serve their country one last time and make the rest of their lives count," the lawmaker added. "They won't be able to tell their loved ones. In exchange, their families would be taken care of for life.

"After the staged attack, we have to let him 'escape' to Pakistan or Afghanistan and make contact with as-Sirat. He'll carry some sort of hidden homing device that will allow us to track him in the hopes that he will be taken to an as-Sirat stronghold as the guy who attacked his own country and swore allegiance to the group," Hearst said, leaning back in his chair.

"The first time I heard his idea, I thought it was interesting but could never work. I've been thinking about it ever since and, the more I do, the more I like it. I'm not even saying that it has a high rate of success or that we'll ever get much beyond the planning stage, but everything else we're doing right now in terms of trying to find Omar Bashir doesn't even get us close to him. We have tried for years and haven't had as much as a whiff of him."

The congressman had paused, taken another cheese bread and looked at his old friend.

McClintock seized the opportunity to jump in, his voice rife with sarcasm. Though some aspects of the plan had intrigued him, he was sure that he'd eventually think of many reasons why this could never work.

"So, all we really have to do is put together a massive government operation that we have to keep secret from everybody while finding a few people who don't mind getting blown to bits? Then we have to lie to the entire country for a while. And then, if we don't find somebody more suitable for the job, we have to trust some high school senior you just met to be able to infiltrate as-Sirat and then all that is left is that we have to swoop in and get Omar Bashir?" McClintock said.

"It sounds so simple that I'm shocked that we hadn't thought of it," he added. "And the best thing is that it'll cost nothing and there is no way that it could go wrong. Shit, let's put something like this together for next week, kill Omar Bashir, dismantle as-Sirat and then we never again have to worry about the threat of terrorism."

Hearst just shrugged off his friend's sarcasm.

"Funny, Bob, that's exactly how I reacted," he replied in the same tone. "And then I pulled my head out of my own ass and thought about it. You always preach this 'outside the box' thinking and here is an 'outside the box' idea. So let's at least discuss why you believe this couldn't work."

"Well, let's start out with your constituent," McClintock said. "What makes you think he is the right candidate and not one of our guys?"

"Because, as soon as our guy is declared a suspect, the media will go through every single aspect of his life. So if it's somebody who is already with the CIA, there is no way they won't find that out. This kid is a blank sheet."

Despite the sarcasm he displayed earlier, McClintock was intrigued by the idea in itself. He had been listening intently, leaning forward as though he wanted to hear the words coming out of the lawmaker's mouth a little bit sooner. The piece of lamb, his favorite dish at Fogo, was getting cold on his plate.

"I asked Hassan why it should be him, and he said that he didn't care if we did not pick him as long as there is a more qualified candidate," Hearst added. "But where will we find somebody like that? We can't even get enough Arabic speakers to translate the calls we are recording. Here, we have a volunteer who is currently in high school, a devout Muslim who is willing to spend the next couple of years to pretend to be increasingly radicalized. I thought about it a lot, and I think we can build a cover story around him that will hold up, at least for a while. And while we slowly groom him to become our terrorist, we can teach him what he needs to know with regard to espionage trade craft."

For the first time really McClintock thought that maybe there was something about the idea that could work. Maybe it could be taken and tweaked into something better. They continued debating the idea at their lunch table and the piece of lamb never got eaten. In the subsequent days and weeks, they kept talking about Hassan's idea on a regular basis, brainstorming and alternately playing devil's advocate.

But no matter how many holes they both tried to poke into that initial plan in the subsequent days and weeks, it never changed much and their discussions only helped refine it.

Eventually, they had taken the plan directly to President Sweeney, who had authorized it after much deliberation.

***

Now, four years later, they were about to find out if it would work.

McClintock was sitting in his office, waiting for the president to call. The two had been in almost constant contact to discuss what they could do to keep everything running as smoothly as it had been. They knew that, eventually, there would be problems and it was their job to identify them before they could put the mission at risk. They already had to bring in a couple of people involved in the investigation who had gotten suspicious, such as the two forensics guys from the FBI lab who were looking into the type of explosive that was used. They had been invited to the White House under the pretense that some of the president's staff wanted to be briefed on the status of the investigation.

Instead of meeting some low-level White House staffers, they had been taken to the Oval Office. There, the president had told the FBI guys that he needed to discuss a matter of national security with them and that it was their duty as patriotic Americans to change their report on the kind of explosives used in the bus bombing.

"I'm not sure if your analysis is complete yet, but I do know that both of you suspect that a military-grade explosive was used to blow up the bus," Sweeney had told the flabbergasted analysts.

"Let me spare you the suspense. The bus was blown up with the help of RDX, more specifically Composition C RDX," the president added. "It is very important that you don't pass on this information. I'm hereby classifying it and you may speak to nobody about this. The reasons for this will become apparent soon enough."

The president had also classified the entire surveillance video. They did not want anybody to pay close attention to what happened after Hassan left the bus. An astute observer would have wondered why so many of the passengers appeared to be slumped over ahead of the explosion. The volunteers all had taken a drug cocktail that first caused them to lose consciousness and then die quickly. The explosion was only for show. By the time the bus blew up, everybody on board was already dead.

Fortunately, so far those had been the only holes that needed to be plucked. From the beginning on, everybody involved in the plan knew that it could only succeed if as few people as possible were aware of what was going on. Over time, the circle of people in the know would necessarily have to keep expanding until it would become too big and porous to contain the secret any longer. At that point, the mission would have to be completed or Hassan would be exposed and killed.

The DNI closed his eyes and thought with fondness of the young man who was their great hope to deal a massive blow to as-Sirat. To McClintock, who had worked with all kinds of people who put their lives on the line for the United States, Hassan was the latest in a tradition of great American heroes. He had taken to him with an almost paternal affection.

Sure, there were some significant political risks for the president and maybe McClintock would have to retire if the plan failed, but Hassan, who sometimes jokingly referred to himself as the "reverse suicide bomber," was putting his life in harm's way.

Not only that, but over the past four years he had alienated all of his old friends as he had pretended to become more and more radicalized. Hassan had lost his soccer scholarship in the hope that he might be able to gain some early credibility with Islamic radicals. Now, he had temporarily shattered his parent's lives and likely caused his father's heart attack. McClintock hoped that everybody would soon know the entire truth.

To the DNI, Hassan was the very definition of a hero. Not only was he risking his life but he also got no accolades for what he did. Right now, he was the most hated man in the country that he was willing to sacrifice everything for.

The ringing phone ripped McClintock from his thoughts and the DNI answered the secure line.

"Mr. President," he said. "How is the kid holding up?"

Friday, 8:05 am ET

The small plane had landed on a private airfield not far from Islamabad. The Gulfstream V can cover great distances, but since it was registered in Spain, a stop in Madrid was made part of the trip to maintain cover. Several men exited the plane and loaded a stretcher into an SUV with tinted glass. They wore jeans and t-shirts and could have been employed in a variety of fields. The only thing a close observer would have noticed is that they were all in extraordinarily good shape. But there were no observers – they had made sure of that. A couple more SUVs were loaded with luggage, although most of their equipment was already in place.

All in all, the team consisted of 26 men. Most of them, apart from Hassan al-Zaid and the intelligence officer in charge, had been training for this mission for a little more than two years. In fact, they had given up any other aspect of their lives for "Operation Pathfinder." They had all learned some Urdu and each of them had a number of special skills. In order not to risk success of the mission if something were to happen to any of them, at least three of the men had received the same training in any of the areas, such as operating the remote-controlled replica of the Metro bus. It had been one of the trickiest parts of the entire operation and a grave concern to all of them. Although the time and route had been picked to minimize the chance of anybody getting seriously injured during the attack, something could have gone wrong. But the team had pulled off that part of the mission without a hitch, In fact, up until now, everything had gone almost too well.

Members of the team had been on Hassan's flight to the Bahamas and from there to Bogotá. Had anything gone wrong, they were prepared to step in, flash their IDs and keep him out of trouble. A number of cover stories had been invented that would have been told if anybody had recognized Hassan but none of them were needed.

Once in Colombia, they had to switch from public flights to the Gulftstream because there was no way that he would not have been recognized in 30 hours of commercial travel.

While they had done as much as possible to create the cover story that Hassan was a terrorist and as-Sirat sympathizer, they all knew that the plan had holes. Eventually, enough people would put the pieces of the puzzle together in a way that would lead them to ask questions for which there were no answers. They were estimating that Hassan had about ten days before his cover would be compromised. By that time, he had to complete the task of convincing the world that he was a terrorist, make contact with as-Sirat and hopefully manage to be taken to the place were Omar Bashir was hiding.

If Hassan had not infiltrated as-Sirat within that small window of time, he never would.

The mission would be deemed a partial success if they managed to find another as-Sirat stronghold, but it had been designed to deliver a death knell to the leadership of the terrorist organization.

They had not all given a couple of years of their lives, and the U.S. government had not invested significant resources in this project, for it to lead to the death or capture of some mid-level terrorists.

So far so good, all the men had thought when they landed in Pakistan. They had convinced the world that Hassan al-Zaid was a terrorist and Omar Bashir had already praised him in a new audio tape. They had gotten Hassan to Pakistan without a hitch and, very importantly, nobody had been harmed during the bombing. Now the hard part was about to begin. Everybody involved in "Operation Pathfinder" knew of the personal risks they ran but accepted them as part of the job. Right now, they were part of a black operation in a country that had recently not been on the friendliest of terms with the United States. But the men all knew that the greatest risk would be undertaken by Hassan, for whom they all had begun to care like a younger brother.

Next in line with regard to who had the most to lose was President Sweeney. As the one ultimately giving the green light for the mission, he would be blamed if it failed. He had authorized the staging of a terrorist attack right next to the Pentagon and misled the American people about it.

Before Sweeney decided to sign off on "Pathfinder," McClintock and Hearst had sat down with him to give the president an honest assessment of what they thought the damage would be to him.

"If this fails, plenty of people in Congress are going to ask for your head. And they may get it," they had told the commander-in-chief. "Somebody is going to call for impeachment and there will be a lot of people in this country who won't appreciate being deceived by their president."

"There will be endless investigations and this is what you will be remembered for. Your legacy would be tarnished," Hearst had told the president.

"Heck, even if it is a full success, there might be an awful lot of people who will question our methods," McClintock had chimed in. "Also, there is no way you'll be able to manage not to perjure yourself. Sure, you can say later that you did it in the name of national security, but if we want this to look real, then you'll have to knowingly give the American people false information at some point."

They also pointed out that the mission would likely not just result in domestic fallout but could also have international consequences, but Sweeney had deemed those as manageable.

"It's not as though anybody likes us over there anyways and Pakistan and Afghanistan are getting gazillions in aid from us," the president had argued. "I'm sure they'll raise a big stink but it'll pass."

Sweeney had taken a week to decide before he made the call to go ahead with "Pathfinder." The only condition he tied to his support was that the public would be fully informed about the mission, whether it was a success or not. The American people would learn the truth from their president as soon as possible, not when documents were declassified 50 years after the fact.

"You know that the fallout from coming clean will be huge, right?" Hearst had asked. "Unless Pathfinder is an absolutely rousing success, you'll have to weather a tough storm."

"I have to do it that way," Sweeney had argued. "I have to explain to the people why we did what we did. If I don't come clean, how could they ever trust me or another president again?

"Besides, we have people who risk their lives for this country every day, so I'm sure as hell willing to not worry about my legacy if it means we get a crack at Omar Bashir."

McClintock had always admired the president for his decision and for being an unwavering supporter of the mission once he had approved it.

FBI Director Stevenson learned of the arson of the al-Zaid residence when he arrived at the office at 6:00 am. After another night with too little sleep, the strain of fatigue mixed with the frustration of failure was showing more each day and the latest news did little to make him feel any better.

Stevenson was sustaining himself on a diet of soft drinks, coffee, quick bites to eat at his desk and aspirin. What was getting to him was not only that Hassan al-Zaid had gotten away but also the feeling that he was missing something important.

The FBI director had spoken to his daughter, who was finishing up her senior year at Stanford, the previous night. Even the work-related stress would not keep him for checking in with his little girl in college at least once a week. He had vaguely discussed the case with her before she launched into a litany of little problems she was having to deal with, including her grad school applications and some trouble in her sorority.

While he listened to her, Stevenson's mind kept returning to an issue that had become a central point for him the case.

"Nina, if you wanted to get a fake passport, where would you go?" he asked his daughter when he was able to get a word in.

"Dad," she chastised him while also giggling. "I'm a college senior, not a crime lord. Wait, can you order them online? If not, I'd have no idea."

Nina Stevenson heard her father sigh on the other end of the line. She could tell from his voice how much pressure he was under.

"If you really wanna know how I'd get one, I guess I would have to ask a person. You know, like, a guy who knows a guy. But I wouldn't even know how to find that first guy. All the fake IDs my friends use are normally ones that they get from older girls. But they often get taken away.

"Of course I never did that," she added quickly.

Her father was always quite adamant about her staying out of trouble, saying it would not be good if the FBI director would have to bail out his daughter.

"Thanks, Nina," he said. "Sorry that this case is so much on my mind, but you know how important it is. Now tell me more about that sorority event."

Sitting at his desk at the Hoover Building and drinking one of many caffeine-containing beverages that helped him get through the day, Stevenson replayed that part of the conversation with his daughter in his mind.

He grabbed a piece of paper and began scribbling notes.

In the middle of the page he wrote the words "How does a college kid …?" in bold letters. From there, he drew arrows to various empty spaces and began asking himself some questions. First, he wrote "... obtain multiple passports that withstand scrutiny at immigration," then "...get his hands on good explosives." The page was quickly filled with unanswered questions. The last thought Stevenson put on paper was "... do all of the little things right and manage to not screw up once."

He stared at the page for a while, trying to make sense of it all.

Then he drew a couple of lines at the bottom as though he was solving an equation. Underneath, he wrote: "He doesn't" and circled the words several times.

***

The safe house in Islamabad was in an area where many Westerners lived, located close to the diplomatic enclave that bordered the Rawal Lake. The team had transformed the house into mission control for "Operation Pathfinder." They each had taken turns living there, preparing for the Pakistan part of the mission, improving their Urdu and getting used to the city and the climate. Some of the electronics and telecommunications expert had done most of the prep work in the previous weeks, setting up secure communications links and protecting it against any sort of surveillance. It had taken a long time to find the perfect place. The house was isolated enough so that the team could work at all hours of the day without suspicion. It featured a high wall and a large garden with many trees that obstructed the view from the main road. In addition, there was a main and a service entrance, allowing the team to move people and equipment more easily. The garden was now full of hidden surveillance equipment and motion detectors. The team was split in three groups, each with a team leader, so that they could work around the clock. One third of them would be fulfilling the primary mission, monitoring Hassan's movements, assisting him in any way possible and maintaining communications with Washington. The second part of the group was responsible for security and maintenance of the equipment as well as for support functions, such as cooking. The last third was in an eight-hour rest cycle. They would need to be fully alert. Getting at least six hours of sleep, except for during emergencies, was mandatory.

The basement of the house had been filled not only with enough supplies to last a month but also housed several generators that would power the electronic equipment in case of an outage. There was a backup for every backup and everybody hoped that the team would be prepared for anything unexpected.

After his arrival in Pakistan, Hassan had been taken to the safe house to get rest one last time. Since the Gulfstream had been faster than a commercial plane would have been, he did not want to arouse suspicion by showing up at the madrasah too soon.

On the way to Pakistan, the team had spent some time altering Hassan's appearance to make it believable that he managed to fly halfway around the world without being recognized. His long hair had been cut short and dyed and he wore blue contact lenses. This was done to make it look reasonable to as-Sirat that he managed to escape the United States.

After a brief rest, roughly 48 hours after the staged attack, Hassan was ready to go. He carried three tiny global positioning devices that would allow the team to monitor his location. One was hidden inside his belt buckle, another in his shoe and the last was built into his watch. Another chip had been surgically inserted in his thigh more than a year ago. It was a prototype of a product that was supposed to monitor a person's vital signs to provide doctors with more information in case of an emergency. Unfortunately, it had stopped working the day before the attack, the mission's single largest setback so far. The decision had been made not to replace it. The consensus had been that there was no time for the surgery. In addition, a new wound might raise too many questions and it could pose health risks to Hassan once he was on his own in Waziristan. They hoped that the three external GPS devices would be enough to track him.

The entire team was assembled when it was time to drop off Hassan. Every one of them hugged him, silently praying that it would not be the last time. Then he got in the back of one of the SUVs and they took off.

***

FBI Director Stevenson stormed through the White House hallways, his pace reflecting his racing thoughts. It bothered him that he had failed the president and his country. The FBI had not been able to make any significant headway in the case. Worst of all, Stevenson had the feeling that he was overlooking something big. Sometimes, as he was poring over all of the information he had on the attack, he felt as though he was close to putting it together, but he could never quite get there. One thing he was convinced of was that Hassan al-Zaid hadn't acted alone. What had been a growing suspicion at first was now a firm belief. It was simply not possible for him to pull of this attack by himself.

But there was something else that had been eating away at him. It was the same feeling one got when trying to remember a name or a place, knowing that the information was right there but unable to pinpoint it. Unfortunately, this was not about coming up with the name of an actor or a song, this was about national security and a terrorist attack that had cost American lives.

When Stevenson had finally admitted to himself that he was absolutely convinced that Hassan al-Zaid could not have acted on his own, he had requested a face-to-face meeting with the president. He hated disagreeing with Jack Sweeney, but in this case the president and people like DNI McClintock were wrong in insisting that this was a lone wolf attack.

It was time that somebody made that clear to them, but he wanted to do it in a personal meeting with his old friend. Though they might have lost valuable time, widening the scope of the investigation could still turn this case around. His request for a meeting had been granted and he was given 15 minutes with the president.

He entered the Oval Office after being waved in by the president's secretary.

"What's up Chris?" Sweeney asked his FBI director.

"There is something wrong about this bombing. I'm not entirely sure what it is, but I'm getting close," the FBI director said. "I'm convinced that al-Zaid didn't act alone. I may not have evidence for this yet, but I just know he had accomplices."

Stevenson leaned forward and forgot the formalities he normally used to address the president.

"Jack, you have to listen to me," he pleaded. "With all due respect, you're wrong about this being a lone wolf attack. Maybe we bungled the beginning of this investigation, but there is still time to recover."

The president looked at his friend of 30 years for a long time, making Stevenson shift uncomfortably in his chair. To fill the silence, he just kept talking.

"With your permission, I'm going to use the entire available force of the Bureau to look for these co-conspirators. It's not like the FBI is doing much good right now anyways with al-Zaid out of the country."

There was more silence but Stevenson felt a sense of relief. He might be reprimanded, but at least he had spoken the kind of truth that he thought the president needed to hear.

Finally, Sweeney spoke.

"You'll do no such thing, Chris," the president said. Stevenson was about to object when Sweeney lifted his hand, indicating him to be quiet. He picked up the phone and directed his secretary to clear his schedule for the next 30 minutes and be prepared to rearrange it further if necessary.

"I owe you an apology, my friend," he said, turning his attention back to Stevenson, "And I applaud your instincts. We were on the fence for a long time about how much we should tell you, but in the end I decided it would be best to keep you in the dark. We knew that you'd be the one who had to brief the media and the public on the investigation, and we needed it to look real. You're a good friend and an excellent public servant but a dreadful actor, so we simply couldn't let you in on it."

Stevenson's face did nothing to hide his confusion.

"My only comfort in you not knowing about this beforehand is that it will shield you from criticism if Operation Pathfinder fails," the president continued. "You're absolutely right. Hassan didn't act alone. He had co-conspirators and one of them is sitting in front of you right now."

Understandably, Sweeney's last statement exceeded the FBI director's comprehension. Stevenson's mouth fell open and his heart seemed to skip a beat before beginning to pound in his chest.

Over the next few minutes, the president gave his stunned and speechless friend an overview of Pathfinder. When he was finished, Stevenson sat in his chair for a while, trying to come to terms with what he had heard and with all the thoughts in his head.

"Jack, I'm asking you this as an old friend, not as the director of the FBI," he finally said. "Are you fucking nuts?

"You are the president of the United States and you're telling me, here, in the Oval Office, where Lincoln worked and FDR and JFK, that you authorized this?" Stevenson added, his agitation showing. Sweeney realized that his was the first time anybody had ever raised their voice to him inside the White House but he let his friend carry on.

"I'm not even mad about you keeping this from me. God knows you didn't want a voice of reason involved in this," the FBI director said. "But you are deceiving the American people. You made them think that there was an attack. You scared the shit out of them."

"I know," Sweeney said, "I wish there had been another way, but I think that, if we're successful, this will save American lives."

"And if it fails? You'll be torn to shreds. You've done so many good things as president but this is all you'll be remembered for," Stevenson said.

"Chris, this isn't about my legacy, it's about many people putting their country ahead of themselves, making sacrifices for the common good of our nation," the president said.

"I also think you aren't giving the American people enough credit. They want to get Omar Bashir as much as I do and I'll come clean as soon as I can," he added.

"They'll see that Pathfinder wasn't designed to be kept from them. It has always been the plan to tell them about it once we didn't put more lives at risk."

The president removed a key from his pocket, opened the top drawer of a dresser next to his desk and used the key to unlock a small safe.

"I had this put in a few weeks ago, just for this purpose," Sweeney said and pulled a box from the safe.

"In here are videotaped testimonials of Hassan al-Zaid and some of the people on the bus," he told Stevenson. "They will be the ones explaining to the country what Pathfinder was and why they decided to participate in it. Of course the people on the bus didn't know all of the details but Hassan's video is very good. We taped it after the fake confession and I think he says it better than I ever could have."

He took out a bundle of letters from the box.

"These are farewell letters from the people who died on the bus. Unlike the videos, these are obviously not for the public. Instead, I plan on hand-delivering them to all of the families, along with the thanks of a grateful nation.

"For none of them, it was about making sure their families are being taken care of. That was just a bonus, Chris. Instead, it was about doing something for their country. Let's make sure their sacrifices were not made in vain."

He walked over to where Stevenson was sitting and handed him the bundle of letters.

"Jack, I'm not questioning what they did. It's a beautiful and brave thing," the FBI director said. "I'm questioning what you did."

"Chris, we'll be friends for a long time after getting out of government. You can criticize me then and second-guess my decisions to your heart's content," the president said. "But now you have to put those thoughts aside. Pathfinder is underway and Hassan is in Pakistan. Now that you know about the mission, we need your help."

"You know that I'm not gonna let you down," Stevenson replied. "No matter what kind of reservations I might have about all of this and on what kind of thin ice we'll be skating here."

"Hey, it's not my fault that you were close to figuring it out," the president said, causing the FBI director to smile. "I would've been perfectly fine to keep you clueless and looking that part on TV."

They laughed and both men knew that their friendship would be alright.

"You're lucky that you're the president and that the Secret Service is outside or I'd beat some sense into you," Stevenson quipped. He paused for a second before adding, "Admit it, you were pretty damn impressed that I was figuring out your little secret."

The president laughed.

"I was impressed, although it's not like you were close to putting everything together. But you would've kept pushing this 'Hassan had help' angle and we can't have that. We'll actually need you to steer the investigation away from trouble for us. I already talked to a couple of your forensics experts, but eventually, there will be others. We have to continue to control the flow of information and the news cycles for as long as possible."

"How do you plan on doing that?" Stevenson asked.

"We have been doing it. For example, Robert McClintock's 'outburst' at the cocktail party was planned," Sweeney noted with a chuckle. "Hassan also made sure to be captured by different surveillance cameras and we've been slowly leaking information to the media so that they focus on the manhunt and the escape instead of on the bombing itself. Pathfinder can only succeed as long as the world believes Hassan is a terrorist who managed to get away and that we are leaving no stone unturned to find him. Sadly, that cover won't stand up to scrutiny forever."

"So what do you want me to do, Mr. President?" Stevenson said, falling back into his more respectful, professional persona.

Sweeney had taken back the letters from the FBI director. As he put the bundle back into the safe, it felt very heavy in his hands. With the letters once again locked away, the president looked up.

"I think I want you to offer your resignation."

***

The SUV with Hassan in it found a spot in the rear of the lowest level of the Islamabad airport garage. The team had scouted out the location beforehand to make sure there were no closed circuit cameras anywhere. They had chosen the SUV and not one of the other vehicles they had available because of its tinted windows. Now, two team members had gotten out of the car and were walking around the garage, making sure nobody was around.

A second vehicle was waiting in the level above. In it, one of the team members gave the "all clear" signal. "You're good to go," the driver said.

Hassan grabbed his bags. The bigger one had been outfitted with a luggage tag showing that it had been checked in Bogotá. He also had the remnants of a boarding pass from a Zürich-Islamabad flight that had landed 30 minutes earlier, just in case anybody would check for these things. It was placed casually as a bookmark in a novel that had been purchased at the Madrid airport. A receipt was in the pocket of Hassan's jeans, along with some euros. They had left nothing to chance.

Before Hassan could get out of the car, the driver stopped him.

"See you in a few days, kid," he said. "Good luck."

"No worries," Hassan responded. "I owe you a rematch on Madden."

Then he was gone and on his own.

The team would keep monitoring his movement with the help of the high-tech GPS devices and using old-fashioned surveillance, but they would have no more direct contact until the end of the mission.

Hassan made his way up a staircase. Once he was on the street level, he headed for a cab stand.

"Please take me to the Faisal Mosque," he told the cab driver in Arabic. The mosque was not far from the madrasah that was his next destination.

The cab sped off and Hassan leaned back. He let out a deep breath and closed his eyes. Though he was now on his own and headed straight into danger, Hassan felt surprisingly calm. He had been working toward this moment for a long time, and he was happy that it had finally come.

Like an athlete who had gone through two-a-days, sparring sessions, spring training or endless scrimmages, it was time for game day. Hassan knew that he could not be more ready. The mission could be derailed by any number of things, including those that were completely out of his control, but he would not fail because of a lack of preparation.

Hassan looked out of the window to get a feeling for Pakistan. The cab was surrounded by some cars and scores of mopeds. The smell of their exhaust crept into the taxi even though the windows were closed.

It was late in the evening and Islamabad was bustling with activity. The cab had air conditioning but it didn't seem to be working properly. Hassan had arrived at the tail end of the rainy season and the humidity, mixed with temperatures of more than 85 degrees, made for an uncomfortable ride. At the end of the trip, he was drenched in sweat but didn't mind. He wanted to show up at the madrasah looking as though he had actually been on the run for a couple of days.

They reached the Faisal Mosque, the largest in the city.

"200 Rupees," the driver said.

Hassan handed him five dollars, about twice what he had asked for, and stepped into the street, which was lined with food carts.

He had a map of this part of the city memorized and headed east. After a brief walk he arrived at the madrasah that the as-Sirat-supporting Los Angeles restaurant owner had told him about. It was a large, slightly run down building that was painted white like so many other structures in Islamabad.

The madrasah had been under surveillance for weeks and intelligence officials believed that it would be possible for Hassan to make contact with the terrorist group here.

Hassan walked through the open gate into an atrium. It was filled with children who were participating in their evening lessons. They were sitting on the ground, hunched over small tables. Each of them was wearing white headgear. A teacher was discussing Islamic ethics with them and two more men with long white kaftans were hovering nearby.

Hassan turned to them.

"Salam Aleikum," he said, again speaking Arabic. "I'm in need of assistance and was told I could come here for help."

The two men gave him a curious look.

"Who has told you that?" one of them said in a tone that was neither friendly nor hostile.

"Waqar Navaz in Los Angeles gave me the name of Hanif Younis and said he could help me find some friends. I'm in dire need of them," Hassan said.

"And who are you?" the elder of the two asked.

"I'm a good Muslim in need of help," Hassan responded, handing the two men his Algerian passport and meeting their gazes. "He will not recognize this name, but I think he may know me by another. Please tell me if I can speak to him or if I have traveled here in vain."

"Follow me," the first man said gruffly.

Together, they entered the bowels of the madrasah. The man led Hassan two floors down and through a small maze of hallways and finally stopped at a closed door.

"Go in there and leave your bags," the man said. Hassan followed the order and walked through the door into a space that was more of a cell than a room. It was illuminated by a single, bright light bulb dangling from the ceiling. He heard the door being locked behind him and the sound of footsteps walking away from the cell. Hassan had nowhere to go and he wondered if they were on to him already. That would be really anticlimactic, he thought.

Then he reminded himself that this was a new stage of the mission. Things were now not mapped out and under his control anymore and there would inevitably be times when he would have to improvise.

Though it seemed longer to Hassan, within a couple of minutes, there were sounds outside the door and a panel was removed, allowing a pair of eyes to gaze into the cell. He turned to face the stare.

"Step under the light," a voice said.

"I had to change my hair," Hassan responded as he stepped backwards and allowed the observer to get a good look at him.

"Be patient a little bit longer," the voice said. "I have to make a call."

"I've been running for three days and I don't mind the rest. But I would like some water and I hope you will allow me to observe the Isha," Hassan replied, referencing the last of the five daily prayers that Muslims observed. "For obvious reasons, I've had to be negligent with regard to my prayers on the trip."

"It won't take long," the voice said. Hassan thought it sounded friendlier now.

A short time later, the door was being unlocked and the man who had accompanied Hassan to the cell asked him to follow. This time, they walked up a flight of stairs before arriving at another room.

The man knocked twice and heard a response from the inside.

"Hanif awaits you," he said and stepped aside.

Hassan entered the chamber. It was fairly dark apart from a lamp sitting on a desk in the back of the room. Behind it sat a large man with an impressive beard, also dressed in a white kaftan.

"Salam Aleikum," the man said. He then twisted the lamp so the light shone on Hassan.

The man looked at his visitor and then at the Algerian passport in his hands. Then his eyes wandered to a newspaper on his desk that had a picture of Hassan on the front page.

"Allahu Akbar, it is really you," he mumbled. He got up from his chair and rushed around his desk to embrace Hassan. "Allah is truly great to have brought you here. Waqar has contacted me and let me know that you might try to reach me but I never imagined you would make it. When Fariq told me a stranger was upstairs, asked to see me and invoked the name of Waqar, I dared to dream but I still did not believe that it would be you. Welcome to the madrasah, brother, you will be safe here."

"Praise be to Allah, who has allowed me to reach you, and to Waqar for remembering me. He gave me your name and this place as a contact two years ago and I was worried that you wouldn't be here anymore or that his information had been wrong. My escape plan ends here with you and I'm putting my life in your hands." Hassan bowed before the man.

"I'll be grateful for any help you can provide. If you can do only one thing, point me into the direction of where to find as-Sirat. But I also don't want to place you in danger by being associated with me. I imagine that anybody who assists me in any way will become an enemy of the United States."

"I am already an enemy of America," Hanif Younis said. "And you have found as-Sirat. As soon as we thought there was an opportunity that you might try to come here, we started thinking about what to do if you made it. You'll stay here for a day so that we can make preparations to safely move you away from here to a different place.

"Fariq will show you to a room where you can get some rest," he added, barking an order to the man waiting outside. "If you need anything, just let him know."

Hassan was taken for another short walk through the narrow hallways before Fariq stopped at a door and swung it open. Though it was not much, the room, which had a bed, some carpets and a couple of pieces of furniture, was a vast improvement over the cell he had found himself in at first.

"It is not much," Fariq said with a shrug. "But it is the best we have. I'll be outside if you need anything."

"Shukran – Thank you," Hassan said.

The door closed and he was left alone with his thoughts. So far so good.

Friday, 2:33 pm ET

When Art Kempner checked the Drudge Report, he mostly saw items he was familiar with. Life had not returned to normal and the attack continued to dominate the news. Hassan al-Zaid was still at large and the administration was increasingly under fire for how it was handling the attack.

The latest blunder and the big story of the day, which Art had also reported, was that the FBI had apparently misplaced the surveillance videos from Metro Bus 2405. Because they were evidence in a criminal investigation, Washington Metro had also handed over any backup data to the Bureau, so the only clips available were those the media were still playing over and over.

"I would like to know what the heck is going on at the FBI," an unnamed opposition senator was quoted in the Reuters story. "I think it is high time that Stevenson rights this ship. This is not a time to fumble around and lose evidence."

Another story linked to on Drudge was about the executive director of the ACLU criticizing DNI McClintock for his thinly veiled threat to want to torture Hassan al-Zaid once he was found.

Apart from that, there were links to several columns criticizing the administration for having been too lax on homeland security in the past few years and to a couple of stories about unrest in Afghanistan. At demonstrations against the pro-American president, people had carried signs with Hassan's picture and the words "al-Zaid for president" through Kabul. The pictures of the rallies had been repeated over and over on the American morning shows, in turn causing outrage in the United States.

Art was about to navigate away from the site when he saw another link at the bottom of the page.

"Funerals for terror victims begin"

He clicked on the link and it took him to a story from a small Ohio paper.

The Van Wert Times Bulletin had an article on the funeral of one of the people who were killed in the attack.

> *Van Wert Terror Victim Laid to Rest*
> *Van Wert, Ohio – Hundreds of people gathered here Thursday to attended the funeral service of Van Wert resident Brian Barnes, a victim of Wednesday's terrorist attack on Washington, DC.*
> *He was 47 and leaves behind a wife, Cindy. The deceased had traveled to Washington to attend a seminar. Shortly after his arrival at Ronald Reagan National Airport, he was among the unfortunate people who had been on board of the bus that was the target of the attack.*
> *Suspected terrorist Hassan al-Zaid is still at large.*

"I was worried right away when I heard about the attack and couldn't get through to Brian," his widow Cindy, 43, said. "I keep thinking back about the way he had said goodbye that morning. It is almost as if he had known. As a former military guy, he wasn't the most affectionate person in public, but he gave me the biggest hug when I dropped him off at the airport and said that he loved me. It was the sweetest thing and I'm glad that he gave me such a nice memory to remember him by."

Barnes, a veteran of the first Gulf War, was laid to rest with military honors.

In addition to family and friends who paid their respects, many Van Wert residents, whose life Barnes touched as a volunteer basketball coach for the YMCA, attended the funeral.

"It's a tragedy that this cowardly attack took one of our best," Van Wert Mayor Betty Sassman, who spoke at the service, said. "We will remember Brian Barnes as an outstanding member of our community who was always willing to help others. He will be missed."

The YMCA announced that it would rename its annual 3-on-3 basketball tournament in Barnes' honor. It will now be known as the Brian Barnes Classic.

Van Wert High School announced Thursday that its varsity football team would wear patches on its jersey with the number 14, which Barnes had worn as a Cougar. Midwest

Meats, where the deceased had worked as a
regional vice president said it would
establish a college scholarship for outstanding
students in Barnes' name.
"I was very touched by the outpouring of
support. This community has always meant
a lot to Brian," Cindy Barnes said.

The phone on Art's desk rang just as he had finished
reading the article. It was a source with a major scoop.

***

Congressman Jim Hearst, Jr. walked into the chamber
of the House of Representatives. He slid his card into
the voting station nearest to the Speaker's Lobby and
voted "Yea" on the New Zealand Free Trade
Agreement.

There would be another vote after this one, and Hearst
didn't want to deal with the reporters in the hallway, so
he walked toward his assigned seat. On the way, he
was stopped by fellow Virginia Congressman Charles
"Chuck" Nelson, the ranking member of the
Homeland Security Committee.

Though the partisan divide in Congress had increased
in recent years and Hearst and Nelson were from
opposite parties, the two had become close friends
over the past couple of decades. Side by side, they had
fought many battles for Virginia, trying to get more
money for their state or prevent military base closures.
They got together for dinner at least once a month,
talking about the good old days and shaking their
heads at the partisan warriors that were elected to
Congress nowadays. It seemed they were more
interested in sound bites than getting stuff done.

"I gotta talk to you, Jim," Nelson now said, tugging on the jacket sleeve of his friend. "Let's find a quiet corner."

The two moved to the back of the chamber and each sat at an empty desk.

"What's up?" Hearst asked. "You know I'm not gonna change my vote on this free trade thing. It's a good deal for my district."

Nelson leaned closer to his friend.

"It's not about that," he said. "I want to give you a heads up on something that's probably gonna start happening pretty soon … as a friend.

"Some of our young members plan on going after the president and Homeland Security. They will argue that the administration was responsible for the terrorist escaping because Dulles was not shut down after the bombing," Nelson whispered. "I don't agree with it. Back in the day, when there was a crisis like this, we used to all work together, not try to score political points. Sadly, that time has passed. They're trying to get me to join because I'm our top guy on Homeland Security. I, on the other hand, am trying to stop them but I don't think I can. But at least I want you to know it's coming."

"I appreciate it, Chuck," Hearst said, wanting to add more but he was cut off by his friend.

"I'm not doing this for you. The administration has enough to deal with right now, trying to find al-Zaid. I don't want them to have to waste time to defend themselves against political attacks. There will be time for that later," Nelson added, beginning to get up.

"Wait," Hearst said, the wheels spinning in his head.

On the one hand, it would be a good thing if Sweeney's opponents were to go after the president on this. It would generate the kind of news that would keep the media focused on something other than the details of the bombing. In addition, he wouldn't mind at all if some of those young, brash opposition lawmakers would get their face rubbed into the mess they were about to make. If Pathfinder was successful, they would look foolish for having attacked the administration.

But there were other political considerations in play. If Pathfinder failed, the president would need all of the help he could get. Hearst could generate some good will among the opposition by not allowing them to take a position now that could be embarrassing down the road.

Maybe there was a way he could accomplish both, he thought.

"Chuck, do you trust me?" he asked his friend.

"As much as anybody in Congress. Take that for what it's worth," Nelson responded with his trademark dry humor.

"What I'm about to ask you to do won't make any sense but I want you to trust me," Hearst said. "More importantly, you have to give me your word that this conversation will only stay between the two of us."

"You know I'm not one of those blabbermouths," Nelson said.

"Yeah, but this is different. I need to hear you say it," Hearst whispered.

"Okay, I promise that I will not divulge anything you're going to tell me."

"Good," Hearst said. "It would be politically foolish for them to call out the president on this. I can't tell you yet why that is, but you have to believe me. Instead, I want you to do it. Call a big press conference and really go after the administration on security."

"Excuse me?"

"I know it doesn't seem to make sense, but you have to believe me that this would do the country a favor. It helps your party and it even helps the president," Hearst said. "You'll understand soon enough."

"Jim, have you lost your mind?" Nelson asked.

"You gotta trust me on this Chuck."

"How do you expect me to do that if you're not telling me what this is about?" Nelson said. "I may be willing to go along with whatever it is that you're cooking up here, but you need to give me more than your word."

"Okay, let me think about," Hearst said and the two Congressmen broke their huddle just as the next vote started.

While Nelson headed to his own seat, trying to make sense of what had just happened, Hearst ducked into one of the rooms adjacent to the House chamber. He reappeared after a couple of minutes and headed straight for Nelson.

"Come with me," he said. "And don't forget your phone."

The pair headed for the same room and Hearst pulled out his cell.

"He is with me now, sir," he said and hung up.

Within a few seconds, Nelson's phone began to buzz and he flipped it open.

"This is Chuck Nelson," he answered.

"Congressman, thanks for taking the call. This is Jack Sweeney."

Hearing the president's voice almost caused Nelson to drop the phone but he composed himself.

"Mr. President, it's good to talk to you," he said.

"Jim told me about your situation and thought it might be best if I spoke to you," Sweeney said. "I just ducked out of a Cabinet meeting to make this call and don't have much time, but I wanted you to know that I think you'd be doing the country a tremendous service if you'd hold that press conference and really lay it on thick. I give you my word that this will not have any negative consequences for you or your party. I don't know if that'll be enough or if you need some kind of other assurance ..." Sweeney's voice trailed off.

"That won't be necessary, Mr. President," Nelson said. "I have your word and Jim's. More than that, if he can get you on the phone within a couple of minutes, this must be important, so I'll do it."

"Terrific, Congressman," the president said. "I really appreciate it. Listen, I gotta run but please consult with Jim about how to best go about doing this. Maybe I could have you over for dinner in a couple of weeks to thank you for agreeing to help the country out."

With that, Sweeney hung up, leaving Congressman Nelson wondering what the hell was going on.

Friday, 6:24 pm ET

It was one of the most uncomfortable nights of
Hassan's life -- the perfect storm of insomnia. Though
it was cooler in his room than on the ground level, it
was still much warmer than he was used to. It would
have been nice to have a fan but no such luck. In
addition, with his luggage taken from him, he could
not change and was forced to go to bed with the same
clothes he had been wearing on the long flight from
Bogotá. All of this, coupled with the large time
difference from Washington to Islamabad, would have
made for an unpleasant night for just about anybody,
but what kept Hassan awake more than anything was
his thoughts.

He tossed and turned, wondering what was ahead for
him and reflecting on the past four years.

Hassan remembered how he had first come up with the
plan of staging a terrorist attack as a means to
infiltrating as-Sirat and he smiled at his younger self
for having had the audacity to pitch the idea to a
Member of Congress and the arrogance to think he
could bring down the terrorist network. Over the past
four years, he had changed so much, but what had not
changed was his firm belief that the plan would work.
At first, it was probably youthful exuberance mixed
with a little bit of foolishness that led him to feel that
way. Later, after the idea had been tossed around at the
highest levels of power and eventually been given the
green light, Hassan's confidence came from seeing
firsthand the kind of preparation that went into
Operation Pathfinder.

He could have never pulled this off as a high school senior, but now he knew that he was ready. Over the past four years, he had dedicated his life to the mission. He had never minded the long hours of training, the countless lessons and practice sessions. Hassan had even done torture training once a month, in which he had been given a code and members of the team then tried to force it out of him.

He had undergone waterboarding and sleep deprivation, toughening his mind with each session. In the beginning he had cracked within the first few minutes, now he could suffer through various forms of torture for hours. McClintock believed that it was possible for as-Sirat to torture him a little upon his arrival, just to see if he was legit.

"I'll be so disappointed if they don't end up torturing me," Hassan had said during his last conversation with the DNI. "But I tell you what: If they don't and I make it back alive, I'm gonna waterboard you for a whole day just for putting me through this."

The comment had made McClintock laugh so hard that he snorted pink lemonade through his nose before agreeing.

No, Hassan thought in his small chamber in Islamabad, it wasn't the rigorous training or the torture that had been most difficult for him, or even the constant awareness that he was heading into a mission that could easily cost him his life.

The toughest part had been abandoning and disappointing his family and friends to build his cover identity. It had been a long and gradual transition from all-American high school athlete to pretend radical.

The slow change had been mapped out by an expert on radicalism and Hassan had followed it to a tee. When the plan called for alienating his best friend in Virginia, he did so. When it called for reducing the frequency with which he should speak to his parents, then he cut back on the phone calls.

The only good part was the distance from UCLA to home. That way he didn't have to face his parents in person and see the disappointment on their faces. Hassan was not sure he could have kept up the charade if he had seen how sad it made his parents to see him slipping away from them into radicalism.

When he envisioned the success of the mission, he did not imagine Omar Bashir being killed or taken away by Special Forces soldiers or the president slapping him on the back at a White House ceremony. To Hassan, success was getting the job done and making it home alive so that he could embrace his parents and tell them how sorry he was for what he put them through.

Whenever he ignored another e-mail from them, begging him for information about how things were going at UCLA or urging him to rethink the path he was taking, the thought that kept him going was that, when everything was unveiled, they would be so proud of him.

It was only when he pictured that moment that he finally found some sleep.

***

Art Kempner checked the New York Times' website to make sure they had not beaten him to the punch. He wasn't really worried about anybody else but also pulled up the Wall Street Journal and Yahoo News. With great satisfaction, he saw that the scoop was his alone.

"Stevenson offers resignation, Sweeney says 'no'"

A breaking news e-mail alert had been sent to tens of thousands of people and the headline was splashed in bold font across the Post's website.

It had been a long afternoon for Art. After getting the scoop that Stevenson had offered his resignation in a private meeting with the president that morning, he had been trying to confirm the story. Sure, some of the younger reporters would have just ran with that rumor but that wasn't good journalism and it certainly wasn't Art's style. He wanted two sources for just about every story, no matter how tricky it was to get them. The veteran reporter felt that it was good to be fast in journalism, but it was better to be right. It was a mantra that he shared with fewer and fewer of his colleagues.

After getting the call from a White House aide about the meeting and the offered resignation, Art had gone to work. It had not taken him long to determine that Stevenson had indeed visited Sweeney at the White House and another source told him that the president had cleared his schedule not long into that meeting. Another source, who had seen the FBI director arrive, told Art that Stevenson seemed agitated. While that could serve as circumstantial evidence and would certainly make for an interesting tidbit for the story, it wasn't the confirmation the reporter needed.

So Art had everybody he could think of who was close to either Stevenson or Sweeney. It was the kind of article that was extremely difficult to nail down because he was reporting on a meeting that involved only two people, neither of whom would talk to him. What he had to do was to find a source who would have talked about the conversation with either of the participants.

It took him four hours to find that person. In the end, a lawyer who had gone to school with Sweeney and Stevenson had called him back.

"Listen, I can talk to you about what happened this morning, but it can't be traced back to me," the lawyer had said. "I don't want any trouble."

Art assured the man that any information he received would be "on background," meaning that the lawyer's name would not be used. Instead, his quotes would be attributed to "a person familiar with the meeting." With that out of the way, they had spoken for 15 minutes, and his source gave Art all the information he needed for his story.

The article hit Washington like a bombshell.

People could not agree on what was more fascinating. Some felt that Stevenson's offer to resign, a move always seen as an admission of guilt of some sort, was the bigger story. Others believed that Sweeney's decision to refuse the offer was even bigger news. For whatever reason, possibly out of loyalty to an old friend, the president had let an opportunity pass to deflect the blame for a bungled response to the terrorist attack from himself.

The story made for great TV and the cable news pundits were all over it.

"I think many people have felt that this attack rattled the Sweeney administration and that they have not been up to the task," a commentator on Fox News opined. "And I think this is the clearest evidence so far of this. Basically, what the FBI director said by handing in his resignation is: 'I really screwed this up'."

A conservative talk show host who was a guest on the same program was even more candid in his criticism of the administration.

"Many Americans have felt for a long time that President Sweeney has weakened our country. He cut homeland security funds, he has done very little to go after as-Sirat and other radicals, and he put his frat brother at the helm of the FBI," the talk show host said, using the kind of language that had made him a staple on AM radio. "It seems to me that the only thing he has not done was to personally invite Hassan al-Zaid to bomb one of our buses and kill Americans." McClintock, who was monitoring the news from his office, caught the remark and laughed out loud.

***

Fariq banged on the door to wake up Hassan in time for Fajr – the morning prayer that was observed before sunrise. In all, Hassan had gotten only a couple hours of uneasy sleep but tried not to let it show when he opened his door.

"How was your rest?" Fariq inquired, handing him a bundle of clothes.

"Knowing that I had reached safety put my mind at ease," Hassan replied. He unwrapped a long white shirt and head gear of the same color.

"I will wait outside," Fariq said and closed the door behind him.

Hassan splashed some cold water in his face and got dressed quickly. Then he joined Fariq in the hallway and the two of them made their way up to the ground level where Hanif Younis was already waiting. With the help of some sheets, a section of the atrium had been closed off.

"While you are now with friends, we thought it would be good to not let too many eyes see you," he explained.

"I appreciate your thoughtfulness," Hassan said. Any additional conversation was cut off by the call to prayer. The three men turned toward Mecca and began their Fajr.

When the prayer was finished, they went back into the bowels of the madrasah and to the room of Hanif Younis, where some tea and breakfast awaited them.

"This is Halwa Puri Cholay, a traditional Pakistani breakfast dish," Younif explained. "It's made from sweet halwa, chick peas and a bread we call puris. You better get used to our food. There won't be any cheeseburgers where you are going."

The large man laughed at his own joke.

"So I'm to move elsewhere?" Hassan asked, knowing how much was riding on the answer.

In planning Pathfinder, the consensus was that they would have a fairly high chance of success if Hassan managed to get close to the as-Sirat leaders within a week or at least found out where they were located. Once that first window of opportunity closed, the chance of failure increased rapidly with each day, along with the likelihood that his cover would be blown.

McClintock, who knew a thing or two about being involved in clandestine activities in enemy territory, had repeatedly tried to drill into Hassan's head that it was alright to walk away from the mission at that point.

"If you think your life is in danger at any point, and especially as time passes, nobody will think less of you and what you have done for our country if you abort the mission," the DNI had said, even though he felt that his warnings would fall on deaf ears.

McClintock privately believed that Pathfinder would end either in success or the death of Hassan, possibly both. He hoped that all of the specialists were right who predicted that it would take less than a week for Hassan to complete the main objective.

Taking into account Omar Bashir's media savvy and his penchant for wanting to make a big splash, the consensus of the intelligence analysts was that he would want to meet Hassan quickly and that it would take less than a week to make contact.

Sitting across from a lower level as-Sirat member in a madrasah in Islamabad, Hassan was about to find out if they were right.

"I do not know where exactly you will be taken, but I know it is a place out west in Waziristan," Younis said. "Today, you will remain here so we can make the necessary preparations to move you there. Tomorrow, you will travel and the day after that, you will be enjoying your Halwa Puri Cholay with Omar Bashir." Hassan could not conceal a wide smile.

"Allah is great," he said. "It will be my proudest day."

"Before you can leave, I want you to stay out of sight. One can never be too cautious," Younis said. "Of course you will be able to join me for the daily prayers and Fariq and I will be around should you need anything. We will provide you with new clothing for the trip. Oh, and wash that hair color out. It might have served you on your trip but you'll stick out here with the light color."

"I thank you for all of your help," Hassan responded, unable to speak much more. He was still trying to come to terms with what he just heard and didn't want his voice to give away his feelings. The plan was working. In just three days, it might all be over, and the sacrifices of the past four years would have paid off. If everything went well, he'd be home within a week.

"Also, we have to take and destroy all of your belongings," Younis said. "We don't want there to be anything that will link you to your identity as you cross the country. Again, one can never be too cautious."

Just like that, Hassan's elation from a second ago turned into a pit that quickly grew in his stomach. If the GPS devices would be destroyed, he was screwed.

"You mean you want to destroy my fake passport and my clothes?" he asked, thinking of the belt, the shoes and the watch with the GPS devices.

"Everything," Younis repeated. "We don't want there to be a trace of you."

Hassan's mind was racing. He had to figure out a way to take at least one of the devices with him without arousing suspicion.

"I hope you will not destroy everything," he said, forcing a smile. "I brought a present for as-Sirat. There are several thousand dollars hidden in my luggage. It's money I had set aside for bribes during my trip but I never needed it."

In fact, the cash had been marked, an idea that McClintock had come up with. It would be widely known that Hassan had escaped with a lot of money, so the thinking was that it would not arouse suspicion. Then, when the money was being spent, it would give them another way of tracking as-Sirat's activities.

"We have already found it," Younis said. "I hope you don't mind, but we carefully examined your belongings."

"I don't mind," Hassan replied. He was not worried about the GPS devices being discovered. They were top of the line pieces of equipment that even an electronics specialist would have a tough time finding. "Like you said, one can never be too cautious."

With a smile, Hassan added: "At least now you know I'm not keeping anything from you."

"I was not worried about that," Younis said. "But the American devils are very good at tracking electronics. We have taken anything they might use to find you and destroyed it already."

There goes the watch, Hassan thought.

"Thanks, that was smart of you," he said out loud.

"So all of my things will be destroyed?" Hassan asked. "I can't keep any memento?"

"I am afraid not." Younis said with some regret in his voice. "I have my orders and they are already being carried out. One of the brothers works as a glass blower here and your things have been taken to his shop and thrown into the furnace. It will be hot enough to burn anything that could be used to identify or track you, so don't worry."

"That's good to know. Thank you again," Hassan said. He was screwed. At least a small ray of hope for him was that the guys would figure out that the devices had been destroyed once they went offline. It would have been worse had they just been stored somewhere in the madrasah when he was being moved. Still, that wasn't much of a consolation.

***

"What the fuck just happened?" Electronics expert Craig Byelick shot up from his seat, staring at the screen that had, until a few seconds before, shown the location of Hassan's three GPS devices. There had been some movement to a point not far from the madrasah and then, in quick succession, one by one went dark. The technician checked all of his equipment but everything was working fine.

"Mike, get over here ASAP," Byelick yelled into the other room, where team leader Mike Sheahan was finishing up breakfast. "We just lost all three GPS signals."

Within moments, Sheahan rushed into the room. "What was that?" he asked.

"We lost the signal all three GPS devices and I don't think the problem is on our end," Byelick said. "There is either something wrong with the satellite or with Hassan's equipment. There had been some movement but then they just went dead."

"It can't be a coincidence if it's Hassan's right?" Sheahan wanted to know.

"It would be extremely unlikely that all of the devices stop working on their own at the same time," Byelick said. "If the problem is with Hassan's equipment, then it was something external."

"Let's get McClintock on the phone."

***

Art Kempner liked to have some water by his bedside, so he grabbed an Evian bottle from the fridge and was ready to call it a night. Breaking news was fun and rewarding but it was also tiring. The exhausting part wasn't really chasing information. What was much more draining was having to constantly worry if the competition would beat him to the punch.

It had been another good day for him and for the Post, Art thought as he was getting ready to shut down his laptop. The reporter checked his e-mail one last time and saw that the intern he worked with over the summer had written him.

Art took pride in tutoring promising journalists that went through the Post's internship program. He never felt that, as the newspaper's top reporter, he was above helping the next generation. After all, he had been given much help and many breaks on his way to the top.

He decided to see what she had written before turning in.

> "Dear Mr. Kempner,
> Sorry that I have been out of touch. Things
> have been crazy since I moved back to
> Oregon and I didn't want to bother you with all
> of the stuff going on in Washington.
> Nice scoop on the FBI director's resignation
> offer, by the way.
> I'm just writing to let you know that I got a
> job!!! I'm working for the Cottage Grove
> Sentinel, a small paper in my home town.
> There are only three reporters, so I get to

cover everything from high school sports to
city politics, at least that's what they
promised me.
Since you have been working so much on the
bombing, I thought I'd send you one of
my first stories. It's on the funeral from one of
the victims, a former Special Forces
soldier who lived here.
I hope everything is going well and thank you
again for all of your help this summer. I
hope I can make you proud.
Sincerely, Meghan"

"Good for you, kiddo," he thought to himself. It was
nice to see people still being able to get jobs in print
journalism, an industry that was slowly dying.
He checked the clock on the bottom right corner of the
screen. It was still a few minutes until "Entourage"
started, one of his guilty pleasures, so he decided to
check out the story Meghan had sent.

Cottage Grove Bids Farewell to Terror Victim
In what Mayor Joey Srnka called "the clearest
sign of what he meant to our community,"
hundreds showed up Friday to pay their last
respects to Cottage Grove resident Tom
Gorsula, 52, a victim of Wednesday's terrorist
attack in the nation's capital.
Some businesses had closed for the funeral and
Sheriff Lenny Baxter estimated that
about 10 percent of the town's population had
taken the time to bid farewell to Gorsula,
the owner of Cottage Grove Grill on Main
Street.
"To my generation, Tom will always be the guy
who took our football team to the state

championship as a standout linebacker and running back. Instead of playing college ball, he joined the military and became a highly decorated member of our Special Forces," Srnka said. "A younger generation will miss Tom as the man who offered everybody with a 4.0 grade point average a free ice cream sundae. And to our youngest, he is just Coach Tom. We will all miss him."

Gorsula is leaving behind wife Holly and twin girls Molly and Libby.

To those who knew him, it is not surprising that it was an act of compassion that led him to Washington on Wednesday. On short notice, he had decided to make the trip to the the nation's capital after hearing that one of the men he served with was being treated for a serious illness at Walter Reed Medical Center. Gorsula never made it there. He got on Metro Bus 2405 shortly after arriving in Washington.

"It just showed what Tom was all about," Srnka, a longtime friend, said after the ceremony.

It was his kindness and compassion that had initially drawn Holly Gorsula to her future husband. The two began dating in high school.

"I never cared about his football records," she said. "What I loved about him was that he cared so deeply about everything he was engaged in, whether it was sports or protecting the country or taking care of his family.

> *"Before Tom left, it was almost like he gave me one last present," she added. "On the way out of the door, he said some of the nicest things, it was almost as though he had a premonition that something was about to happen. I'll never forget that moment, along with so many other happy memories he gave me."*

The quote stopped Art cold. He was pretty sure that the story he had read earlier about one of the victims was not about the same man despite both articles sounding very much alike. It was late and he was ready for bed, but somewhere in the back of his head an alarm bell was beginning to ring.

> *Holly Gorsula voiced dismay that the military had not made it possible to allow her nephew Ken Gorsula, who followed his uncle's example and is currently serving in Afghanistan, to attend the funeral.*
> *"Apparently they don't allow them to take leave right now, but it seems there could have been an exception, seeing how my husband was a decorated combat veteran," she said.*

Art quickly responded to Meghan, telling her that he liked the story and encouraging her to keep up the good work. Then he wrote a post-it note and pasted it to the screen of his laptop before closing it.

"Check funeral stories from local papers," he reminded himself.

Saturday, 1:18 am ET

The loss of the GPS signals had caused a flurry of activity in Islamabad and Washington. The equipment in the safe house was switched with one of the backup machines, and satellites were checked and double-checked. It quickly became clear that the technician's initial assessment had been correct – there was a problem with the transmitters.

In the end it was the Director of National Intelligence who prevented the team from panicking. They all respected him as a veteran who had seen it all and lived to tell about it.

"I think we have to continue our work under the assumption that the GPS devices Hassan was carrying will no longer be of help to us," McClintock said, speaking on a secure line with Mike Sheahan. "But that doesn't mean that Hassan is in trouble. In fact, while the loss of the equipment will make things more difficult for us, the fact that the transmitters have been destroyed might be a good sign."

"How is that a good sign, sir?" the team leader asked.

"Think about it. It's highly unlikely that some third-rate as-Sirat operative would be able to find the transmitters that, according to our techies, are virtually undetectable," McClintock explained. "If they were sophisticated enough to find them, then they would know better than to simply destroy them. In that case, they would use that knowledge against us, maybe to lure us into a trap or something.

"The way I see it, they just destroyed all of Hassan's stuff," the DNI opined. "Maybe they burned it or threw it in a lake or something. If that's what they're doing, then it's a good sign because it means that they believe that anything associated with Hassan is potentially dangerous. And they'd only think that if they're buying the cover story."

McClintock's analysis calmed everybody down, but having lost the ability to track Hassan electronically was a major problem. During a conference call in which the DNI discussed the new situation with the team, several of the men voiced regret that they hadn't switched out the transmitter transplanted in Hassan's leg.

"There's no point crying over spilled milk," McClintock said, again the voice of reason. "Thinking about it will just distract us from the task at hand, which has gotten much more difficult now. Since we've lost our ability to monitor Hassan electronically, we're gonna have to do it the old-fashioned way."

The team spent the next hour going over how they could most effectively track Hassan. Fortunately, they had planned for this contingency and had some assets in place to conduct in-person surveillance. First, they had rented the apartment with a view on the entrance of the madrasah when it was determined that the school should be Hassan's starting point. In addition, several of the Pathfinder members were of Middle Eastern descent and could pass as Pashtun or one of the other groups of ethnic minorities living in Pakistan. They would be able to follow Hassan when he was being moved without arousing immediate suspicion.

Their car park not only included the nice SUVs but also several cars that could be used for surveillance, for example a couple of beat-up taxis and a well-used 4x4. Of course none of the vehicles were American made.

The team quickly devised a new rotation that would allow them to have some people near the madrasah at all times. The school was located at a busy part of the city, making around-the-clock surveillance possible. Once they got a glimpse of Hassan, they hoped to be able to follow him.

"If they take him out west, or up north into the mountains, you have to be very careful about following him too closely," McClintock cautioned the team. "There won't be many cars out there and it'll be very difficult to tail somebody. Whatever you do, don't take any risks that would allow them to figure out that they're being followed. We have a lot of satellites in this part of the world and drones, so if you know the general direction of where they're taking Hassan, I hope we'll be able to pick him up from the air."

The DNI ended the call by reminding them to stay calm. Not everything was going to go as planned, the loss of the GPS signal was just the first of many things that would cause them to have to think on their feet. "You're the best of the best and you've trained years for this week," McClintock said. "Trust in your ability and your preparation and everything will work out."

***

The alarm bells that had begun ringing in Art Kempner's head before he went to sleep had not stopped throughout the night and forced him to wake up at 6:00 am on Saturday, the one day on which he normally liked to sleep in.

The reporter also broke with his routine of spending the better part of the morning eating a long breakfast and reading the four newspapers he subscribed to. Instead, he planted himself on his favorite chair with his laptop, a plate full of toast with Nutella, some orange juice and coffee.

"Breakfast of champions," he mumbled to himself and went to work.

Whenever Art talked to young journalists, he was inevitably asked what made a good reporter. He usually responded by giving them the kind of answer they were expecting to hear, saying that it took hard work, persistence, great sources and excellent news judgment. It was his way of testing them because, most often, it wasn't the first question in an interview that yielded the best news. Instead, it was normally a follow-up that built on a previous answer.

So when he was pressed on what he thought the single most important quality was that a journalist needed, or if he was asked what he thought made him the Pulitzer Prize winner he had become, Art would always give the "real" answer, which was that he believed that his "nose" for news had gotten him to the top of the profession.

Sure, there were times when his gut feeling was wrong, but most often the alarm bells were right and led him to a huge story.

For now, Art had no idea what that story could be in this case. All he knew was that it was odd that the two local news stories from different parts of the country sounded so similar. He had read both of them carefully and then jotted down the similarities.

Both terror victims were male veterans. They were of similar age, married and active in their communities. While that description would fit any number of people, what had really caught Art's attention and caused the alarm bells to ring was how each of their wives had described their last moments together. Basically, they had both indicated that their husbands had acted in an unusual way and as though they knew this would be their final farewell.

The reporter spent the next three hours searching local newspapers for stories about the funerals of the other victims. When he was finished, the alarm bells had turned into air raid sirens.

Art had found articles on 30 of the passengers, a dozen of which made references to the victims having some affiliation with the military. That was a rate of 40 percent, making it a statistical anomaly. What alarmed him even more was that the spouses of at least five more of the victims said something to the extent that the final farewell had been especially heartfelt. That was a figure of about 20 percent. And those calculations only took into account the stories that mentioned military affiliation and final farewells.

His coffee had long gotten cold and Art got up to brew another pot and stretch his legs. He needed to think. His instincts told him that there was something going on here but he didn't know what it was. Yet!

***

Hassan had spent most of his day in the chamber of Hanif Younis. His host was adamant about keeping him out of his students' sight.

"They're devout young Muslims and I believe they'll grow up to become warriors for the cause," he explained. "But they have much to learn, such as keeping their little mouths shut. I worry that they'd trumpet the news all over the city if they learned who you are or even that there is a special guest staying with me."

Younis kept Hassan company for much of the morning, asking his guest question after question about his life in America, the bombing and the subsequent escape. This gave Hassan the chance to try out his cover story, and he was delighted to see that Younis never seemed to doubt the tale of a young American Muslim who grew disenchanted with his country and aspired to join as-Sirat.

Hassan appreciated the opportunity to test his cover but would have rather spent time alone to process everything that happened since his arrival. He remained elated that it seemed as though he would be able to fulfill his primary objective – to be taken to Omar Bashir. However, the loss of his transmitters was a grave concern. If the team was unable to track him, then the discovery of the as-Sirat headquarter was pretty much for naught unless he was able to somehow make contact and relay the location. He needed time to think.

"Would it be possible for me to get some rest, Hanif?" he finally asked. "I enjoy our conversation but the jet lag is getting to me and I want to be well rested for tomorrow's journey."

"Certainly," his host said. "I'll escort you back to your chamber."

Once he was alone in his room, Hassan made a mental checklist of what he knew and did not know.

He was now without a working transmitter, meaning that the team would have to rely on other means to track him. They had planned for the possibility of the electronic surveillance failing and Hassan knew that assets were in place at the safe house that would allow them to follow him in person. He also knew that the team was watching the madrasah right now from across the street. Putting two and two together, he determined that the fact that they hadn't stormed into the madrasah with guns blazing was an indication that they had figured out that the destroyed GPS devices didn't mean that Hassan was in trouble. Maybe he would get the chance to give them a signal when he was leaving Islamabad. Unfortunately, he hadn't been given any information about his trip, so there was nothing he could pass on to the team even if he found a way to do so.

He racked his brain trying to figure out how he could make contact, not only on tomorrow's journey but also from his final destination but he came up with nothing that resembled a viable plan. The best he could think of was trying to swipe a cellphone before leaving but he had not seen one yet.

The more he thought about the situation, the clearer it became to Hassan that he might have to improvise once he reached the as-Sirat headquarters. Certainly there would be phones there, he would just have to find a way to use one.

***

Art Kempner was sitting in his favorite chair in the living room of his Capitol Hill home. His feet were up on an Ottoman and some classical music was playing softly in the background. In his hand, Art held a digital recording device and spoke into it occasionally.

He had spent most of his day thinking about the similarities of the terror victim's stories. As he liked to do on weekends, Art had set out before noon for a stroll around his neighborhood. He often walked to the Supreme Court and the Capitol as he was thinking about stories. Sometimes he made it down to the national mall and, on rare occasions, he even hiked all the way to the White House, especially if the articles dealt with the president.

This time, deep in thoughts, his walk ended when Art looked up and, much to his own surprise, realized that he had hiked past the Vietnam Memorial, the Lincoln Memorial and then across the Memorial Bridge toward Arlington Cemetery.

What had kept him so occupied was that he could not make sense of the information he had about the bus attack. Art estimated that the normal rate of people associated with the military in a group of 36 adults should have been much lower than 40 percent. Of course, he had reminded himself, the attack had taken place near the Pentagon where there was a much higher concentration of military personnel. Still, that figure seemed much too high. It was not as though the victims were all going to a veterans convention. Another reason for such a high concentration could have been that the terrorist had specifically targeted them but many of the victims were retired, so it was not apparent that they were associated with the military. In addition, many had just arrived at National Airport, so there was no way this could have been planned. Another possible explanation Art had come up with was that Hassan al-Zaid had simply targeted a bus that was scheduled to go by the Pentagon, but that seemed unlikely to the reporter.

The spouses' descriptions of the final farewells especially bothered him. He had done some more research and found out that there were many claims about premonition of death, including the dream Abraham Lincoln reportedly had about his assassination. In addition, some studies showed that people were more likely to cancel their tickets or not show up for flights that ended up crashing. One such case Art read about was that of former Olympic tennis champion Marc Rosset, who decided to stay another day at the U.S. Open in 1998 rather than to take a Swissair flight that crashed. So maybe that explained the hints at premonition.

Another possible reason could simply be wishful thinking on the part of the spouses. Maybe they just wanted to believe that those final farewells were especially tender and heartfelt. Art had decided that he would check with a psychologist first thing Monday, hoping that this would help him make sense of the information he had collected.

* * *

After two hours of basketball in the still potent afternoon sun, Captain Ken Gorsula was exhausted. Having grown up in Oregon, he felt that he would never get used to the kind of weather he had experienced in Iraq and Afghanistan. Here at Bagram Air Base, it had rained only a couple of times in the last three months and the temperatures were just now coming down a bit in the evenings.

Gorsula debated between taking a shower and going to one of the computer terminals that allowed the soldiers to stay in close touch with home. Seeing how he hadn't been online in a couple of days, he decided to check his e-mail first. There were only a few messages from family and friends.

"Out of sight, out of mind," he thought. At least he could count on spammers writing him on a regular basis. In between offers for penile enhancements, "get rich quick" schemes and a variety of prescriptions, he found an e-mail from his mother.

"Wish you could have been here, Kenny. It was a beautiful service."

His mom was not much of a writer. At least she had finally gotten the hang of e-mail. This time, she even managed to attach a file. It was the same article about his uncle's funeral that had gotten Art Kempner so excited. For Gorsula, it only served as a reminder that he hadn't been allowed to go home. He was still pissed off about the decision and had fired off a letter to the editor to the Army Times, which had printed it in its online version.

While he could have gone to the funeral in Oregon and made it back by the following day, he instead had been sitting at Bagram, playing poker for nickles, watching movies and shooting hoops.

In his letter, he had called the decision a "way to lower morale" that had "no foundation in their current mission."

"What would the military rather want me to do, spend some time with my family, recharge my batteries and say farewell to the man who inspired me to join special ops or sit around in Afghanistan with nothing to do? My example isn't even the worst. Another member of the unit was not allowed to go home for the birth of his child and a third was denied the chance to see his mother before she started chemo. How do I know? Because we have been sitting around with nothing to do other than complaining about this dumb decision. I would hope that the military will quickly rethink and rescind this order."

Gorsula had felt better after firing off his letter and publicly expressing his anger with the Pentagon leadership. But he also realized that his frustration was fueled by not being able to fight as-Sirat in Pakistan and he was just lashing out at the Pentagon because he couldn't get his hands on the terrorists. All he could do was pummel the pictures of Omar Bashir and Hassan al-Zaid that he had taped to the dart board by his bed. The e-mail from his mother stoked his anger and frustration again and he figured he would probably break the dart board later that night.

"Fuck 'em all," he said to himself, logged off and headed for the shower.

Sunday, 4:12 am ET

It had been another short night for Hassan. This time it was nervous excitement that kept him awake. When he finally admitted to himself that he wouldn't be able to sleep anymore, Hassan got up and ready for the day. The feeling of anticipation reminded him of how he felt the nights before his birthday as a kid. Farouk al-Zaid was a generous father and never spared any expense to make his only child happy. He always made sure to not only buy most of the items on the wish list but to also surprise his son. When Hassan turned six, he awoke to a basketball hoop in the driveway. When he turned nine, his father took the family to Disney World. However, Hassan's favorite birthday was his thirteenth. His father woke him up early and they drove to the airport. They boarded a flight to Chicago but his father still refused to tell him what their final destination was. A fancy town car was waiting for them at the airport and took them to Soldier Field, where the U.S. soccer team took on Brazil. The al-Zaid's had great seats and it was the best day in Hassan's life. At the time, he had already been identified as a standout soccer player, and watching the game made him practice harder than ever because he swore to himself that he would one day wear the U.S. jersey.

"Well, that didn't happen," Hassan thought to himself, looking down on the kaftan he was wearing.

This time, he was excited for another type of trip and he again didn't know where it was going to take him. Hassan hoped that the day's journey would indeed lead him to Omar Bashir and that he would be able to serve his country in a more meaningful way than playing a soccer game. The excitement by far overshadowed his concerns over the lost transmitters. Over night, Hassan had grown more confident that he would figure out some way to make contact. And, if that was not possible, he would find another way to make sure that all of the sacrifices he and others made were not for naught.

Hassan sat on his bed, waiting for the knock from Fariq. When it finally came, he jumped up, eager to start his day. He opened the door and Fariq was surprised to see their guest dressed and ready to go.

After the early prayers, Hassan ate breakfast with Hanif Younis and the two spent the morning trading questions. Hassan was eager to learn about as-Sirat while his host wanted to find out more about the United States.

After Dhuhr, the noon prayer, the two men walked to Younis' chamber and Hassan saw that another man was waiting for them.

"This is Nasir," Younis said. "He is part of the brotherhood and will accompany you from here on." They exchanged greetings and took a second to look each other up and down.

Nasir appeared like a man not to be trifled with. It was tough to say how old he was but Hassan guessed that he was in his 30s. While he couldn't really see the voluminous Hanif fighting for as-Sirat in any capacity other than as the shaper of impressionable young minds, Hassan had no doubt that Nasir had seen combat. He was wiry and not very big, but there was just something about him that oozed danger and he had the same determined look that Hassan had observed so many times when he was training with the other Pathfinder guys.

"Thanks for everything, Hanif," Hassan said, embracing his host. "Are you not coming with us?"

"Oh no. I'm just a very small piece in a large machine, not important enough to go where you're traveling to. But it has been a privilege to play a part in your journey."

"Are you ready to go?" Nasir said.

"Yes."

"Then follow me."

The group walked to the ground level of the madrasah and out of the front gate. Hassan, hoping that the team was watching, looked around so that they would be able to recognize his face. Nasir opened the back door of an old Land Rover that was idling at the curb. Hassan got in the car and greeted the driver with a Salam Aleikum. The man turned his head and returned the greeting.

One look had told Hassan that Nasir was not the kind of man anybody should mess with unless they were ready to face the repercussions. Still, he seemed like a pansy compared to the driver of the Land Rover. The man was probably going on 50 but he was in excellent shape. The hairy hands that gripped the steering wheel looked as though they could easily crush it, and Hassan could not miss the scars on the man's arms and across his left cheek.

"Fawad has fought countless battles for us, starting with the Soviets when he was just a boy," Nasir, who had gotten in the passenger seat, said as though he had read Hassan's mind.

"He has killed many more men than you but, I must admit, in less spectacular fashion."

Nasir said something in a language Hassan didn't recognize, and Fawad put the car in motion.

"It's Pashto," Nasir explained, again interpreting Hassan's expression correctly. "Fawad grew up in Afghanistan and the constant fighting never left him with much of a chance to go to school and learn other languages. It has his advantages. He won't know what we'll be talking about and we won't distract his driving."

"Can you tell me where we're going?" Hassan asked.

"Fawad will drive us to the edge of South Waziristan, to a city called Zhob. It's where he lives. His fighting days for the brotherhood are over but he still helps us as a driver and a courier," Nasir said. "From Zhob, you and I will meet up with somebody else and then move on to our final destination.

"It'll take a while to get there," he added with a smile that did not reach his eyes. "That will give us some time to talk and get to know each other."

Then Nasir began bombarding Hassan with questions about the bombing, his escape, and life in America. On the surface, they were similar to the ones Hanif Younis had asked the previous morning but Hassan immediately noticed a subtle but unmistakable difference. While the madrasah teacher had asked out of pure curiosity, Nasir was interrogating him. Hassan vowed to be careful but he was not worried. He had been practicing for this type of thing.

The traffic was light and they soon reached Tarnol, from where Fawad took national highway 80 West toward Bannu.

Almost a kilometer behind them, an old taxi was following the Land Rover, relaying back any information to the safe house in Islamabad and to the beat-up 4x4 following even further behind, ready to take up the pursuit of Hassan at any time.

Sunday, 8:00 am ET

The reason that Art Kempner normally only got to sleep in on Saturdays was that he would wake up early on Sundays to be able to watch the morning talk shows. "Meet the Press" would always remain his favorite, partially for nostalgic reasons and because he was a somewhat frequent guest. He still enjoyed watching the shows on the other networks. Fox, which was always first to be aired in the Washington area, had made great strides with its program and Art also liked ABC's show, which aired next at 10:00 am.

All of the networks this week were obviously focusing their broadcasts on the terrorist attack. The vice president was the exclusive headliner on "Meet the Press" while Fox and ABC each had booked the National Security Adviser and the Senate Minority Leader. CBS had the bipartisan duo of Jim Hearst and Chuck Nelson. While they were veteran Members of Congress, the two Virginia lawmakers were certainly not a high profile combo. Still, the network had let it leak that the show would be worth watching and had promoted it heavily.

The earlier shows were fairly predictable. The administration officials strongly defended the president and the opposition leader stressed that this was a time in which everybody had to work together. Then the CBS's Face the Nation began and it was clear within minutes that this one would actually deliver some news.

"I understand that you have some misgivings with regard to how the aftermath of the terrorist attack was handled," the host said as a lead in, directing his question to Chuck Nelson.

"I sure do. The bottom line is that the administration should have closed both Dulles and BWI airports. The failure to do so, in my view, allowed the terrorist to get away," Nelson said.

Art actually heard himself gasping. Coming from a veteran lawmaker, that kind of rhetoric was a slap in the face of the president, whom Nelson had pretty much just blamed for letting Hassan al-Zaid get away. Just as stunning as this attack on the Sweeney administration was also that it came less than a week after the bombing.

"As the ranking member of the Homeland Security Committee, it is my responsibility to speak out about this," Nelson continued. "Maybe it will serve as a wakeup call to the Sweeney administration so that they can get their act together and find the terrorist."

"Wouldn't you say that it is unusual to voice this criticism so soon after the attack?" the host asked.

"That may be true, but there is no time to waste. I'm also comforted by the fact that I have the backing on this from a member of the president's own party, my dear friend and colleague Jim Hearst."

Art straightened up. Certainly Hearst wouldn't criticize the president. When he saw who had been booked for the show, the reporter had figured that Hearst was there to counter anything negative Nelson said about the administration.

"Let's turn to Congressman Hearst then," the host said. "Do you also feel that the administration bungled the response?"

"I regret saying that I do," Hearst said. "You know I'm one of President Sweeney's most loyal supporters, but in this case the administration has done an awful job."

Art could barely believe what he was hearing. Hearst stabbing the president in the back like that was unprecedented.

"I'm a member of President Sweeney's party, but my primary responsibility is to serve my constituents and that is why I feel compelled to speak out along with Chuck.

"Of course, I'm in a unique position because I represent the district in which the terrorist grew up. I think the administration should have done more to keep the people in my district and across the country safe."

The host could barely conceal his glee when he asked the next question. Nobody would be talking about any of the other morning shows on this day or the next because all the news had been made on CBS.

It kept getting better for him because the two Virginia Congressmen continued their tag team beating of the administration for the entire time they were on. Every now and then they sounded a conciliatory note before continuing their assault on the president and his team. During a commercial break, Art headed to get his laptop and his blackberry. The Post had people assigned to write about what was said in the Sunday morning talk shows, but the Pulitzer Prize winner knew that he would be called into action on this day. What was taking place here was just too stunning and, at the very least, he would be asked to provide his thoughts on the matter. Now he just had to figure out what exactly his thoughts were.

It didn't make a whole lot of sense. Nelson was a veteran lawmaker with a history of building bridges, not burning them. It seemed even less conceivable that

Hearst would go after his own president. The election was more than a year away and there was no way he was getting this much heat from constituents just because a terrorist had lived among them.

For the second time in as many days, Art was stumped, unable to make sense of a situation. He was wondering if he was slowly losing his edge.

***

The Land Rover had been plowing through Pakistan for almost three hours when they reached Bannu. Nasir had spent about half of that time peppering Hassan with questions. Then, apparently pleased with the answers he received, Nasir thawed considerably and he and Hassan carried on a more normal conversation for the rest of the drive.

From Bannu, they headed north on National Highway 55 to Dera Ismail Khan, which they reached shortly before noon. They stopped for some food before resuming their trip west. This time, they took National Highway 50, which took them toward Zhob.

"We're almost there," Nasir said when they reached the outskirts of this city of about 50,000. "You have to play close attention now. Fawad will take us under an overpass. Once I give the signal, we have to get out of this car and jump into the back of a truck that is waiting on our right side. Got it?"

"Sure, when you tell me, I'll get out on the right and follow you to a truck."

"Exactly. Don't mind the two men who will be standing on the road. They're going to take our places, just in case somebody was following us."

They drove through Zhob for a few minutes. There was some sort of a large market going on and the city was bustling with activity. Eventually, Fawad turned into a side street and the reached an area that was quieter. When they got to an overpass, the Land Rover stopped and Nasir said "Now."

He and Hassan hurried out of the car and climbed onto the platform of a pickup that was idling on the other side of the street. To Hassan's surprise, they were not the only people there. The pickup had been modified into a sort of bus with benches on each side and metal bars that kept people from falling out. What appeared to be a family of three was sitting on one of the benches. The man and the woman looked impassively at the two new passengers and a child that could not be older than four paid them no attention at all.

"Lay down under the bench, facing front, and I'll cover you with some blankets," Nasir said. Hassan complied. "Unfortunately, this part of the trip will be a little bit uncomfortable but it is for your safety and ours. We'll likely come up on a checkpoint or two. They shouldn't be any trouble but you never know."

"I don't mind," Hassan said, his voice muffled by the blanket over his head. While Nasir may be speaking the truth about checkpoints, Hassan figured that this method of transporting him had also been chosen to not allow him to recognize where they were going. "From now on, only speak when I'm talking to you and listen to all of my commands," Nasir said. "When you hear other voices, just lay still."

Hassan could feel the truck moving and soon became uncomfortably hot under the blankets. He hated to admit it, but the simple maneuver Nasir pulled off would likely shake anybody following them. As he was stewing underneath the blankets, Hassan forced himself to come to terms with the fact that he was going to be on his own wherever he was headed. He took some comfort in thinking that as-Sirat would not go through so much trouble if he was not going to a place that the military would view as a high value target.

Hassan tried to keep track of how long the trip took and also made mental notes of when the truck seemed to be going uphill for extended periods of time. While he could not see where they were going, he wanted to gather as many clues as possible.

After what he estimated to be thirty minutes, there indeed appeared to be some kind of checkpoint. The truck stopped and he could hear voices. All seemed in order, though, because the vehicle began moving again after a few seconds.

***

McClintock had spent all weekend in his office, monitoring the situation from there once the transmitters had gone dark. His inability to affect the outcome of events added to his nervousness. Most of the time, he was pacing up and down his office, running countless scenarios of "what ifs" through his head.

He was still hopeful that Pathfinder would succeed, but the loss of all means of electronically tracking Hassan had put a damper on the mission's chances. He was dreading the next phone call he got from Pakistan, and when the phone rang, his fears were confirmed.

"We lost him, sir," Dan Helbig, the team leader of the second shift said. "We were able to follow him to

Zhob but then they got away. We're hoping that the satellites might have picked something up but that's doubtful. Sorry."

McClintock was already checking out a map of the area.

"Well, that's something. We always felt that the as-Sirat leaders might be located a little more toward the east, but if they took him this far west, maybe that'll give us a clue as to where they might take him," the DNI said.

"And Zhob isn't too far from the border, so we can probably blanket the area pretty well with satellites and drones and hope to pick up his trail that way," McClintock added, speaking as much to himself as to the Pathfinder member.

"What do you want us to do now?" Helbig asked.

"Well, you can't hang around in Zhob because you'd attract attention," McClintock said. "I suggest you fall back to the safe house in Islamabad and hang tight. You guys are the people Hassan will contact if he has the chance, so you should be where he expects you to be. Once you assemble the whole team, let's talk about how else you can contribute."

***

Hassan estimated that they had driven for a little over an hour when the truck stopped.

"It's safe to come out," Nasir said. "Sorry for the inconvenience but it was for your safety and for ours."

"I understand," Hassan said. He looked around as he climbed off the truck. As far as he could tell, they were in a mid-sized town. There were some different level buildings and he also spotted a supermarket. Based on the position of the sun, he estimated that it was about 5:30 pm, meaning that he was right about how long it had taken to get here. Of course, that information was only partially helpful in determining where he was because he had no idea in which direction they had traveled, how fast they had been driving or whether they had gone in a straight line or not. Besides, before any of the information he was gathering became useful, he would have to find a way to make contact.

"We'll have tea here and then we'll move on," Nasir said. He led Hassan to a little tea house nearby and they sat at the table in the back.

"We'll be here for a few minutes," he explained. "The driver is just waiting to see if anybody followed us. You just have one more leg to go and then we're there. I'm sorry to say that we'll be walking the rest of the way."

"You're so concerned about security, but what about the family in the truck?" Hassan asked. "Aren't you worried about people talking."

"This isn't Islamabad, where we had to be more careful. You're in our country now, Hassan," Nasir said. "If these people would figure out who you were, they would shower you with presents and carry you to our final destination on their shoulders. You're a hero here."

"Maybe we should tell them who I am," Hassan said and grinned. "That way I wouldn't have to walk."

Nasir threw back his head and laughed.

Just then, the driver of the truck stuck his head in the door and gave Nasir a nod.

"Time to go," said Hassan's companion before starting to grin. "By the way, growing up in America, how much experience do you have with leading mules?"

"Are you joking?" Hassan asked, and Nasir laughed again before explaining.

"See, we could drive but we try not to do that so much. Cars attract more attention. Nobody watching from above seems to care about a few people using mules to move goods from one town to another. So today, you'll pretend to be a fabric merchant. The place we're going to is known for its dyes, so we use that as a cover to move people and supplies.

"Oh, and don't worry about the mules, a couple of our people will do all of the work," Nasir added.

They walked to the outskirts of the town where they met up with a small caravan. It consisted of six men and about a dozen mules that were carrying large baskets and boxes. Nasir greeted the men and they began walking down a dirt road out of town. The late afternoon sun was in their backs and provided pleasant warmth.

"So, what are these mules actually carrying?" Hassan asked.

"Dyes and fabric," Nasir responded. "This time, you're our precious cargo. All the men are armed and will protect you with their life if necessary. But it won't come to that. Like I said, this is our country. The Pakistani military does not bother us and the Americans are not allowed to come here anymore. We're perfectly safe."

***

The Conspiracy Club, as Art Kempner had privately named them, was reconvening at Alan Hausman's favorite Mexican restaurant. The reporter was looking forward to the meal, not only because food and company were good but also because he wanted to hear what Alan's friends had come up with in response to the challenge he had posed. After the first dinner, he had contemplated using the experience to write a story about conspiracy theorists but now that he himself found a couple of things odd that were connected to the bombing, he really wanted to know what they thought.

Art had made the decision not to tell them about the disproportionate number of people associated with the military on the bus. As a reporter, he had always been careful with how much information he would hand out before printing it. After all, he made money because the Post was selling news and not giving it away for free. But there was something else. Art really felt like he was on to something but he had to figure out what it was first.

The group quickly picked up where it had left off, playful insults were flying across the room that was soon filled with laughter.

When the food arrived, conversation ceased shortly as everybody dug in. After taking a few bites, Art used the silence to get a word in.

"So, I hope you guys remembered my challenge," he said. "Is there something about this attack that you think is odd? And I hope you don't mind that I'm recording this. Like I said, this might come in handy for a story down the road. But no worries, I won't use any of the information unless I specifically get your approval."

They all indicated that this wouldn't be a problem and Art placed his digital recorder on the table.

"Surely you must have figured out on your own that the government is behind this," Rick, who was wearing a different GW t-shirt this time, quipped. "The way I see it, the attack has been filmed in a Hollywood studio and the images were somehow projected on Alan's windshield with secret technology, or maybe they controlled his memories somehow," he continued in a conspiratorial tone. "You forgot to wear your saran wrap hat, didn't you Alan?"

"Guilty as charged," Alan Hausman said amid their laughter.

"But seriously," Rick said. "There are a lot of things about this attack that would alarm a good conspiracy theorist. First of all, they claim that they lost the complete surveillance tapes. How the hell does that happen? Losing evidence or not sharing records, like the footage from cameras on 9/11, will always alarm a good conspiracy theorist."

Some of the others nodded.

"But here is something that I actually found odd, all conspiracy theory stuff aside," Rick said. "For the past few years it has been drilled into our heads to be on the lookout for 'suspicious packages' and stuff, and here you have a bus full of people and none of them said anything when a Middle Eastern kid leaves his backpack behind. I think all of us are a little bit guilty of profiling in a situation like that. I know I'm eyeballing people with turbans more closely when I get on a plane, but here nobody seemed to do anything."

"Okay," Art said. "Lemme take the other side. First of all, with regard to the tapes. The administration are the ones who came out and told the public that they had misplaced the tapes, even though they knew they would be ridiculed and criticized for it. It seems like they had nothing to gain by admitting that. And with regard to the luggage, it seems like a lot of these people had just arrived in DC so there were probably a lot of bags on the bus and quite a bit of confusion because they had to get off the Metro and on a shuttle bus. Who is next?"

They all started talking at the same time. When order was restored, Art went around the table and asked them what they found most odd about the bombing. One of them questioned how the bomb was triggered so that it exploded right at the Pentagon. If it was a timer, it would have been a lucky coincidence.

The next man said he found it odd that the terrorist had decided to blow up a bus instead of just leaving the bomb on the Metro.

"Maybe that was his plan all along but the Pentagon station was closed, dumbass," Rick said to laughter. "Now that in itself is highly suspicious. But I find any sentence suspicious that involves the word 'Pentagon'."

When most of them had weighed in, Art spoke again. "I can understand how some of those things look odd, and I guess that was the point of the exercise," he said. "But nothing you brought up is really an indication that something isn't as it seems, right? I mean, after all we know that the bus exploded. Alan saw it happen and we know there were people on it who died. So does this mean that the attack is above conspiracy theories?"

"It better be," Alan said. "I mean, if those military cars hadn't slowed me down, I wouldn't be sitting here, so you guys better believe it was real."

"We all know that the bus really blew up, I don't think there is any debate about that, Alan," said Steve, the older man with the beard. "But I do have a question about the whole thing that has been bothering me for a few days. I just can't make sense of it, and I think it is just the kind of thing that Mr. Kempner was referring to when he was saying that you can find something odd about anything."

Steve looked in the round to make sure he had everybody's attention. Satisfied that they were all listening, he continued.

"Mr. Kempner, I don't believe in subsidizing the oil industry, so I don't own a car," he explained to Art. "I use my bike a lot and the bus for longer trips. I've been living here for more than 30 years and I guess I'm averaging at least one bus trip every day in that time.

"That comes out to more than 10,000 bus rides in and around DC and that is a pretty conservative figure. It could easily be 15,000 or even 20,000. Anyways, I looked at the demographics of the passengers when they released the list of victims and I can tell you one thing for certain. I have never, ever been on a bus with almost 40 people on it and none of them was under 30 or an immigrant. Maybe it is because they all came from the airport, but if I didn't know better, I'd call the demographics of that bus suspicious."

The others began debating what Steve had said but Art paid their discussion little attention. His mind was elsewhere. So here was yet another thing that was odd about Metro Bus 2405 and its passengers and it was not just him feeling that way.

The sense that there was a huge story somewhere close kept getting stronger and he also had the feeling that something else had been said at dinner that was important. He just couldn't quite put his finger on what it was. At least he had the conversation on tape. Maybe if he listened to it again he would be able to connect whatever dots there were.

The alarm bells were louder than ever and Art vowed that he would start thinking of asking the right questions and getting some answers to them.

***

The beginning of their trek hadn't been too arduous, but after a march of over four hours, Hassan was beginning to feel his legs. While some uncertainty was gnawing at him, overall he was buoyant. If Nasir and the others had figured out who he was, he'd be dead by now. Hassan believed the fact that he was still alive meant that he was actually being taken somewhere important.

After the sun set shortly after the last leg of the journey began, temperatures dropped quickly, although the workout of the hike kept him warm. Hassan figured that they were at least a mile above sea level. Mountain ranges surrounded the path on which the men and their mules had been marching. So far he had seen only one car, an old bus that had blanketed them in a cloud of dust. It found its way into Hassan's nose and mouth and he coughed and spit, trying to get rid of the taste.

"I forgot that you are new here," Nasir said with an apologetic smile and handed Hassan a scarf. "Wrap it around your head and cover your face if you see dust coming our way. And turn when a car approaches. Don't worry, you'll pick up everything quickly."

The only other person they encountered was an old man who was taking a mule in the direction they had come from. They greeted him and he bowed deferentially.

"The locals living around the base are strong supporters of as-Sirat," Nasir explained. "We provide them with goods and money. Omar Bashir is a strong believer in improving their lives to strengthen the bonds between them and us. He has funded several schools in the area and every now and then we go there for guest lectures.

"I know America is intent on trying to win the hearts and minds of its enemies," Nasir added, spitting on the ground. "It will never work here. We're sharpening their minds and they have given us their hearts in return."

The rest of the march had been uneventful. The men had chatted throughout as though they didn't have a worry in the world. After Hassan's coughing attacking, each of them had taken some time to walk and talk with him, dispensing advice on various aspects of living in the mountains.

Finally, Hassan saw a town appear in the distance and the pace of the men quickened.

"There is your new home," Nasir said.

"You live in a town?" Hassan asked, his surprise not an act. "Funny, at home the government is telling people that as-Sirat is cowering in caves. Just more of the lies they are feeding people in America, I guess."

"Be patient, you'll see soon enough how we live," Nasir said. He pointed to the mules, which were clearly excited. "Look, even they know we're home. I hope the Americans never catch one of them because the mules could show them the way to our headquarters."

He laughed and slapped Hassan on the back, clearly giddy to get home and relieved that he had succeeded in bringing his precious cargo along.

"You made it, brother."

They entered the town. Although the darkness made it difficult for him to take in the environment, Hassan estimated that there were about four dozen buildings, none of them taller than two floors. He saw no phone lines going into town, which was a concern. The town of Andan was well protected by its surroundings with mountains flanking it on two sides. The road seemed to be the only way a car could get into the town and a well-positioned sentry could probably spot anybody who was approaching from a long way out.

The group turned toward a building that looked like a warehouse. A few men were waiting there and helped unload the mules.

"Follow me," Nasir said and ducked into a door.

Hassan saw that the storage facility was built right into the mountainside. They entered a large room that was barely lit. It was filled with bolts of fabric and containers for what Hassan thought were dyeing chemicals based on the smell in the room.

When his eyes got used to the darkness, he looked around some more, trying to take in all of the details and figuring out why he had been taken here. Hassan was just about to ask when he heard a sound from the back wall, the one that was built into the mountain, and a shelf swung open.

"Welcome," Nasir said and stepped into the narrow passageway that had appeared out of nowhere. He allowed Hassan to pass and closed the door behind them.

"The door can only be opened from the inside once it is bolted," Nasir explained, pointing to a sturdy bolt. "There are others throughout town. You'll see that it is a very large network."

They went through a long tunnel and Hassan saw others branch off from time to time. In addition, there were several rooms, some with mattresses on the floor and others that seemed to be used as storage. He also saw one that was filled with weapons. None of them had doors. Instead, curtains were used to separate the rooms from the tunnel.

It was noticeably cooler inside of the mountain and the grim-looking men Hassan saw in the various rooms were dressed warmly. At their feet, cables were running along the tunnel, splitting off into the rooms and providing the lamps that lit the passage with electricity. Hassan could hear the distant rumbling of generators and the smell of diesel hung faintly in the air.

Finally they reached a metal door. Nasir banged against it and a pair of eyes appeared in a small opening. The door was unlocked and, when it opened, Hassan could see that it was massive.

Two men were standing in the next tunnel.

"We're a brotherhood and have no need for doors other than this one. It's his last line of defense," Nasir explained. "I'm sure he'll explain its purpose to you in due time. Let these guys search you. One can never be too cautious."

The bodyguards thoroughly patted Hassan down before they waved them on. It was good that they hadn't checked his pulse because it was racing and butterflies were fluttering in his stomach. They reached another door and Nasir again knocked.

"Enter," they heard a voice say.

Nasir opened the door and allowed Hassan to walk in first. There, in the middle of the room with a cup of tea in his hand, stood Omar Bashir.

"Allah is great," Hassan shouted and lunged forward. Nasir and the bodyguards immediately reacted to the sudden movement and rushed into the chamber. They saw Hassan, kneeling on the ground, clasping the hem of Omar Bashir's kaftan.

With a flick of his hand, the as-Sirat leader waved his bodyguards and Nasir away.

"Rise, my American brother," Omar Bashir said. "There is no need for such a display. We are all family. I praise Allah for guiding you to us."

Hassan looked up at the terrorist leader. The tears of joy that were gleaming in his eyes were real. All of the hard work and the sacrifices of the past four years had paid off. The plan was working.

"The plan isn't working," Jack Sweeney thought. He had been in office for six years and experienced a lot of ups and downs in that time, but the current day was one of his bleakest as president.

Ever since DNI McClintock had called to let him know that they had lost Hassan, doubts had come crashing down on Sweeney.

"I think I've made a terrible mistake," the president told his wife over dinner. Vocalizing his fear made him feel even worse and things didn't get better when the first lady asked what he was referring to.

She was not cleared to receive that kind of information, so the president told her that he could not elaborate, at which point she got upset with him and they had a rare fight. Normally, when there was such a quarrel, he would try to make her laugh by making some kind of joke about "first couple counseling," pretending to call the Secret Service for help or complaining that he could not possibly be expected to have an argument without his speech writer and a teleprompter present. This time, however, he just let her berate him for a few minutes before mumbling: "You'll understand soon enough," and fleeing to the Oval Office.

Back at his desk, Sweeney tried to get some work done but his mind kept returning to Pathfinder.

When he authorized the mission, the president truly felt that he was not worried about his legacy. Instead, he believed that he made the decision that was best for the United States. Now, thinking that the plan was falling apart, he realized that a complete failure would make things much more difficult for him.

Still, while he was becoming painfully aware of what could be ahead for him, such as congressional hearings, calls for impeachment or his resignation and a pissed off Pakistan, his primary anguish was for the people who had sacrificed so much for Pathfinder.

He hoped that, if the mission truly was a failure, Hassan and the other men would make it home okay, but it was too late for the 37 men and women who had died on the bus.

Sure, they had all been terminally ill, but each of them still had given up the last few months of their lives for their country and this mission, instead of spending the time with their loved ones.

Sweeney regretted that he never got the chance to speak to them. He had wanted to but, logistically, there was no way it could be done without putting the mission at risk.

Finding the volunteers had been one of the trickiest aspects of Pathfinder. The challenge had been to identify candidates, get them to agree to be part of the mission before they could tell anybody else about their condition and then find reasons for all of them to come to Washington.

They quickly had to discard the hope that there would be enough people in the DC area who fit the profile. In fact, they had to search the entire country to find their 50 volunteers.

The only way it could be done was through the health care systems of the Defense Department and the Department of Veterans Affairs. The president authorized a couple of doctors to gain access to the results of certain medical tests within that system. Basically, whenever someone was deemed to have a terminal illness, the tests were flagged and these doctors would review the case to see if the patient could be a potential volunteer. In effect, they knew of the patient's condition before the patients themselves found out about it.

The list of possible volunteers then went to McClintock, who reviewed their entire military file. As a former top spy, he knew the profile of people willing to risk their lives for their country. He had to quickly decide in each case whether the person was a possible candidate because they had to get to them before anybody found out about the terminal illness. They could not risk spouses or others telling the media after the attack that those who died only had a couple of months left to live anyways.

To add pressure to the search, McClintock could not afford to make many mistakes in his selections. Basically, he had to be certain that the people they approached would agree to become victims in a staged terrorist attack to give the United States a chance to cripple as-Sirat. Otherwise, those who rejected him might start telling stories about how the government had tried to recruit them for a daredevil mission.

In the end, McClintock had batted a clean 1,000. He had selected people with excellent service records, strong leadership skills and who volunteered in their communities. A last criterion was that he approached people who did not have too much money saved up.

As an added incentive, McClintock dangled the possibility of financial security in front of his potential volunteers. If they agreed to become part of the mission, their families would receive $1 million once the details of Pathfinder had been made public. McClintock was fairly certain that appealing to the candidates' sense of patriotism would be enough to get them to sign on, but providing financial security for their loved ones was not only the right thing to do, it also made their decisions much easier.

The selection process had begun four months ago when the president made plans to visit the Middle East to see one last time if there was another way to stop terrorism, even in light of the worsening situations in Pakistan and Afghanistan. If Pathfinder got the final green light, the staged bombing was to take place right after Sweeney's return.

They contacted 50 people and none of them turned them down. Thirteen of them died prior to the day of the attack. The others had shown up as promised and given their country the last weeks or months of their lives, including the man who had taken a job as a Metro bus driver. He was the one who steered the bus out of Crystal City until the Humvees could take over remotely.

Sweeney opened his safe and took out the bundle of letters. He weighed it in his hands and then leafed through the stack and looking at the names on the envelopes.

"Please don't let it all have been in vain," the president prayed. Eventually, he put the letters back and headed for the residence for a long and uncomfortable night.

***

In Andan, Hassan was feeling just the opposite. He was exhilarated and the adrenalin pumping through his veins prevented him from falling asleep, even though he was worn out from the long hike to Andan and the thin mountain air.

Hassan was still coming to terms with the fact that he had successfully made contact. Sure, he had always been confident that the plan would work, but to actually be in as-Sirat's headquarters, only a few feet away from Omar Bashir, gave him an overwhelming sense of accomplishment. He shifted around on his straw mattress, wrapped the coarse blanket more tightly around his body, listened to the snoring of the men he shared the room with and tried to give his mind time to catch up with the events of the previous days.

It was obvious that Omar Bashir was delighted to see him. He embraced Hassan repeatedly and insisted that they share the evening meal. Then the as-Sirat leader had personally given him a tour of the "bunker," which was his name for the cave complex the group called home. Omar Bashir introduced Hassan to many of the as-Sirat members currently living in Andan, including Khalid el-Jeffe and his other top lieutenants. The entire time, the terrorist leader kept saying how happy he was that Hassan made it to Pakistan, lauding him for the Washington attack and predicting that they would achieve "big things together." He also indicated twice that his group was planning a major attack on the United States in the near future without providing details.

After giving him some time to settle in, the as-Sirat leader invited Hassan back to his quarters so the two of them could talk. Omar Bashir turned out to be an attentive and pleasant host. A couple of times Hassan felt as though he must be dreaming. It was simply too surreal to be sitting in a cave next to the world's most wanted man, sipping on tea and chatting about a variety of subjects.

Hassan told him all about the bombing and his escape and the as-Sirat leader often interrupted him with questions to get additional details, such as whether the reports were true that Hassan had originally targeted the Pentagon Metro Station.

"That was the plan but the power outage made me quickly change objectives," Hassan explained, rehashing his cover story again. "So I got off the train and selected the bus as a new target. Sadly, Washington's poor infrastructure prevented me from doing more damage."

He shrugged but the as-Sirat leader assured Hassan that he had done well.

But Omar Bashir didn't just want to talk about the attack and the escape. He seemed just as interested in life in the United States and what caused Hassan to want to join his group. The as-Sirat leader even managed to completely surprise his guest with a question Hassan never expected to hear in this setting.

"I heard you were a very good football player and I want to ask your opinion of something. Can you believe Madrid paid all of this money for a defender? I admit Banjano is a great talent, but 80 million euros?" The as-Sirat leader laughed when he added: "They are paying more for this young Brazilian than the Americans are offering for you and me together. Of course, he probably plays better."

"I'm surprised we are talking about soccer ... I mean football," Hassan replied. "Everybody else has been asking only about the attack. For the record, I think Banjano is worth it if they win the Champions League."

"Don't be surprised," Omar Bashir said. "We all love football but have no opportunities to play. So wait until I tell everybody that you were one of your country's best. They will have many questions for you. "Here, we all know what it feels like to kill infidels," the as-Sirat leader added, almost as an afterthought, "but we can only dream of playing football in front of thousands of fans."

They continued discussing a series of soccer trades and the start of the European leagues for a little while before Omar Bashir returned to business, sharing with Hassan his vision of finding more young men like him in America.

"Imagine how effective we could be if there were only a few more like you," he said. "And I think you can help us find and convince other young men to follow your example. You have proven that it is possible to hit the United States from the inside and to get away. Now we just have to let the world know about it. Tomorrow, we will leak to the media a rumor that you made it to Pakistan. Then, we will follow it up with a joint video message that will embarrass America and shake the world. Now go get some rest and think about what you want to say to the infidels."

Omar Bashir embraced his guest again.

"Trust me, you making it to here will change everything," he said.

Hassan smiled into the darkness of the room when he recalled those words from the as-Sirat leader.

"I hope you're right," he thought.

Hassan then willed his mind to tackle the task at hand. Though his main objective of locating the as-Sirat headquarters had been completed, the loss of the transmitters meant that there was more work to be done. He had to figure out a way to make contact and he had to do so quickly and without alerting the people in Andan.

During the tour of the "bunker," Omar Bashir had told him that, as a security measure, there were no phones in the entire town. The as-Sirat leader did not mention the two satellite phones that he and el-Jeffe kept under lock and key for extreme emergencies. The numbers were only known to a handful of people, including a mole in Pakistan's defense department and Shareef Wahed in the United States.

So Hassan knew that he wouldn't be able to use a phone to get the word out. He would have to think of some other way to make contact.

**

Before calling it a night, Art Kempner e-mailed his former intern again.

> *"Meghan, can you please get me in touch with Holly Gorsula? I'm working on*
> *a story and I have to talk to her about it."*

Art made a list of the things he wanted to get done the next day. First of all, he planned on speaking to some of the spouses of the victims. Before hearing from them directly, he wanted to find a psychologist to discuss whether people could imagine that a final farewell was especially heartfelt just because they wished it had been.

He felt that the key to whatever it was that caused his alarm bells to ring had something to do with the bus, so he wanted to find out as much as possible about it and its passengers. Art made a note to call the Pentagon in the morning to see if he could talk to the soldiers in the Humvee. They were closest to the bus, so maybe they had noticed something out of the ordinary.

Another item on the list was to talk to Washington Metro to figure out if there was a way that the terrorist could have targeted the bus specifically. He wanted to get a time line of the events that led to the shuttle buses being used.

Art recalled that he had read an Associated Press story in which Stacey Harper had been identified as the last person to have seen Hassan al-Zaid before the bombing. He dug up the story and was pleased to see that there was a line in there about how she had chased the bus unsuccessfully and felt blessed because she had been close to getting on it. Art wanted to talk to her specifically about that.

The last thing he did before turning in was to send out an e-mail to all of the people he knew who used Metro buses in the DC area. He was a little bit nervous about involving so many people because he didn't want anybody to suspect what he was working on, but to have any statistical relevancy, he needed a lot of data. Art agonized over the text of the e-mail for a few minutes before settling on a version that he felt was not an outright lie but obscured what he really wanted to get out of the survey.

> *"I'm doing research on a story on transportation patterns for different demographic groups. Can you please e-mail me tomorrow and the next day and give me an estimate of*
> *the share of people under the age of 30 who use the buses you ride. Also, please give me a rough estimate of the percentage of white*

males, African American woman and
immigrants on your buses. This doesn't have to
be a scientific poll, so you don't need to talk to
people and ask them their age or anything, I'm
really just looking for some rough figures.
Thanks, Art."

When he hit the "send" button, the Pulitzer Prize winner felt the familiar sensation of nervous excitement that he experienced whenever he thought he was on to a big story.

"I guess I'm gonna find out if I still have my instinct or if I have turned into a conspiracy theorist myself," Art thought with a smile on the way to get his water bottle from the fridge.

***

When he woke up, Hassan sought out Nasir and asked whether he could walk around town for a little bit.

"Sure, it's no problem. It's not like we are hiding in the tunnels all day. We just don't all go out at once or carry weapons around. Even then it probably wouldn't be too much of a problem since everybody in Waziristan is armed," Nasir said. "The beauty of the town is that it provides us with perfect cover and we can do normal things. There are even some places nearby where we can train and that are protected from sight. You'll see them soon enough."

Hassan followed Nasir to the door that led to the storage room and showed him how to open the secret door.

"Don't ever bolt it during the day time unless you want to annoy the others," he said. "If you ever come here and you can't open the door, push this button here and it will set off a bell in the cave and somebody will come for you."

Before he allowed Hassan to walk around Andan, Nasir made him open the door a couple of times.

"Why don't you come with and show me around?" Hassan asked.

"Sure, why not," Nasir said, and the two made their way outside.

It was a gorgeous day. The air was clear and the sun mixed with the altitude and a breeze made for a perfect temperature.

"It's so beautiful here," Hassan said as they walked among the buildings. He pointed to the mountains that rose in a steep angle on both sides of the town. "Can we climb these mountains?"

"I wouldn't do it without equipment," Nasir said. "I don't think I have ever heard of anybody going up there. We're not mountain goats and even they would have a tough time with these cliffs. If you want to climb rocks, we can find another place for you. I think Omar would not be happy if we found that you had fallen."

The two kept on going and Nasir tried to teach Hassan as much as possible about Andan. He showed him other buildings from which he could gain entrance into the caves and where the doors were hidden.

Nasir then led Hassan to a food storage room that was located next to a well.

"We have our own storage room in the bunker, but there is always some food here to replenish our own supplies," Nasir said. "With 40 men in the hideout and our stocks at half capacity, we could remain here for a month. Toward the back, on the other side of the mountain, we have air filters. The only real problem would be the diesel for the generators."

"So are you worried about being attacked?" Hassan asked.

"Of course we have to be vigilant," Nasir responded, "But I think most of us aren't too worried. The main threat is the Americans and the new Pakistani president has forbidden them to strike here without his approval. We have nothing to fear from the Pakistani military. So you need not be worried."

"I'm not," Hassan said. "After all, you've been here for a long time already without anything happening."

"Even if there was some sort of attack, there are many of us and we are all experienced fighters and well-armed. It would take a large force to defeat us here," Nasir added. "As you can see, the town is only accessible from two sides. You have the road in the front and then a trail in the back and we have sentries overlooking them both. In a few weeks, once we have trained you, you'll become part of the rotation and do guard duty like everybody else. Unless Omar thinks otherwise, of course."

"I don't want special treatment," Hassan said. "I just want to be one of the brothers."

"Don't worry, we'll all like you. Ready to go back?" Hassan nodded and they headed back for the bunker. As he had done all morning, he tried to take in every little detail, knowing that it might be useful information down the road.

Monday, 8:15 am ET

The president's glum mood had carried over into the morning. He brooded over breakfast and the first lady knew her husband well enough to keep conversation to a minimum. Jack Sweeney was a news junkie and he began each morning by watching cable news, always rotating between CNN, Fox and MSNBC so he could not be accused of favoritism, and scanning several of the major newspapers.

He was just reading an article on the Sunday "attack" on him from Congressmen Nelson and Hearst, which brightened his mood slightly, when he heard the CNN anchor announce that regular programming would be interrupted for a breaking news update.

"CNN has just learned that al-Jazeera is reporting that Hassan al-Zaid, the man who has claimed responsibility for last week's terrorist attack, is in Pakistan," the anchor said. "Again, Hassan al-Zaid is believed to be in Pakistan, according to an al-Jazeera report."

On a normal day, Sweeney might have smiled at the fact that one network was announcing "breaking news" only to then parrot what another network was reporting. But it was not a normal day, and instead the news provided him with a valve to release some of the pressure that had been building up since he began fearing that Pathfinder had failed. The president walked into an adjacent room, picked up a phone and demanded, with barely concealed anger, to speak to the Director of National Intelligence. McClintock was on the line within seconds.

"What the hell, Bob?" Sweeney fumed, finally being able to blow off some steam. "I thought we agreed that we wouldn't leak the Pakistan stuff for another day or so since we're already dominating the news cycle with the Hearst-Nelson thing. How can we salvage this mission if we're not on the same page?"

To Sweeney's surprise, McClintock's voice was cheerful without a hint of contrition.

"Mr. President, it wasn't our leak. Hassan did it! He made contact!"

"What do you mean?"

"I mean that we didn't leak it. Somebody beat us to the punch," the DNI said giddily. "And there is only one possible source this could come from and that's as-Sirat. They are the only ones apart from us who know that Hassan is in Pakistan."

"Couldn't it be somebody who saw him in Islamabad?" Sweeney asked.

"No, anybody who saw him there would not call al-Jazeera, they'd call us and try to get that $25 million that we promised anybody who could give us clues about Hassan's whereabouts," the DNI said. "Also, al-Jazeera would not run with the information unless it came from one of their reliable as-Sirat sources. Hassan did it, sir. As-Sirat thinks this is a major victory for them and they want to trumpet it to the world and make us look like idiots. He did it! We did it!"

"Are you sure, Bob?"

"Mr. President, look, there are no certainties in this line of work, but this is the only explanation that makes any kind of sense. I'm positive that Hassan is now with as-Sirat."

Sweeney's mood had brightened significantly but he was not ready yet to be as excited as the DNI.

"Well, there is still the matter of us not knowing where Hassan is," he said.

"True," McClintock conceded. "But our men followed him to a town that is not far from the border. It gives us a target to focus on. We will cover the entire area with satellites and drones. It's a big target, but at least it's a target.

"And, Mr. President," he added. "Don't count out Hassan. I have spoken to him many times and monitored him during the training for the mission. This kid is really smart and, if there is a way to make contact from wherever he is, he'll find it."

***

Seeing the al-Jazeera report made McClintock's heart leap and gave him a much needed boost. Prior to the news out of Pakistan, he had been just as worried as the president about the status of Pathfinder but he was determined not to show it. The DNI didn't want team members to feel like they had failed and lose confidence in their abilities. He needed them to be sharp and to believe in the mission.

While President Sweeney was understandably concerned about the fallout that would follow a failure of Pathfinder, the DNI was primarily worried about Hassan. McClintock had spent his entire adult life in the service of his country, and at an age when others started their families, he was spying on the Soviet Union. He never contemplated marriage. There was no way he would want to put anybody he loved through the agony of worrying about his life every day. But, if he had a family, he would want a son just like Hassan. Over the past four years that McClintock had overlooked Pathfinder, he developed something akin to paternal feelings for him. They spoke frequently. At first, McClintock wanted to find out if the kid was up to the task. Then, he wanted to pass on his own knowledge of being undercover in enemy territory. Whenever they spoke, they always discussed the mission, but their conversations increasingly covered other areas. They talked about UCLA, politics and sports. In addition, Hassan, who had to sever the ties to his own parents for the sake of the mission, often turned to the DNI for advice and help in situations in which he normally would have asked his dad. McClintock could not have been more proud of his charge and the way he had grown into the job. Hassan was bright, brave and ambitious. He was willing to sacrifice everything for his country, had a good sense of humor and did what he was told without ever complaining. In short, he was everything McClintock would have wanted in a son.

When the team lost Hassan in Zhob, the DNI was worried about Pathfinder, but he was devastated when he thought about Hassan being on his own among men who would take delight in killing him if they found out who he really was. Worst of all, there was nothing that McClintock could do to help.

The previous night, he had dreamed that Hassan had been beheaded, just like the last guy he had sent to infiltrate as-Sirat. When he woke up, the DNI was as depressed as he had been in a long time. Losing Hassan would be devastating. It would be tough on a professional level but possibly worse on a personal one. The welcome news from Pakistan was just what he needed.

McClintock thought back to the last conversation he and Hassan had before the bombing. He had really wanted to meet in person to see his charge one last time but managed to resist that urge. It would have been bad trade craft. Instead, they had talked on the phone for over an hour.

The DNI dispensed last minute advice and urged Hassan to stay calm, no matter what happened.

"Remember that luck favors the prepared," he had told him. "You are as well prepared as you'll ever be and you have a great team backing you up. Trust them and trust yourself. Most of these missions fail because people freak out and make a mistake. And remember, you can always get away if you feel they are on to you."

In some ways, McClintock now thought, he had been trying to reassure himself as much as Hassan, who had been calm and collected as always. Maybe Hassan sensed that the DNI himself was worried because he did his best to take the edge off the moment.

"Are you scared?" McClintock had asked at one point.

"Bob, to be completely honest, I'm petrified," Hassan had said. He was the only person on the team who used the DNI's first name, and he never did it in front of anybody else. But the two had developed an undeniable rapport and he felt stupid to call him "sir," "director" or "Mr. McClintock."

"I'm so scared," Hassan said and then paused. "Here we are, it's the beginning of September and the Yankees are five games out in the East and only lead the wild card race by one. How could I not be scared?"

The little joke had caused McClintock to laugh and be reassured that Hassan was in the right mindset for the mission.

In one of their earliest discussions, they had found out that they shared a love for the New York Yankees and they often talked about the team's fortunes. This year, it wasn't looking so good for the Bronx Bombers. McClintock had promised that he would get them great tickets to watch a game at Yankee Stadium, to which Hassan had only responded: "You think I need you to get me tickets once all this is over and I'm a hero? Heck, the only reason I agreed to this crazy plan was so that I could throw out the first pitch in a game after I bring down as-Sirat."

In that last conversation, after joking around for a little bit longer, Hassan had eventually discussed some of his concerns. He wasn't worried about himself, he just wanted McClintock to promise him again that he would be there when the president delivered the message to his parents if something went wrong. "They're gonna want answers to things that the letter doesn't provide. I think you are the best person to give them those answers," Hassan had said.

The DNI assured him that he would. They had discussed this before and, in retrospect, McClintock believed that Hassan only brought it up again to help him overcome a sense of helplessness.

Now, alone in his office after the phone call with the president, he was beginning to feel the same way again. The Pathfinder team was idle in Islamabad and there was not much McClintock could do in Washington other than to redirect all available drones and satellites to the area around Zhob. Of course, this would have to be done in a way that wouldn't let all of the reconnaissance teams know that they were looking in the same place. They couldn't afford to let word leak out about that.

McClintock just had to trust that Hassan would find a way to let them know where he was. The DNI hoped that his boy would come through.

***

Art Kempner was on the hunt. He was twirling a pencil in his hand as he checked the latest round of responses to his informal bus survey. He had received more than 50 by mid-morning and all of them basically said the same thing. There were no buses that didn't have a healthy percentage of young people and likely immigrants on them. As Steve had asserted during dinner the previous night, the demographics of Metro Bus 2405 were absolutely unique. No other bus with a comparable number of passengers came even close.

Now Art had to find out if there was a logical explanation for that, if it was a freakish coincidence or if there was an altogether different reason for it – one that he couldn't figure out.

The reporter had arrived at work before 7:00 am, trying to start checking off things from his to-do list. Since it was still too early to call anybody, he had begun his day by e-mailing psychologists, asking them for their input on final farewells and premonitions. He kept his inquiry vague, hoping that he would be able to explore the topic in greater depth once he got them on the phone.

Then he called the Pentagon, one of the few places in the federal government where it was possible to reach somebody just about any time and not just from 10ish to "I think I'll head home early today," as was often the case in other agencies and departments. It often frustrated Art that bureaucrats couldn't even stick around for their nine-to-five schedule. The answer he got from the Pentagon was predictable. The Department of Defense would not release the names of the soldiers from the Humvees. Art hoped that he could find another way to contact them and sent an e-mail to the Post's defense reporter, asking if she had an idea on how he could get in touch with the soldiers.

At 9:00 am, he was finally able to start making some calls. First on his list was the Washington Metro. He was told by an operator that nobody was in the office yet. Art wasn't surprised. He left a voicemail for the head of public affairs, stressing that he expected to be called back in the morning. There were some advantages to being a Pulitzer Prize winner working for the Washington Post. One of them being that it was easier to get calls returned and he was certain that he would hear from them before noon.

Art wanted to start calling the families of the terror victims but thought better of it. He didn't want to harass them and would likely be able to ask better questions after he talked to a psychologist. Instead, he called Stacey Harper's parents in Woodbridge. Like many young people, she didn't have a land line and he was unable to find a cellphone number for her, so he wanted to get in touch with the young woman through her parents. He talked briefly to Amanda Harper, explained who he was and politely asked if it would be possible for Stacey to get in touch with him. Amanda

Harper said she would pass on the message but noted that her daughter was very flaky about that kind of stuff.

Now that Art had contacted the people he wanted to get in touch with, it was pretty much a waiting game for him. He spent the time sifting through the documents he had compiled on the story and listened again to the part of the dinner he had recorded.

The phone finally rang. It was a Harvard psychology professor who had written several books on dying, including one on dealing with the loss of a loved one.

"Let's assume I have a group of 300 people who die in a plane crash," Art said. "And you spoke to their spouses or next of kin. How many of them would likely say something to the effect that their final farewells had been especially warm and heartfelt, as though the deceased had a hunch that they would not return?"

"Research would indicate that the number of people would be fairly small," the Harvard scholar said. "The normal reaction immediately after such a sudden death is a feeling of regret and possibly of guilt. If you love somebody, you often wish it was you who had died and the thing that goes through your head will more likely be that you wished you had told the deceased one last time how much you cared for them."

"So a figure of more than 20 percent would be too high?" Art asked.

"For a random event? Much too high," the professor responded emphatically. "We're talking about accidents or natural disasters like an earthquake, right? In that case it would be much lower. Maybe a handful people out of 100 would perceive that a farewell was especially warm. The others would regret that it had been a normal goodbye and so much was left unsaid."

"So what could be a reason for a greater percentage of people claiming that some sort of premonition made that last goodbye special?" Art followed up.

"That's not exactly my field of expertise, but I would say the only reason you would have for such a farewell is not premonition, it is that the person leaving knew for a fact that they were heading into danger," the professor said, going into teaching mode. "For example a firefighter might say goodbye to his wife differently than a school teacher. Somebody who remained in New Orleans for Hurricane Katrina probably had the urge to call up their family and friends and say some nice things because they knew that danger was coming their way. I'd imagine that astronauts say their goodbyes differently than school bus drivers and that somebody deploying to Afghanistan would want to say something especially nice and reassuring to the loved ones they leave behind. So if you asked those spouses, the percentage would go up."

"Thanks for your insight, professor," Art said, excitement in his voice. "It's been very helpful. I hope I can call you back if I have any follow up questions."

"Absolutely, I'm glad I could be of assistance," the professor replied and hung up.

Art leaned back, the phone still in his hand. Even as the professor spoke, a theory had begun forming in the reporter's head. Now, he closed his eyes to allow the pieces of a puzzle to fall into place. Art went over the information he already had: There was a group of people, many of them associated with the military. They all happened to be on the same bus, coming to Washington from different parts of the country. Before they left their homes, a disproportionate number of them said the kind of goodbyes that people say who are headed into harm's way.

The wheels started spinning in Art's head. Maybe they were part of a secret military mission, and a dangerous one at that. It would explain their common backgrounds and the farewells. But what kind of dangerous mission would they be selected for, Art asked himself. After all, most of the people on the bus had been over 40. Maybe they had been selected for a certain type of expertise. But, if they were some sort of analysts, why would they be worried about their lives? Maybe they were about to travel to a place like Iran to do some undercover work for the United States.

So did Hassan al-Zaid's attack unknowingly derail a covert U.S. operation? Or had he found out about it somehow and the bombing was designed to take out the team?

Art sighed. He had the beginnings of a theory that answered some questions but raised others. Of course, he could also be on a completely wrong track.

Hassan sat in the room he shared with three as-Sirat fighters. None of them were there at the moment and Hassan appreciated a brief moment of solitude. His day had been spent with getting to know Andan, the bunker and the as-Sirat members who currently lived there.

Everybody was eager to talk to him. The men slapped him on the back, congratulated him on the bombing and expressed how happy they were that he was one of them now. Many of them had words of advice for him and some of the older as-Sirat fighters started telling him about the rules of the hideout.

At the armory, a man named Yezem gave him a quick lesson on weapon safety.

In the kitchen, he was told that large quantities of food were cooked for breakfast, lunch and dinner but that he could also eat at other times. He was expected to help with the meal preparation one day out of the month.

"Don't worry, you won't go hungry here," a Bosnian Muslim named Kemal Zlatan told him.

Khalid el-Jeffe, Omar Bashir's top lieutenant, spoke to Hassan for some time about some of the rules.

Fighting among the men was strictly forbidden and any conflict that could not easily be settled was to be taken before Omar Bashir. Leaving Andan alone without telling anybody was also prohibited.

"We always want to know who is here," el-Jeffe said. "But it is also for your protection. The sentries might shoot you if they see you wandering around and nobody told them that you have been given permission to leave.

"I know our rules might seem burdensome at first but they have kept us safe for many years and you will learn to appreciate them," el-Jeffe added.

Had he actually aspired to join the group, the warm reception would have been great but Hassan only wanted some peace and quiet so he could think. After the elation of having accomplished his primary target, reality had begun to sink in. The knowledge of the location of as-Sirat's headquarter was useless information unless he managed to relay it back to the team in Islamabad somehow. And that was going to be a problem.

Andan had no phones and no Internet, so calling or e-mailing were out of the question. Hassan had contemplated just taking off and following the road, but that also seemed futile. There was no car here, so he would have to leave on foot, and it seemed like a long shot that such an escape could succeed. First of all, the sentries might see him and even if they didn't, he really had no idea where he was going. On the way here, they had not always stayed on the road and there had been some intersections, so he might not find his way back to Zhob. Even if he did, Nasir was probably right about this being as-Sirat country. If he just disappeared, they would hunt him down and the rest of the local population would probably merrily join in. Earlier in the day, when Hassan had toured Andan, he had come up with a sliver of an idea, but he would have to improve on it. As it stood, it was more likely suicide than a way to communicate his position, so he would just have to think of some other way to make contact.

Nasir stuck his head in the room.

"Hassan, Omar wants to get started on the video in half an hour."

"I'll be there," Hassan said. He smiled to himself because inspiration had just struck.

***

Nicole Delgado, the Washington Metropolitan Area Transit Authority's press secretary, finally returned Art's phone call. The reporter was tempted to ask if the press office operated on the same schedule as the notoriously delay-plagued Red Line but he thought better of it. He needed some answers so there was no point in pissing off the woman who could give them to him.

"Thanks for getting back to me."

"No problem. What can we do for you Mr. Kempner?"

"I'm just trying to get a better understanding of what happened last week. At some point, the power went out in the Pentagon Station, correct?"

"Yes, that's right. We lost power for about 30 minutes," Delgado said. "At the time it happened we were already on our non-rush hour schedule so there weren't as many trains on the track. Still, when we couldn't figure out right away what the problem was and didn't know how long it would take to fix it, we followed protocol and unloaded the inbound trains in Crystal City and the outbound trains in L'Enfant Plaza and Rosslyn respectively."

"So the problem was fixed after 30 minutes? Did you ever figure out what happened?" Art asked. "How many trains were affected going into the city during the outage?"

"We first unloaded a Blue Line train going into DC, then two Yellow Line trains and then another Blue Line train. But we found out about the attack right after unloading that one and stopped service altogether for a while."

"And in this type of situation, you put people on buses?" Art asked.

"Sure," the press officer replied. "One of our main bus depots is nearby on Jefferson Davis Highway, so it didn't take long for them to arrive."

"It seems like all of these events were kind of random, would it have been possible for somebody to anticipate everything that happened and target Bus 2405 or one of its passengers specifically?" Art asked.

"I don't think anybody could target a shuttle bus because we only use those as needed," Delgado explained. "Now, with regard to targeting a person, I guess that is possible. I mean, all someone would have to do is follow them onto a train or a bus."

On a whim, Art asked another question.

"Okay, one more. With the kind of explosive power that this bomb had, would it have caused more damage had it gone off in the train?"

"Absolutely. If it goes off in the train, you not only have the victims from the blast but you're also dealing with derailment. So in that regard, we caught a break."

"Thanks," Art said. "Oh, wait, did you ever figure out what caused the problem at the Pentagon?"

"I'm not sure. I'll get back to you."

"Great, thanks. I may also call you again with follow up questions."

Art tried to reconcile the new information with his theory. So it might be possible that the terrorist had followed the victims from National Airport to the Metro. But they might not all have been in the same car on the train. And, it seemed that Hassan al-Zaid wanted to get away, so maybe using a bus was the better way to accomplish that. But how did he know that there was going to be a shuttle bus in the first place, Art thought. He couldn't have. So maybe he wanted to explode the bomb at Pentagon station and then was forced to change plans when the power went out.

Again, for every one of his questions that was answered, a couple new ones popped up but Art still felt that he was making progress.

***

Hassan and Omar Bashir were huddled together in the quarters of the as-Sirat leader. They sat next to each other in front of a small table that had nothing on it apart from several blank sheets of paper and a pencil.

"Do you think you will feel more comfortable writing an entire script and just reading it on camera or do you want to prepare some notes and work with those?" Omar Bashir asked. The as-Sirat leader had summoned Hassan so that they could discuss what they wanted to say in the video. Omar Bashir was clearly giddy about the impact it would have.

"I always find your messages very effective, so which do you prefer?" Hassan asked.

"I rarely script an entire speech. I think reading from a piece of paper makes it more difficult to speak with passion. I also prefer to finish the video in one take to preserve the authenticity of what I am saying."

"Then I'll follow your example and try using some notes. Do you want me to speak English or Arabic?"

"I usually speak Arabic because I'm addressing our brothers," Omar Bashir said. "You, however, should speak English because we are sending a message to America."

The as-Sirat leader gave Hassan an outline of what he wanted him to say.

"I want you to taunt America because they were not able to catch you," Omar Bashir said. "And you have to inspire others to follow your example. You are not appealing to the masses, you are appealing to a select few who might have aspirations of striking against the United States but have not acted on them."

Both of them spent the next few minutes working on what they wanted to say with Hassan only occasionally interrupting to ask questions.

"I'm curious about one thing," Hassan said. "For years, they have told us that your videos and recordings are laced with hidden messages. Is that true?"

"We have more reliable ways to communicate," Omar Bashir said. "But it is ironic that you would ask because this time, I am sending a message to one of us who has been living in America for many years and is preparing a major strike. He needs to check his e-mail because I have sent him his attack orders.

"Shall we begin?" the as-Sirat leader asked before Hassan could follow up and they went to the filming area.

Omar Bashir wanted to start the video with himself speaking and then have the camera zoom out so that Hassan came into view.

"I call on all followers of the one true faith to rejoice with us on this most glorious of days. The fight against the great Satan and the Zionists has been long and difficult, but we have witnessed the beginning of the end of the imperialistic oppressors," Omar Bashir said. The change in his personality was remarkable to Hassan. A minute ago, the as-Sirat leader had calmly discussed the logistics of the video in his chamber. Now, sitting in front of a cave background with an AK 47 leaning against the wall to his left, he had become a fire and brimstone preacher who spoke with great passion and intensity.

"One man has shown America its own weakness and ushered in a new phase in this fight. He has shown that the hundreds of billions of dollars America spends each year on killing Muslims everywhere in the world does not provide protection within its own borders," Omar Bashir continued. "The time has come for others in America to pick up weapons and follow the example of Hassan al-Zaid. He has shown to us all what is possible for somebody who has Allah on his side, along with the determination of not allowing the great devil to keep oppressing his brothers. Hassan al-Zaid was the first American to defy his country but he believes that he will not be the last."

Omar Bashir smiled and could not resist reveling in this moment.

"How do I know this? Because he told me over breakfast."

With that, the camera zoomed out and panned over to Hassan but also still showed Omar Bashir, who was beaming.

"I'm Hassan al-Zaid, responsible for last week's strike against Washington. I am proud of what I have done. It is time for young Muslims to follow my lead. My message to them is simple: The tide is turning. Maybe you were once afraid of what America would do to you if you acted on your convictions. Times have changed because now America is afraid of you," Hassan tried to speak with the same passion and conviction as Omar Bashir and also sought to copy the as-Sirat's leader sometimes rambling style. Hassan's eyes kept glancing at his notes. He had to get his speech just right.

"The U.S. government perpetuates nothing but lies. It wants you to believe that America is strong, but that is not so. For many years, the United States has spent untold sums of money on protecting itself and even more on finding our leader, who is sitting next to me in good health. Despite all of the billions invested in homeland security, which is just another name for allowing the government to spy on its citizens, Allah allowed me to strike at America right next to the Pentagon. Then, even though I was the most wanted man in the country, I got away. After that, I managed to accomplish what the supposedly awesome U.S. military has not been able to do. I found Omar Bashir. All this should show you that you, too, can do what I did. America is weak and you have Allah on your side. I have another message. This one is to the government of the United States. The writing is on the wall, Yankees, your time is coming to an end. I could only make you look like fools because that is what you are.

You think that killing my brothers will make you safer but the opposite is true. With every one of us that you kill, ten more will rise and take up arms against you. It is a tide you cannot stop. You couldn't even stop me from striking at your heart. You couldn't even find me after I did. Mark my words, America, your time is running out."

The red light on the camera went off and Omar Bashir clapped his hands.

"Very good," he said. "The entire world will be watching this by tomorrow. Let's look at it to make sure we don't have to do a second take."

Omar Bashir was even more pleased when he saw the video and Hassan knew that it would make quite a splash.

"Perfect," the as-Sirat leader said. "A courier will take this to Islamabad and it will be played all over the world by tomorrow morning. Truly a good day's work."

***

Ken Gorsula put the clippers down and looked at his handiwork. The special ops soldiers had taken turns cutting each other's hair, and Gorsula now picked up a mirror to hold it in front of the poor man whose head he had just shaved.

"I think it looks marvelous," Gorsula said in his best effeminate voice.

"Captain, no disrespect, but you can't cut hair worth shit," his "victim" responded. "I think I gotta report this to an officer so they can take your expert marksmanship badge away. Seriously, you're telling me you can hit any target from a quarter mile away and yet you missed this large patch of hair behind my ear?"

"My bad," Gorsula laughed and picked up the clippers to rectify his mistake. "It's not like it's gonna make a difference with your face. Maybe a bad haircut will distract people from noticing that train wreck you call a smile."

It had been another quiet day for the special ops forces at Bagram. They played hoops to stay in shape and some of them had staged a shooting competition, but they were growing more restless by the day.

"Did you guys see that al-Zaid supposedly made it to Pakistan?" one of the men asked. "I hope that motherfucker is dumb enough to try to make it here so we can get him."

"I don't give a shit if he is in Pakistan and what the politics are," Gorsula said. "If we find out he is there, they better let us go after him and don't rely on the Pakistanis. Half of them are as-Sirat anyways."

The other soldiers nodded. They knew that Tom Gorsula had died in the Washington attack and that his nephew was itching even more than the rest of them to find Hassan al-Zaid.

"I'm sure that, if we get intelligence on where he is, the Pakistanis will allow us to go in," one of the men said. "Otherwise, there would be serious repercussions."

"If our intelligence people find out where he is, I'm not gonna wait for permission from another country to go after him, I'll tell you that," Gorsula said. "I owe my uncle that much. I just want a chance to get al-Zaid in my cross hairs."

***

It had been a productive day for Art Kempner. He talked to a few more psychologists, all of whom had pretty much confirmed what the Harvard professor told him in the morning.

More importantly, in the course of the afternoon, Art had spoken to a dozen of the spouses of Bus 2405 passengers and asked each of them why the victims had been in Washington and whether the trip had been planned for a long time. The answers gave credence to his theory that the victims were in the nation's capital as part of a coordinated and secret effort.

All of the trips appeared to have been planned on fairly short notice and were booked at roughly the same time. In each case, the victim had told their spouses about ten days before the bombing that they had to go to Washington. Almost uniformly, they had said that the reasons for the trips were work-related, with most of them explaining that they had to attend a conference for a few days. Art always inquired about the profession of the victims and compiled a list.

He then called the Washington Convention Center and all of the area hotels that were most commonly used to host conferences to ask what kind of events they had scheduled last week. Just to be sure, he also called the various industry organizations of the victims' professions to ask if they had anything special scheduled the previous week. Art really wasn't surprised to find that there were no matches. There wasn't a single conference scheduled in DC that any of the victims would have had reason to attend.

The evidence suggested that, in a coordinated effort, several of them had booked their trips at about the same time and lied to their spouses about why they were traveling to Washington. Art wondered where they had really been headed when they got on the bus and he was determined to find out. He had the feeling that the answer had something to do with national security. Why else did they all lie?

Throughout the day, Art had kept thinking about his theory and he felt strongly that Hassan meant to blow up a Metro train, probably right underneath the Pentagon, and only switched targets because of the power failure. The reporter wondered if the terrorist had, unknowingly, done more damage to the United States than he could have dreamed of by taking out some sort of undercover unit.

Monday, 6:00 pm ET

Apart from the faint humming of the generators and air filters as well as the sounds the as-Sirat fighters next to him made in their sleep, it was quiet in the cave when Hassan got up. Although some of the lamps were turned off at night, the tunnel was lit well enough so that he could find his way to the door through which he had first entered the "bunker."

He unbolted and unlocked it and stepped into the storage room. It was darker there, with only some light coming from the open door to the tunnel and the moonlight that shone through. Hassan reached behind a crate near the entrance and pulled out the flashlight he had stored there earlier in the day. He turned it on, locked the secret door and looked for the small bag with the two other things he would need. When he found that as well and hid it inside the folds of his kaftan, he stepped outside.

The air was so cold in the middle of the night that the first deep breath Hassan took tingled in his lungs. He used his hand to cover the flashlight, not wanting to alert the sentries. If he was found, he would just use jet lag and the need for fresh air as an excuse for his nightly stroll. Hassan hoped that this would be enough to satisfy a sentry's curiosity and avoid suspicion. If he was searched, he would have a hard time explaining why he carried around the items in the bag.

In his exploration of Andan earlier in the day, he had found the perfect place he needed to carry out his plan and memorized how to get there. Now, he walked in that direction slowly but not in a way that indicated that he was worried about discovery. If anybody was watching, he did not want to appear as a man who has something to hide.

In Hassan's own estimation, the plan he had come up with didn't have a favorable risk-to-reward ratio. He would have preferred waiting until he thought of something better but time was a luxury he didn't have. For now, this was his only idea with any chance of success. At least it was something.

After a short walk through the darkness that took him up a small incline to the highest point of the town, Hassan reached a two-floor storage building that he noticed earlier. He went to work. The next few minutes would be crucial. If anybody saw him now, he would have no excuse.

Fortunately he was able to complete the task unnoticed. He tucked away his supplies again and headed back toward the bunker.

Once there, Hassan first hid the bag and then put the flashlight behind the crate again. He might need it again. Without being seen, he safely made his way back to the chamber.

Hassan lay awake for a long time. He figured that he would have just a few more days to make contact before he had to start taking greater risks. Maybe he would have to try to escape on foot, hoping that he would get by the sentries at night and then make his way to a settlement.

Another thought began taking hold in his head. Maybe it would have to come down to Hassan trading his life for that of Omar Bashir. Subconsciously, that idea might have been there all along. Hassan always knew that there was a good chance he would not return from the mission alive. At least if he sacrificed himself, he could guarantee that Pathfinder would not be a total failure.

The only reason that he was thinking about leaving Andan was not self-preservation, it was to get word to the U.S. military so that they could take out all of as-Sirat's leaders. If he acted alone, the damage to the terrorist group would not be as comprehensive. Hassan estimated that, at best, he would be able to kill Omar Bashir and maybe a couple more men before they would get to him.

The way he saw it, there were three options. He could stay put, try to think of a better way to communicate his position and risk getting a bullet in the head once his cover was blown. Hassan almost immediately dismissed that option. That left him with two choices. He could try to escape and get word to the U.S. military that the terrorists were in Andan. The upside to that option was that, if it succeeded, it would almost certainly result in the entire as-Sirat leadership being neutralized. And, of course, that he would live. The downside was that, if he never made it to safety, they would have nothing.

The second choice was to grab one of the weapons, shoot Omar Bashir in the head and take as many as-Sirat fighters as possible to the grave with him. In that scenario, the damage to the terrorist group would be great but likely not fatal. That option would also end in his certain death.

Hassan thought of all of the risks that had been taken and sacrifices that had been made to get him to this point. It was up to him now to make sure all of that was not in vain.

The way he saw it, he had a window of opportunity of maybe 48 hours before he had to choose.

Omar Bashir was right. The impact of the video was enormous. Within minutes of it being aired on al-Jazeera and posted on aljazeera.net, the website crashed because the servers could not keep up with the demand. And that was hours before most Americans were waking up.

Over the past years, the world had gotten used to seeing charred bus carcasses, craters in roads and blood on streets. Last week's attack had been special because it had taken place right next to the Pentagon and was the first time the U.S. had been hit since 9/11. Still, everybody had anticipated that the United States would eventually be targeted again and it was no surprise that it happened.

The video, on the other hand, showed something that had never been seen before – the world's foremost terrorist chatting with Hassan al-Zaid, who was currently the most hunted person on the planet. And the two acted like they didn't have anything to worry about, seemingly unfazed that they were the top targets of the only remaining superpower and all of its might. The fact that Hassan looked like the recent college graduate he was and spoke in accent-free English only added to the intrigue of the video, as did the fact that he taunted America for letting him get away.

President Sweeney was woken up by his staff at 2:00 am, ten minutes after the clip first aired on al-Jazeera. DNI McClintock was already waiting by the phone and it didn't take long for the commander-in-chief to call.

"He really did it," Sweeney said. "I mean, we were all

hoping that he could, but seeing it with my own eyes is … wow!"

"I know, sir. I'm feeling the same way. I was so happy to see him alive," McClintock said. That statement did not do his emotions justice. When he saw Hassan on the video he nearly wept. Although he had exuded confidence when talking to the president and the team in Islamabad, privately he had been very concerned about Hassan. "Now we just have to find him. I was hoping that he was trying to send us some kind of a message through the video, and it seemed to me like he wanted to tell us something, but I can't figure out what it is. Maybe it's just wishful thinking."

"Well, knowing that he is alive and has achieved his objective should boost morale. I know I was in a bit of a funk but that's over now," the president said. "And this will allow us to step up satellite and drone surveillance in Pakistan without it raising questions."

"I agree, sir. And this video is dynamite," McClintock said. "Nobody will talk about anything else for the next couple of days and that should buy us some time. I want to see the person who thinks that this is a setup when this video is out there.

"Well, I want to watch this a few more times and talk to the guys in Islamabad. You should probably get some more sleep, Mr. President. I'll make sure you will be woken up again if anything else happens."

Sweeney agreed and went back to bed.

"Everything alright, dear?" the first lady asked.

"Yeah, finally some good news," the president said.

***

The network producers certainly felt that the video was dynamite.

Between 7:30 and 8:30 in the morning, when many people on the East Coast turned on their TVs for breakfast, CNN aired the four-minute video nine times. It would have been more had it not been for time set aside for commercials. The video spoke for itself but that didn't stop the networks from bringing their security experts again.

"Quite frankly, I'm stunned by what we're seeing here," a former administration official said on Fox. "It's not only that Hassan al-Zaid managed to find and reach Omar Bashir, it's also the brazenness of this video. It's like they are not a bit concerned about our military strength. Wherever they are, they seem to feel perfectly secure."

***

Halfway through the day, it was obvious that the video sparked a new wave of anti-Muslim backlash in the U.S.. More than a dozen assaults had been reported throughout the country in which the attackers made reference to Hassan al-Zaid or as-Sirat. Fortunately, nobody was seriously injured. In addition, there was an attempted arson on a mosque in upstate New York and Islamic web sites were bombarded with hateful comments.

Shareef Wahed was not affected by the violence. The people at Michigan State who believed they were his friends kept going out of their way to let him know that they did not condone the backlash. A group of them had watched the video together while having coffee at the student union and then saw a report of a

cab driver beaten in Boston because he was Muslim.
"It's ridiculous and narrow-minded to think that people
are terrorists just because of where they were born,"
one of them said. "That would mean that hundreds of
millions of people would all be terrorists, even
Shareef."

The as-Sirat sleeper thanked them for their sentiments.
On the inside, he just wanted to laugh. These cretins
and their political correctness. He would love to see
their faces when they found out that he was the one
leading the attack on the nuclear power plant. Maybe
he would call one of them just before it happened.

But now was not the time for daydreaming. There was
a message for him in the video. He had to check his e-
mail account as quickly as possible.

Shareef Wahed had no idea how many American
intelligence analysts dissected Omar Bashir's videos
each time one was released to find out if they had a
hidden meaning, but he doubted that they would ever
figure out the "code." It really couldn't be much more
simple. An AK 47 to Omar Bashir's left meant:
"Check your e-mail." That was it.

He didn't know if there were other clues for other
sleepers, but he doubted it. He was by far the most
difficult to reach, in a country that had the toughest
surveillance and the lowest number of as-Sirat assets.
Shareef Wahed excused himself politely. He had to get
to an Internet cafe to check the account. On his way
out, one of his "friends" caught up with him.

"Don't take it too hard, buddy," the grad student said
and put his arm around Shareef Wahed. "Some people
in this country are assholes."

The as-Sirat sleeper wanted to reply: "Yeah, like all
300 million of you," but instead he just nodded sadly.

He decided to drive to Fort Wayne this time. It would take him a good part of the day to get there and back but he liked to switch cities from time to time. He had the address of several Internet cafes in his wallet and, after an uneventful drive, he chose one in a mall on Interstate 69.

This time, the login was Desmond_T1984@gmx.com and the password was utut1970. There was a message waiting for him in the "drafts" folder.

> *"Hi sis,*
> *It looks like most of us will all be able to get together for Thanksgiving after all.*
> *Kyle and Peter are already making travel arrangements for the whole family. I hope you can accommodate that many people. But don't worry, you don't have to cook for everybody. ;)*
> *Mammie said she would know in ten days if she can come, so let's get in touch then at the latest.*
> *Hugs, Brittany"*

Shareef Wahed's heart leaped. Out of habit, he read the e-mail a couple more times before deleting it. It was easy enough to understand. The attack was on for Thanksgiving and the fighters would start coming into the United States soon. He'd check the next account in ten days to find out how preparations were proceeding. The as-Sirat sleeper wiped any traces of his Internet activity from the hard drive, paid in cash and left.

Less than three months! After all of these years, he finally had a target date. He hoped that the brothers would make it safely across the border. He didn't know exactly how many men Omar Bashir would send him but he knew it would be more than enough to take over the plant and hold it long enough for him to carry out his task. It would be up to him to deliver success and he was ready.

Art Kempner had spent most of his day working on a story about the as-Sirat tape and its impact on Washington. The attack and the aftermath had become an embarrassment for the administration and President Sweeney's team looked like amateurs dealing with it. In fact, a congressional source had said something to that effect in a New York Times story.

"Here we are, saying we're doing everything we can to get this 21-year-old and then he shows up in Pakistan. It made us look like morons," the unnamed Congressman was quoted.

The consensus in the capital was that heads would have to roll and they would have to roll quickly. Sacrificing one Cabinet member alone would no longer suffice. Talk in the nation's capital was that FBI Director Stevenson would definitely need to go and that the President's national security adviser and Homeland Security Secretary deBerg were goners as well. Another thing that would likely have to happen was for the president to step before the country with his hat in hand and admit that massive mistakes had been made.

Americans were always willing to rally around the flag and their president in a time of crisis, but they also expected their elected leaders to not fumble around. Opinion polls showed that Sweeney's approval rating was heading south quickly.

The phone rang and Art picked up.

"This is Art."

"Hi, it's Stacey Harper," a young voice said. "My mom said you wanted to speak to me."

It took the reporter a split second to figure out who was on the line. His story on the as-Sirat video had taken all of his time during the day and he had barely thought about his investigation of the bombing and the victims.

"Oh, yes, Ms. Harper," he said after a brief pause. "Sorry, it's been a crazy day here."

"Please call me Stacey, you make it sound like you're talking to my mom. Do you want me to call back when you're not so busy?"

"No, no. I'm all done with my other work."

"Are you guys writing about the video? It's insane, isn't? I still can't believe it. Hassan and I went to high school together and now he's in a cave somewhere with Omar Bashir. What a mind fuck. Ooops, excuse my language."

Art laughed, both at her cussing and the question of whether the Washington Post was writing about one of the biggest news stories in years.

"Yes, I did write about that, but I want to talk to you about this other thing I'm working on. This might take a few minutes. Do you have time now?"

"Totally," Stacey said.

"Great. To start off, can you please describe everything that happened on your morning commute the day of the bombing? Try to remember every detail, please."

"Sure. I was running kinda late for my class at Georgetown but was hoping that I could still get there on time. But then, of course, there is a problem with the train and we all had to get off at Crystal City."

"Was the train pretty full?" Art asked.

"Nah, I'd say not even half full. There were certainly still empty seats, like, nobody was sitting next to me.

"Anyways, we're stopping in Crystal City and the train operator said there would be shuttle buses available. I know a shortcut to the bus terminal, so I totally thought I'd be able to beat everybody else there and get on a bus quickly. I was feeling lucky, too, because my door opened right at the escalators so I was one of the first ones through the gate."

"What kind of shortcut are you talking about and how do you know about it?" Art asked.

"I interned in Crystal City before. If you get out of the Metro station, you can take the escalators up to get to the bus terminal, but they moved it a couple years back when it was expanded. So, if you take the escalator, it's the long way, but if you turn right when exiting the station, there are some steps that get you there quicker."

"Okay, sorry, I didn't mean to interrupt."

"Anyways, I take my shortcut and I think that my luck is continuing because I see a bus that says 'Rosslyn Shuttle' on it right as I get outside. So I tried to chase it but I guess the bus driver didn't see me, or whatever. I was really pissed at the passengers because one of them looked right at me and he must have known I was trying to get on the bus but he didn't say anything to the driver. I mean, I always say something when I see somebody wanting to get on. I was really annoyed at the time but I guess that saved my life. Pretty crazy how that sometimes works out, huh?"

Stacey waited for a response.

"Are you still there?" she asked after a couple of seconds.

"Oh yes, sorry," Art said. His pulse was racing and he fumbled through his notes. "Just to be sure, you said you were on a Blue Line train?"

"Yeah, I live near Van Dorn Street."

"And the bus, Bus 2405, that must have left from the terminal right before you got there, right?" Art wanted to know.

"No, actually it didn't. It came from a side street near the terminal. Maybe that's where they were loading the shuttles," Stacey said. "So, there I am, all out of breath and so pissed off at the driver that I actually memorized the number because I wanted to call in and complain.

"Anyways, then I saw the bus stop ahead of me and Hassan got off, but I didn't know it was him because it was a ways away. He caught up with me as I was walking back toward the bus terminal. At first I think he didn't recognize me but later he did. Oh, and Hassan said something like that it wasn't so bad that I didn't make the bus. Now I know what he meant."

"Earlier you indicated that you still can't believe that he did this. Why did you say that?"

"Well, he was so normal in high school," Stacey said. "And I never felt that he hated America. I remember one time at a basketball game, he kinda yelled at this guy because he didn't take his hat off during the national anthem. I guess he just became a different person in college but when I saw him last week, he seemed, like, normal."

"Thanks, Stacey. This has been really helpful. Do you mind giving me your cell number so that I can call you back if I have any more questions?"

"Yeah, no problem," she said and gave him her information.

As soon as Art hung up he dialed the number of the Washington Metro press officer, hoping that she was still in the office. He was lucky.

"Hi, it's Art Kempner with the Post again. I just have a couple more questions. Are you absolutely certain that the first train that you unloaded at Crystal City was a Blue Line train?"

"Yup, 100 percent. I even double checked that after I talked to you yesterday."

"So, the people on the train should, in theory, have been the first ones on the shuttles, right?" Art asked.

"Absolutely."

"Those shuttles, did they board right at the bus terminal or was there a separate loading area for people coming from the Metro?"

"If there's a problem with a train, we always provide shuttle service to and from the station. In this case, that means to the Crystal City Bus Terminal. It's always a bit of chaos, but there is some legal reason for it. I think we don't want to have passengers cross too many streets because if they get hit by a car, we'll get sued."

"Okay, I'm sorry to ask this again," Art said, "But you're absolutely sure that the people from the Blue Line were the first off the train?"

"Yes, positive. The Blue Line train was the first one to arrive."

"So the people from Bus 2405 would have been on that train?"

"Yes."

There it was. Art now felt that he had conclusive proof that there was something fishy about Bus 2405. From Stacey's description, she would have been one of the first people off the train and at the bus terminal. There simply was no way that a bunch of people from out of town could have beaten her onto the shuttle. And, according to Stacey, the bus hadn't even originated at the terminal. It just appeared near the station, fully loaded.

"I want to ask you a favor," Art said, choosing his words deliberately. "Actually, it's kind of a deal. If I can correctly predict something about the Crystal City Metro stop that I would have no way of knowing, will you do me a favor?"

"Depends on what the favor is, I guess."

"I did a Metro story not too long ago and am somewhat familiar with your records policy, so I know that you have been trying to make your records more accessible. I also know that I can get the information that I'm seeking eventually. The favor I'm asking is that, if I can get my prediction right, we bypass all of that nonsense and you'll give me access right away."

Delgado laughed.

"Well, go ahead and make your prediction and then we'll see."

"Fair enough," Art said. "I want to see the surveillance tapes from the Crystal City station but my prediction is that you will tell me that the cameras didn't work or that there is some other reason why they would be useless to me."

There was a long pause.

"That's correct. We only had one camera operational and it's at the back of the station, so you can't really see anything," the press officer said. "So what do you want?"

"I want access to the tapes from the station at Reagan National Airport and I need it tonight."

Art had been certain that the Crystal City tapes would not show anything but maybe, whoever had planned this had forgotten that anybody who has to get off a Metro train also has to get on it.

"Are you gonna tell me what you're up to?" Delgado asked Art.

"I can't tonight and I'll have to ask you to keep quiet about this for a little bit."

There was another pause.

"I'll be here for another hour. Bring a letter with your request and I'll see what I can do," she finally said.

"I'm on my way."

***

The Director of National Intelligence was briefing President Sweeney on the surveillance efforts he had ordered. A lot of satellite coverage was directed at the area between Zhob and the Pakistani border and half of the available drones were patrolling the area.

"It's still going to be tough," McClintock said. "There are so many mountains and a million places to hide. But at least having these capabilities will allow us to see more. Maybe we'll get lucky."

The air surveillance was covering an area of over 10,000 square miles, a circle with a radius of more than 50 miles that was centered in Zhob. Their efforts were focused on the mountains near the border, an area that was rich in caves and steep valleys. On this first day of the search, nobody bothered to look at Andan because the consensus was that Omar Bashir would not be living in a town.

"Our plan of distracting the media is working almost too well, Mr. President," the DNI said, shifting subjects. "Have you seen your poll numbers?"

"Yes, they're gonna be Nixonian in a week if this keeps going," Sweeney quipped, sounding more light-hearted than he felt. Privately, and he would never admit this to anybody, it was a good thing that the country had seen Hassan reach Omar Bashir. It showed that the plan could have succeeded, even if it failed. It would help to keep the heat off him. Primarily, he remained focused on the mission but there was a part of him that, in his darkest hours, started worrying about the political implications. One couldn't become president without being a politician, Sweeney thought.

"So, how long do you think we will have?" he asked McClintock.

"We caught a lucky break with this video, no doubt about that. It should buy us at least a day or so more. Then we'll have to figure out something else but it'll get increasingly dicey."

The DNI had grown very close to the president in the past couple of weeks. They relied on each other to keep their spirits up and McClintock sensed that Sweeney might need a smile.

"I have a terrific idea, sir," he said, unable to contain a wide grin and a wink. "I saw a chubby intern in the hallway when I came in. Maybe you should take one for the team because we know the media will focus on nothing else once that is leaked."

"Thanks, Bob," Sweeney said, acknowledging the effort. "I was thinking more along the lines of a Jello wrestling match between you and the former Russian president ... you know, settle some old scores between spies."

"Are you kidding? He'd kill me! Have you seen the pictures of him with his shirt off? I heard he wrestled a bear and a rhino the other day."

They both laughed, thankful for the light-hearted moment.

***

A little earlier than planned, Hassan made up his mind. He had spent the entire day thinking about his choices. His first plan had obviously not worked, at least not yet, and he had not found a viable way to make contact, so it was down to him trying to kill Omar Bashir or attempting to escape and call in the cavalry. In the end, it came down to one simple truth. At this point, he alone had the power to make Pathfinder at least a partial success. Even if there was an 80 percent chance of him being able to make contact, there was still the possibility that he was killed beforehand and that the mission, his mission, would end up a complete failure. And even if he did manage to get out, it would take him a good while, giving Omar Bashir and the other as-Sirat leaders a chance to get away.
Hassan decided to give it another day to make preparations and then he would strike. Weapons were abundant in the "bunker" and Hassan had no problems getting access to the as-Sirat leader. With the decision made, he felt a tremendous sense of relief. Even though he was certain that he would die the next day, Hassan got a good night's rest for the first time in a week.

***

Art Kempner arrived at Metro headquarters at the Jackson Graham building within half an hour. Of course he had used a cab and not Metro. Though he was in a rush, he still took the time to print out the pictures of several of the terror victims. Art was pretty sure that none of them would show up on the video, if the tape even existed.

Nicole Delgado waited for him in the lobby, accepted the letter requesting the release of the surveillance tape and together the two headed to Metro's security department on the third floor. The press officer led him to a video booth and pulled up another chair.

"So, what do you want to see?" she said. "I spoke to a couple of people, and, in light of your reputation, we will expedite your request. Within reason!"

"Sure, I really just need to see two tapes. First, I want to see the ones from the arrival and departure of the Blue Line train from Reagan National Airport. And, just to be sure we're talking about the same train, I want the one from Van Dorn Metro, too."

"Okay, why don't we start with the one from National?"

Delgado typed in a search string and quickly found the right file. She opened it and the screen was separated into four quadrants, each showing the footage of one of the video cameras at the station.

"These seem to be working," Delgado said and she pushed "Play"

They saw the train pull into the station from all angles. It came to a stop and about a dozen people exited the train. Apart from them, there were only a few scattered people on the platform. The videos were a little bit grainy, so Art wasn't sure about a couple of the passengers, but there was no way that all or even a majority of the Bus 2405 victims had entered the train from that station.

"Okay, let's double check the other one," Art said. He picked up the picture of Stacey Harper that he had found on the Internet.

Delgado again found the file and they watched it. One of the cameras filming the entrance gate clearly showed Stacey entering the station and then getting on the train.

"It's the same train?" Art asked one more time.

"Yeah," Delgado didn't quite understand what she had seen but sensed that it was significant. "Do you need anything else?"

"Just for you not to tell anybody about this," Art said.

***

In the cab back to the office, Art was trying to put it all together. It seemed clear that, after arriving at National airport, the victims didn't use the Metro to get to Crystal City. But then there was no reason for them to be on this shuttle bus. Yet somehow they all appeared on it as though they had boarded it somewhere else.

If that was the case, how in the world did Hassan al-Zaid get on the same bus? If Stacey didn't get on it, then there was also no way that the terrorist had been on the Blue Line train. Did he just happen to walk around Crystal City with a massive bomb in his backpack and found a bus that didn't even originate at the terminal? That seemed highly unlikely.

Then there were all of the problems with Metro that day, the power outage at the Pentagon, the surveillance cameras that didn't work and the tapes from the bus that had been misplaced.

Everything just seemed so orchestrated, from the travel plans the victims made at the same time, to all of them arriving at National in a 30-minute span, to the way they appeared to have gotten on the bus, to the surveillance problems.

But what would have been the point? There was no doubt that the terrorist was on the bus and that he left his backpack. There were the clips of the surveillance tapes from the bus, and there was the meeting with Stacey.

For a split-second, Art thought that maybe the bombing was staged. Maybe the bus had been unloaded somewhere and nobody was on it when it exploded. But that wasn't possible.

There was no doubt that the bus had blown up and that there were victims. There was a massive crater on Washington Boulevard and Alan had been right there, seeing body parts fall from the sky. In addition, the remains had been positively identified as belonging to the victims. Heck, Alan could have been dead also if he hadn't been slowed down.

"Wait a minute," the reporter said to himself. He pulled out his cell and called Alan.

"Hey, it's Art. I have a question. Can you please describe to me exactly what happened right before the bus exploded?"

"Sure, I was on Washington Boulevard, listening to the Grateful Dead and then I caught up with a pair of Humvees that were driving kinda slow. I honked so one would move because they were driving side by side, but they didn't budge. Then, when I was about to honk again, the bus blew up."

The cab had reached the Washington Post and Art tossed the driver a twenty, not waiting for the change.

"Okay, let me ask you this. In retrospect, would it be fair to say that the two Humvees blocked you?" the reporter asked.

"Dunno, I mean, they were just driving slowly next to each other."

"Could any car have gotten past them and closer to the bus?" Art inquired.

"No, not the way they were driving."

"So, whether it was on purpose or inadvertently, they were blocking you?"

"I guess you could say that. What's this all about, Art?"

"I think I'm a converted conspiracy theorist. I have to run and get back to work. Please don't mention this conversation. I'll be able to explain soon."

Art had reached his desk, sat down and closed his eyes.

In the background, MSNBC was replaying a clip of Hassan's confessional video, distracting the reporter's thought process.

"... time for somebody to give you a taste of your own bitter medicine. I will prove that you can no longer feel safe on your buses. You also should not feel safe in your malls or believe that your children are safe in their schools."

"He even told us himself," Art thought. "He never planned to detonate his bomb on a train. A bus had always been the target. But had he targeted this specific bus? If yes, how had he found out about it?"

It also seemed as though somebody else knew that the bombing would take place and tried to prevent people like Stacey from getting on and people like Alan from getting too close. That still left the people on the bus who died.

Too bad that the theory of the bus being unloaded beforehand didn't hold water, because then everything kinda would have made sense. If, for example, somebody knew beforehand what Hassan al-Zaid would do, they could have let him carry out his plan, unload the bus after the terrorist got off and let him believe that the attack was successful. That would also explain the "lost" surveillance tapes. Then, whoever knew about the bombing, could follow Hassan al-Zaid and see if he led them to other terrorists.

It would make sense, but there was irrefutable evidence that there had been people on the bus when it exploded. Art knew he would have to keep looking for a theory in which all pieces fit.

Wednesday, 4:00 am ET

Hassan awoke well-rested with his mind at ease about the plan to kill Omar Bashir. He decided to do it sooner rather than later. He didn't want thoughts about death to start creeping up and get him to chicken out. It had to be done, Hassan told himself. There was no other way to ensure that Pathfinder was a success. And it had to be done now, before his cover was blown. He needed to stay strong for just a little bit longer.

Hassan went to one of the rooms in which weapons were stored and looked for a gun small enough to hide inside his clothes. The armory was rich in assault rifles and heavier weapons but there were only a few handguns. After looking around for a little bit, Hassan found three Heckler&Kochs. He took one, regretting that there were no American-made handguns. That would have been more fitting. Hassan made sure that it was loaded with a round chambered and flipped the safety off before hiding the weapon inside his kaftan.

He made his way to Omar Bashir's quarters. When he got there, the as-Sirat leader just stepped out of the heavy door, flanked by one of his body guards.

"Hassan, I was just about to look for you. There is something I want you to hear about."

Hassan felt the weight of the weapon against his body and part of him had the urge to pull it out and get it over with. But the situation wasn't right. The as-Sirat fighters were all highly trained and Hassan could only be assured of getting a single shot off before they would be all over him. That first bullet had to kill Omar Bashir. He certainly didn't want a bodyguard in position to take it for the as-Sirat leader. So, instead of pulling out the gun, he followed Omar Bashir into his room.

Khalid el-Jeffe was already waiting for them. Omar Bashir motioned for everybody to sit down and poured them tea. They were surrounding a table on which documents were piled high. Omar Bashir motioned to his bodyguard who handed him a laptop.

Hassan evaluated the situation and again decided to wait. It would be too difficult to quickly pull the gun from under his kaftan from a sitting position. He would act as soon as everybody got up. Hassan told himself to be patient. He was astonished how calm he was even though he only had a few more moments to live. But Hassan knew that he was doing the right thing.

"I wanted to talk to you about our greatest mission," Omar Bashir said. "Everything else that has been done before will pale in comparison."

That statement managed to tear Hassan's thoughts away from thinking about the assassination. The as-Sirat leader paused for effect before continuing.

"On the American Thanksgiving Day, a group of as-Sirat fighters will seize control of a nuclear power plant. We will then cause a meltdown and release as much radioactive material as possible. If all goes as planned and with Allah's will, we will make the Chernobyl disaster look like a picnic."

"Wow," Hassan said, "I mean, that's great news. Where is the attack going to take place?"

"Near Chicago," the terrorist leader said, tapping on a map. "With the strong winds there and seasonal wind patterns, fallout should reach the city quickly. It's tough to estimate how many people will die right away, but over time, it should be tens of thousands if we get it right. And it will cripple the economy in the area. We believe that Chicago will be severely contaminated."

"But how can you force a nuclear meltdown? Don't they have ways to prevent that?"

"My young brother, we have been planning this for a decade," the as-Sirat leader said with a smile. He saw the concern on Hassan's face, misinterpreting it. "Don't worry, it will work. Three of the men on the mission are nuclear physicists, among them the leader of the team. He has lived and studied in America for many years. He can manufacture a meltdown and override all of the security systems. The team will then blow up something that is called a 'containment building' to release the radioactive material."

Hassan's mind was reeling. The revelation threw a wrench in his assassination plan. All of a sudden, there was a more important mission than killing Omar Bashir. He had to warn people about the attack because it would certainly be carried out whether the as-Sirat leader was dead or not.

Over the next hour, during which Omar Bashir shared some of the documents with him, Hassan tried to learn as much as possible about the attack. But he never managed to steer the conversation in a direction that would get the as-Sirat leader to give away anything that could be used to identify the people who were to carry out the mission. Hassan hoped that it wouldn't matter. If he escaped and made contact, Andan would be stormed and the plot disrupted. He just had to get away.

Omar Bashir served a second round of tea and his bodyguard removed the documents and the laptop.

Hassan made a mental note that he took them to a small room adjacent to the one they were in.

Omar Bashir finished his tea and rose, indicating that the meeting was adjourned. Hassan only remembered that he carried a loaded gun when he got up and it pressed into his stomach. He was eager to get going and to prepare for his escape.

***

"I think you trust him too much," el-Jeffe said after Hassan left. "Most of the men have no idea of the Chicago attack."

"You don't trust him?" Omar Bashir asked.

"I don't know. I didn't like his look when you both entered this room earlier. And I think he asks too many questions."

"He has proven himself sufficiently, don't you think? Reports are that America is in political turmoil because of his actions. He has been everything we could ever have hoped for."

"Yes he has proven himself," el-Jeffe said. "And he has been almost too good to be true."

"My old friend, you sound like a woman."

"I still don't think you should tell him too much. What if he is captured? We won't know if he'll give up our secrets."

"Khalid, how could he be captured? We'll never allow him to leave here again. He is too recognizable. He will end up like you and me, living in the bunker without ever venturing past Andan again."

Wednesday, 9:02 am ET

Art Kempner had long debated whether he should write an article based on the information he had. On the one hand, he didn't have a complete story. There were plenty of unanswered questions. On the other hand, if the people on the bus were supposed to be part of some secret operation, he might never get those answers. In the end, Art spent three hours the previous evening drafting an article because he was too worried that somebody else would beat him to parts of the story. It was the never-ending fear of any journalist sitting on a huge story and there was no doubt in Art's mind that this was what he was dealing with.

He felt he had to write it now or somebody else would figure out some of the same things he had. Art also couldn't rely on people like Delgado or even Alan to keep their mouths shut. The last reason, albeit an important one, of why he wanted to get started on drafting an article was that it would put pressure on whoever had the answers he was looking for. He would go to the White House with some of the information he had and see if that would get him any further.

With the decision made, Art had hammered away on a draft article until 1:00 am. He had to find a delicate balance between giving his readers newsworthy information without delving into areas of analysis and speculation. So he focused on what he knew to be true. It was enough to debunk the theory that both Hassan al-Zaid and his victims arrived on the first Blue Line train.

He also mentioned that the demographics didn't make sense, pointing out that Hassan al-Zaid was the only person under 30 on the bus. He wrote about the security cameras from National Airport Metro stop and pointed to the terrorist's own video statement.

> *Bus Bombing Deserves a Closer Look*
> *A Washington Post investigation into last week's Pentagon bus bombing raises serious questions about the official version of the chain of events that culminated in an attack claiming 37 American lives.*
> *It has been widely accepted that U.S.-born as-Sirat follower Hassan al-Zaid, who has confessed to carrying out the strike, and his victims were forced to leave a Metro train because of a power failure at Pentagon station. It has also been assumed that the original target of the attack was a train and not the shuttle bus.*
> *But al-Zaid's own words and evidence gathered in the process of the Post's probe indicate that neither of these theories is possible and that our view of the events will have to change, in some cases drastically.*
> *The investigation also uncovered some oddities related to the bombing and raises questions about them that have so far not been asked or answered but deserve to be publicly aired as the nation is trying to return to normalcy.*

Art read over the rest of his draft and was pleased with it. He'd have to run it by the managing editor and then take it over to the White House. Art sent a quick e-mail to President Sweeney's press secretary, asking him for a few minutes of his time in the morning. He was sure the request would be granted. Getting face time with top officials was another perk that winning the Pulitzer carried with it.

***

Hassan laid down for a nap, his head resting on a heavy jacket. He felt something hard pressing against his skull. It could be any number of things. Hassan had loaded the jacket with items that could prove useful during his escape. There was, of course the Heckler&Koch and some additional ammunition. He had also taken a couple of knives, some matches, scrap paper that would help him start a fire and a few other knickknacks.

Sadly, Hassan had been unable to find a compass. It would have been especially useful since he expected to have to avoid the few roads in this part of the world because that's where as-Sirat would come looking first. While Hassan had sometimes cursed the rigorous weekends he had spent training with the Pathfinder team, the lessons were about to pay off big time. He figured that he would be able to generally figure out where he was going by the position of the stars if the night sky was cloudless.

The jacket itself was also a new acquisition. He had told one of the older fighters that he had been very cold at night and would like something to cover up with. The man returned shortly with the jacket and another blanket. Hassan gladly accepted both.

He spent the day making several trips to the kitchen, swiping bits and pieces of food each time. Now he had a stock of dried fruit, meat and bread that should last him for several days and also a couple of large canteens of water. Hassan hoped it wouldn't take that long but he wanted to be prepared. It certainly wouldn't be a cakewalk back to territory that could widely be described as friendly. A bag with his food was hidden in the storage room.

Hassan planned to leave Andan around 2:00 am. That way, he would make sure that everybody else was asleep when he got up while also allowing him a couple of hours to put some distance between himself and as-Sirat. The last step in his preparation was to get some rest. He shifted the jacket so that he was more comfortable and quickly fell asleep.

***

Just as Hassan was laying down, DNI McClintock started his first conference call of the morning. The news he received from the heads of the different surveillance agencies was not good. They had found nothing unusual in the area they were searching.

"We need to keep looking," he ordered, "Even some of the areas where we don't think as-Sirat would be, such as on the plains or in towns.

"I want you to look at everything," the DNI said, stressing the last word.

"We're working around the clock, Bob," the head of the National Reconnaissance Office said. "And we have only so many satellites and so many people.

"Can we bring in some additional staff, like recent retirees, contractors with the necessary clearance?" McClintock asked.

"I'll look into it. When are you going to tell us what all this is about?"

"You'll know soon enough," the DNI said, his tone indicating that he did not wish to talk about the subject. He was very frustrated with the lack of progress but at least he felt they still had some time. They were nearing the end of the window during which they felt Hassan should be able to operate, but there had really been no signs that anybody was onto them. At least that part of Pathfinder had gone off without a hitch.

"How about the drones?"

McClintock's question was directed at the CIA and the Air Force, both of which operated unmanned aerial vehicles.

"All the capabilities we can spare are covering the area," the CIA director said.

"Do the teams know that everybody is looking in the same area?" McClintock asked.

"No, we haven't told them and also asked all of the drone operators not to discuss their current target with anybody, including others with the same clearance."

"Good. Let's do another call at 2:30 pm."

After the conference call, McClintock called President Sweeney to let him know that the surveillance teams had not had any luck. Then he contacted the Pathfinder team in Islamabad. The DNI wanted them to prepare to go to Zhob the next day. Maybe having his men in the area would stir the hornets' nest a little.

**

It didn't take Art Kempner long to convince his managing editor that he was on to something really big. He had started the meeting by asking her what she thought the chain of events was that led to the bombing upon which Emily Strauss had recited the widely accepted story.

"What if I were to tell you that the attack never could have happened that way? Is that something you would be interested in?" Art said. Although the "Entourage" reference was lost on the matronly editor, he immediately got her undivided attention.

With each new piece of evidence he presented her with, Strauss got more excited. It was something Art really liked about her. Though she, like him, had seen just about everything in journalism, Strauss still managed to feel enthusiastic about good stories.

Art showed her the draft article and explained why he wrote it the way we did.

"I think people can easily find out some of this stuff on their own. For example, I'd be surprised if some blogger hadn't already written about how the demographics don't fit. So we need to get moving soon to get the ball rolling or somebody will beat us to the punch. At the very least, I can take this to the White House and see if we get a response of some sort."

"What kind of response are you looking for, Art?"

"I think just about anything might be useful. I'd like to ask if they had even considered an alternative version of what happened before the bombing. If not, I'd like to know why the FBI couldn't also figure this out, or, if they did, why we haven't been told. And, I would love to get an answer on why all the people with military history were on that bus."

"Okay, let's bark up that tree and let me know how it goes."

***

Art strolled over to the White House, enjoying a beautiful day. Many Washingtonians do not pay much attention to the scores of landmarks they see every day. They were just buildings that caused inconveniences when there were protests or roadblocks. And they served as endpoints for the annoying motorcades that held up traffic several times per day.

It was even worse for staffers and reporters because for them some of the country's most historically significant buildings were just work places. Back when they still had a weekly touch football game on the National Mall, Art remembered how wide receivers would announce that they would "break toward the House side" or run a "Senate slant."

He always tried to maintain the perspective of how awe-inspiring buildings like the White House and the Capitol really were. Art felt the same way now as he walked across Lafayette Park. The entire world always had an eye on this building because many decisions made here would impact everybody on the planet. When he reached the gate, he handed over his "hard pass," the most coveted of press credentials, and was waved through. He walked up the driveway toward the White House and reached the Brady Press Briefing Room. Art saw that it was sparsely populated at this hour and stuck his head into the hallway next to the podium with the president's seal. He caught the attention of some assistant-under-deputy of something or another, and asked the young man to let the press secretary know that Art Kempner was here now.

Then he sat down in one of the blue chairs and pulled out a copy of the Post. He tried not to have his picture taken while reading the Times. He did that at his home or in the bathroom.

"Art, buddy, good to see you."

It was one of the press secretary's jobs to make reporters like him and, more importantly, his boss. That explained why Kyle Eubanks welcomed Art like a long lost family member and not a guy from work.

Art returned the greeting.

"So, what can I do for you?" the press secretary asked.

"Let's talk in your office."

"Okay, I'll lead the way."

Art followed Eubanks to his office further in the bowels of the White House. He sat down across from the press secretary's desk and pulled a couple sheets of paper from his shirt pocket.

"So, Art, what's up?" Eubanks said after closing the door and making it to his desk.

"I'm working on a story. In my view, it is huge and everything I have found out might only be the beginning. I would normally not write an article in which so many questions remain unanswered, but I think, and my managing editor happens to agree, that the information we already have compels us to run it.

"And we plan on doing it tomorrow," Art added.

"Can you stop with the Chinese water torture and get to the point?" the White House press secretary said. His smile looked a little uneasy now. Press secretaries did not like surprises. They liked to control information.

"Well, the story basically says that not everything about the bombing last week is what it seems. We have evidence showing that it could not have happened the way people think it did ... and the way the Sweeney administration has been portraying it, by the way."

Art laid out his case, trying to stick to the facts and veer as little as possible into the realm of speculation. He also withheld some important pieces of information, not wanting to lay all of his cards on the table.

"I think there are many questions that need to be answered," he concluded. "Did anybody in the administration raise doubts about the accepted version of events? If so, what happened? Also, I know that there is no way you'll come back to me with anything on whether there was a covert team on that bus. But I think this administration should ask itself how Hassan al-Zaid managed to target this particular bus, because it certainly looks like he did."

Art was certain that, if the administration knew more than it had been letting on, it was unlikely that Kyle Eubanks had those answers. It was just not practical to tell the press secretary anything the public was not supposed to find out. After all, he spoke to reporters all day long and conducted two daily briefings. But Eubanks certainly had access to those who did have the answers. Art needed him to take his questions to some of the top people in government and hopefully somebody would then come back to him.

"Art, listen to yourself. Covert team? We're still in the middle of an emergency and you want me to figure out if we knew whether the victims of this attack had been on a Blue or Orange Line train?" Eubanks said. "I don't doubt that your research is solid and I admit that some of the stuff you're telling me sounds interesting, but I'm sure there are explanations for this."

Art was not prepared for that reaction. Obviously, it was part of the press secretary's job to downplay any story that could shed a negative light on the administration but the reporter hadn't expected the press secretary to be this combative. The fact was that he simply caught Eubanks in a bad moment. For a solid week, the press secretary had been forced to defend the administration's actions in the aftermath of the bombing and it was fraying his nerves. Art's inquiry had just come at a bad time, and served the press secretary as a valve to finally be able to release some of the pressure that had been building up.

"Do you want me to walk into a National Security Council meeting and say 'Hey, I know you're talking about the latest as-Sirat video and how we can find the terrorists, but could I just get everybody's attention? Whoever knows about the covert ops team that was on Metro 2405, could you please let me know what's going on with that'?

"Seriously, Art," Eubanks added. "This sounds like it could come from some conspiracy theory blog or something. Missing video cameras and bus demographics? Again, I'm sure there is an explanation for all of this. Are you actually surprised that Metro equipment isn't working or that a station lost power?"

"Kyle, my information is solid and there is a bunch more stuff I'm not telling you. You know me. I'd never come to you with this stuff unless I knew there was a story."

"I'm sorry, it's just been a really long week and, as you know, we're not looking too good," Eubanks said, sounding more exhausted than combative now. "How about this: I'll take the first part of your question to some people and we'll take it from there."

***

What happened next really surprised the White House press secretary. He had shot off an e-mail to his FBI counterpart saying: "You're going to hate me for this and I know it sounds like something from way out there, but Art Kempner from the Post is planning to run with a story that not everything about the bombing is what it seems. He has some evidence and wanted to know whether, as part of the investigation, the FBI ever looked at the possibility that this happened differently from what we thought. Particularly with regard to how people got on the bus and where they came from before that."

The FBI press secretary opened the e-mail two minutes later. He happened to be at a meeting with top Bureau officials that was just concluding and mentioned its contents to the group, which included FBI Director Stevenson. Stevenson said he would deal with this himself and asked them not to worry or talk about the e-mail.

When the room was empty, the FBI Director called President Sweeney, pulled him out of a call with a foreign leader and told him about the problem. The president immediately called for Kyle Eubanks.

Now, just over ten minutes after having sent the e-mail, the White House press secretary stepped into the Oval Office. The president wasted no time.

"I need to know exactly what Art Kempner said."

The press secretary was baffled. "Mr. President, how did you ..."

"There is really no time for that, Kyle," Jack Sweeney said. "I need to know everything that happened."

His press secretary gave the president a brief rundown of the conversation. He could tell that the commander-in-chief was not at all pleased with what he was hearing. At the end of the report, Sweeney let out a deep sigh and said: "Fuck."

It was the first time Eubanks had ever heard his boss swear. He didn't like it one bit and wondered if he had somehow screwed up.

"Okay, that'll be all. Don't talk to anybody else about this."

Sweeney waved his press secretary out with one hand and with the other he already reached for the phone.

"Get me McClintock."

It took a second for the DNI to get on the phone.

"We're screwed, the dam has burst," Sweeney said and explained.

They both knew that time was running out on Pathfinder, even if they managed to plug this leak.

They had reached the kind of territory in which their window of opportunity would be closed in hours, not days.

Wednesday, 12:53 pm ET

The fancy world clock on McClintock's desk showed that it was 12:53 in Washington, and 22:53 in Pakistan. Then it didn't show anything because the DNI had picked it up and flung it at the wall on the opposite side of the office, where it disintegrated with a pop.

McClintock let out an obscenity-laced tirade that made his secretary in the next room blush.

It was all going to unravel and time was running out for Pathfinder. It was not just the Washington Post story. Even if they could do something about that, there would be another and then another.

McClintock's gut feeling, which rarely was wrong, told him that they would have only hours to find Hassan before the mission would blow up in their faces.

He had felt so good about Pathfinder a couple of weeks ago. Hassan was brimming with confidence that had transferred to the other team members. The DNI could only imagine what he was feeling now, alone among enemies, more and more aware that help would not come. They had failed this brave young man.

McClintock also thought about the fallout that was sure to follow. It would be a big, ugly political mess. He was close to retirement and could weather a storm. Of course, the DNI was worried about the president. He had admired Jack Sweeney's courage to authorize a mission that, if unsuccessful, could destroy his presidency.

But Sweeney had not blinked when deciding to go ahead with deceiving his entire country in order to take a shot at as-Sirat. He knew all other approaches had not worked and time was slipping away. With the political climate having changed in Pakistan and it being about to change in Afghanistan as well, this was the last best opportunity to try to deal a fatal blow to the terrorist network.

In McClintock's view, the president should be commended for his decisions, not condemned, even if the mission would end up a disaster.

The DNI chastised himself for thinking along those lines. There was no evidence yet that Pathfinder had already failed. As far as he knew, Hassan was still alive and still trying to make the mission a success. He should do the same. Unless there was incontrovertible evidence that there was no hope, he would do everything in his power to prevent Pathfinder from failing.

McClintock called the team in Islamabad, informed the men of the bad news and ordered them to move toward Zhob. Then he placed calls to the heads of the different surveillance agencies, telling them to squeeze everything they could out of their staffs.

Wednesday, 1:35 pm ET

The phone rang and Art Kempner picked up.

"Art, you have visitors," the receptionist said. "They are in conference room B."

"Who is it?" he asked.

"Some guys from the White House."

Kempner quickly made his way through the newsroom, trying to figure out who had made the way to the Washington Post Building. When he opened the door to the conference room, he saw that his managing editor, White House chief of staff Jared Watkins and a couple of Secret Service agents were waiting for him.

"Both of you, please come with us," Watkins said. "We have a car waiting in the garage. Let's take the back stairs."

The quintet made its way to the basement, with Kempner wondering what the hell was going on. The White House chief of staff didn't often make house calls. When they got to the garage, a couple of large, black SUVs were waiting for them.

"I'm going to have to search both of you for weapons," one of the Secret Service agents said to Kempner and Strauss. Just then, the door to one of the cars opened.

"I don't think that will be necessary, Matt. We are here as guests and I don't think Mr. Kempner and Ms. Strauss would try to harm us … at least not intentionally."

"Of course not, Mr. President," the agent said.

The veteran reporter had seen many things but he was speechless now as he was staring at President Sweeney in the parking garage of his office.

"Please, join me in the car," Sweeney said. "We have the area mostly sealed off but we also can't afford to risk being too visible.

"Besides," he added with a smile. "I wouldn't want any of my political opponents to barge in on us. They already think I'm too close to the press."

Kempner and Strauss got into the spacious SUV and sat down in a row of seats facing the president.

"First of all, for now this conversation is off the record, is that clear?"

The reporter and his editor nodded.

"Mr. Kempner, I understand you contacted my press office earlier today about an article you are working on. I further understand that this story is slated to run tomorrow and would raise some questions about last week's bombing. Is that correct?"

The president paused until Kempner nodded again.

"I'm here to give you answers to some of the questions you probably have," Sweeney continued. "More importantly, I'm here to try to convince both of you to not run that story tomorrow.

"Since I don't have a great deal of time, let me be as frank as possible. Hassan al-Zaid didn't kill anybody on that bus. He is not a terrorist and there was no terrorist attack. What the world witnessed was an act of heroism by patriotic Americans, most of whom sacrificed the last months of their lives for their country. As I'm telling you this, another, Hassan al-Zaid, is putting his own life in the gravest of dangers in defense of the United States. At least I pray that he is still alive."

The president handed a document to the stunned Kempner.

"This is an outline of something called 'Operation Pathfinder.' You may read it as I am speaking but the document cannot leave the vehicle and it is also off the record for now," Sweeney continued.

"I originally authorized the mission in my first term. Basically, Pathfinder is a staged terrorist attack that allows us to place an asset deep within as-Sirat with the aim of letting us deal a serious blow to the group's leadership.

"I gave the final green light after it had become clear that the situations in Afghanistan and Pakistan were not turning in our favor. If Pathfinder is not successful, we have to anticipate that as-Sirat will emerge stronger than ever and quickly become our most serious national security threat since the fall of the Soviet Union.

"At first, everything went according to plan. The attack hurt nobody. The people on the bus were all terminally ill volunteers and they took something that killed them painlessly before the explosive device we planted went off. There was no doubt in anybody's mind as to who was responsible for the attack, thus giving Hassan access to as-Sirat. Unfortunately, we have lost him. A GPS device we had implanted in Hassan stopped working just prior to the attack and three portable transmitters became useless when all of Hassan's possessions were taken from him after he established contact with as-Sirat.

"Despite those setbacks, he obviously managed to achieve his objective and we have no indication that his cover has been blown. We also managed to follow him for quite a bit toward his current location, so we have a general idea where Hassan is. Right now, every reconnaissance asset we can spare is monitoring that area in the hopes of finding a sign from Hassan that will lead us to as-Sirat. Though all of the unfortunate setbacks have made Pathfinder somewhat of a long shot, there is still a chance that the mission will succeed."

The president squinted and pressed his lips together. His eyes found Kempner's.

"However, if you run your story, it'll likely create enough doubt about the attack that it will doom the mission and leave the United States more vulnerable. It would also be a death sentence for Hassan al-Zaid, one of the great heroes in this country's history. I'm asking you … no, I am pleading with you not to run that piece tomorrow.

"If the national security implications are not enough to sway you, I'm willing to sweeten the deal by offering you exclusive access to myself and anybody involved in Pathfinder once the mission is concluded. You, and only you, will get to write the full story and I promise you that we will keep nothing hidden from you.

"I'm well aware that Pathfinder comes with great political risks for my administration. I have authorized and taken part in the deception of our citizens. It wasn't an easy decision but I still believe it was the best one. The American people may not feel the same way, especially if the mission is ultimately unsuccessful. There is no doubt that my opponents will seize on this and they may push for impeachment. As the last part of our deal, should you agree to hold the story, I will promise you this: If my opponents manage to start a credible impeachment movement, I will give you the exclusive story that I will endorse such a step. You can report that I will publicly lay out every aspect of what I have done with regard to Pathfinder and let the Congress and the American people judge my actions."

The president paused for a few seconds to allow his words to sink in.

"This is not about covering anything up. In due time, I will lay out everything to the American people whether Pathfinder is successful or not. It was always planned that way. This is about national security. I implore you, on behalf of our nation and on the behalf of a young man who is alone in enemy territory half a world away, to not run that story. I hate to do anything that can be viewed as obstructing our First Amendment, but we need more time.

"There you go, that's my pitch. What's it gonna be?" Sweeney concluded.

Kempner looked at his editor and then the president. "I think we should be allowed to think about this for a little bit and discuss it," he said.

Sweeney nodded.

"Fair enough. Let's touch base in 30 minutes and see where we stand."

The president knocked on the window and a Secret Service agent opened the door.

Strauss had already exited the SUV when the veteran reporter turned to Sweeney.

"Whatever we decide, I can tell you this. There will be no horse trading. If we do this, it'll be because we believe you that it is in our national interest, not because you are offering me access."

***

Hassan and the other men had gone to bed just before midnight. They sometimes talked a little before going to sleep and Hassan used those conversations to pick up information that could prove valuable down the road. On this night, he learned that three men, including Nasir, had set off for North America the previous day to be part of a major operation. Hassan figured that it was the attack on the power plant.

"Let me get some sleep, guys," he said. It was not in his interest to have them stay up. He wanted at least an hour to pass from the last snippet of conversation to the time he would leave. He wanted to be certain that they were all asleep.

"You've been sleeping all day, Hassan," one of the men mocked him. It was true, Hassan had taken an extensive nap in the afternoon and was wide awake. He didn't want to risk falling asleep and missing the ideal start time.

The as-Sirat fighters didn't do him the favor of going to sleep quickly. Instead, they kept talking for almost an hour longer, excited that another major mission was about to start and anxious when it would be their time to take up arms against the oppressors again.

Not too far away, Omar Bashir had trouble sleeping. He thought about Hassan and something Khalid el-Jeffe had said earlier.

Was the young American too good to be true? The as-Sirat leader did not think so, but for the first time, he started to ask himself some questions. Was it really possible for Hassan to pull off the escape the way he did? With the western world looking for him, he had managed to fly across the globe undetected. He even made it more difficult on himself when he sent that video to the television networks. His forged documents must have been impeccable. How did he obtain them? At the very least, Hassan's forger would be a good man to know and as-Sirat should make use of him in the future.

Omar Bashir thought of other young recruits. They were ignorant idealists. But Hassan was completely different. Hassan was perfect. He was everything the as-Sirat leader could dream of.

On the other hand, what else could he be if not a young man wanting to join the cause? Omar Bashir knew from the daily news reports that America was in turmoil and Hassan was the reason for it.

Maybe it would be best if he and el-Jeffe sat down with Hassan the next morning and go over every little detail of his escape. At the very least, it could ease the concerns of his top lieutenant. It was good to have unity. Allah willing, Hassan and el-Jeffe would have to live together for a long time to come.

***

"Art, Strauss wants to see you."

The reporter checked the time on his computer. It was a little after 2:00 pm and the president had left them about 30 minutes earlier. It didn't take a genius to figure out what Strauss needed him for. He saved the document on his screen before making his way to the managing editor's office. Understandably, he had been having a tough time concentrating on work. The events of the past hour had occupied his mind, preventing him from getting anything done. Though he had seen a lot in his decades of covering American politics, having the president come to the newspaper to ask for a story to be held was just as unbelievable as Jack Sweeney's account of Operation Pathfinder itself.

He and Strauss had not needed much time to decide on what should happen with the story. The Washington Post would not put at risk the life of Hassan al-Zaid and jeopardize an ongoing major counterterrorism operation. Art didn't feel completely at ease with that decision but knew that such was the nature of making a tough call.

Emily Strauss was on the phone. She waved him into her office indicating that he should shut the door. In his haste, Art didn't realize that the cord of the door's blinds got in the way and prevented it from falling shut.

"Art Kempner is here now," she said, then paused and added. "Sure, I'll hold for the president."

She motioned for him to have a seat.

"We're doing the right thing, Art," Strauss said, probably more to herself than the reporter. It was also as much a question as it was a statement. They were in the unenviable position of having to pick between two choices, neither of them right or wrong but both fraught with danger and massive pitfalls.

"Yes, Mr. President, this is Emily Strauss," she said. "I'm here with Art Kempner and I'll put you on speaker phone now."

"Well, what's the call?" President Sweeney asked.

Just then the door opened quietly and, without being noticed by Strauss or Kempner, another Post reporter stuck his head into the office.

"We have decided to hold Art's story for the time being, Mr. President," the Post's managing editor said and Kempner thought he heard a sigh of relief on the other end of the line. "We do not like being put in this position but the reasons you have given us outweigh, in our rushed judgment, the First Amendment considerations. Sadly, there is no time to review all of the issues more thoroughly. We'll have to do that in retrospect."

The door to the office closed as quietly as it had been opened. A stunned young reporter stood in the newsroom, trying to make sense of what he had just heard.

Back in the office, Sweeney expressed his gratitude to Strauss and Kempner.

"Trust me, I hate to have to put you in this situation. I also would understand if you want to report about my visit and my request once all this is over and, if you want to skewer me for my actions, please feel free to do so. Right now, all I care about is the lives involved and protecting this mission for as long as possible.

"I will not forget this," Sweeney added as an afterthought. "I have to get back to work and I know the Post has a hole to fill on the front page."

With that, the president hung up.

***

Jonathan H. Nicklaus sat at his desk in the Post's newsroom with his thoughts reeling. He had just heard the president of the United States of America interfere with the freedom of the press. It also appeared that his newspaper had agreed to the outrageous and, in his mind, possibly unconstitutional request from Jack Sweeney to hold a story from Art Kempner.

Nicklaus had no idea what the veteran reporter was working on, but he was determined to find out.

While Kempner had made his way to the top of the journalism world by putting in long hours as a beat reporter who had covered anything from sports to crime and even entertainment in his early years, Nicklaus was part of a new generation.

Short on actual experience, he had a master's degree in journalism from an Ivy League school. That, and some connections, had gotten him a job with the Washington Post. His academic journalism background had also given him a different, more idealistic view of the profession and the First Amendment. To him, it was untouchable. It was the most important law of the land.

After contemplating what he had learned, Nicklaus decided to take action. If need be, he would blow the whistle on his own paper and expose whatever deal the Post had with the president. He closed his eyes, thinking about what this could do for his own career. Surely he would be hailed as a First Amendment champion.

But first, he had to find out what was going on, starting with figuring out what Art Kempner's story was all about.

Wednesday, 2:25 pm ET

DNI McClintock was on edge, his mind always returning to a picture of Hassan, sitting alone in a cave somewhere and hoping that help would come. They couldn't fail the kid. The president had called to let him know that the Post would hold the story, but that did little to ease McClintock's worries. He just knew that there wasn't much time. Once the dam had shown the first cracks, it would certainly soon burst.

It was almost time for the 2:30 pm conference call. Hopefully, Hassan was asleep somewhere, as safe as one can be in enemy territory. For this briefing on the surveillance efforts, the DNI had demanded that not only the heads of the agencies participate. McClintock also wanted to hear from the men and women who knew the reconnaissance best – the leaders of the various teams that used drones and satellites to monitor the vast target area. When McClintock began to speak, they all understood that something big was going on but none of them knew what it was.

"Please, someone tell me that you have some good news," the DNI began, almost pleading with them. "Has there been anything unusual in the sectors you have been asked to cover? Please, there has to be something."

Those working with McClintock on a regular basis had never seen him this emotional. As he quizzed them one by one about what they had been observing, the DNI looked increasingly weary and old as nobody reported unusual activity.

"I can't tell you why this is so important because it is classified above a level that anybody here is cleared for, but you have to believe me that time is running out for us and I feel you are our last chance," he said.

"If you have seen anything out of the ordinary, no matter how insignificant it might seem to you, please let me know," McClintock continued. An image of Hassan again flashed through his mind. "Anything? Please!"

For an agonizingly long time, McClintock only heard static.

Then, a voice.

"Sir, this is Lieutenant Colonel Amanda Tongan. I head an Air Force squadron of unmanned aerial vehicles. While we also did not have any unusual activity in our sector, there was something a little bit odd that we noticed just a few hours ago. I wouldn't normally bring this up but you're being so insistent ..." her voice trailed off before starting again.

"In the small town of Andan, which is on the Pakistani side of the border to Afghanistan in the Waziristan region, it appears that somebody has painted what appears to be a New York Yankees logo on the rooftop of a building. It wasn't there last time we took a picture of that town, which was a month ago. Obviously, the area is very anti-American so we all were a little surprised to see it there and got a bit of a chuckle out of it. You should be able to see that image on your screen in a second, sir."

McClintock's heart leaped as his last conversation with Hassan, in which they had talked about the Yankees' playoff chances, flashed through his mind.

"A Yankees symbol?" the DNI repeated, his emotions reflected in his voice.

"Yes, sir. Sorry, I would not have brought it up but you wanted to know if there had been anything new," the Lieutenant Colonel apologized, taking McClintock's reaction as a rebuke.

The DNI saw the reconnaissance photo appearing on his screen.

There it was, a crude painting of the Y overlapping an N, drawn on the flat roof of a building.

"'The writing is on the wall, Yankees'. He told us in the video," McClintock stammered, his voice breaking. He had found Hassan. He was sure of it. Now they needed to get him out.

"Get me the president right now," he shouted in the direction of his chief of staff, leaving the other participants of the conference call wondering what the hell was going on. "And the SecDef."

***

"So, I hear you're working on a big story, Art. What's the scoop?" Jonathan H. Nicklaus had strolled over to Art Kempner's workspace and tried to ask the question as casually as possible.

"What?" Art said, torn from deep thought. He looked up and recognized the young reporter whom he regarded as a snotty kid who hadn't earned the right to being a reporter for one of the top newspapers in the country.

"You heard wrong," he grunted. "I got nothing in tomorrow's issue. I was working on something but it fell through."

"That's a bummer," Nicklaus said, feigning sympathy. "I hope it wasn't anything major."

"Nothing really," Art responded trying to be as brief as possible. He didn't feel like elaborating. "Now please excuse me, I gotta head to the john."

"Sure thing," Nicklaus said and walked away.

When Art passed him on the way to the bathroom, Nicklaus returned to the veteran reporter's desk. He looked at the screen and saw that it was not locked and that a few Word documents were open. He clicked on one indicating that it was for the following day's issue and the headline jumped at him: "Bus Bombing Deserves a Closer Look."

The young reporter skimmed through the beginning of the story before minimizing the window again and walking back to his desk.

So the White House was trying to prevent the publication of a story that would show it had bungled this investigation even worse than previously thought. Nicklaus felt that the country deserved to know about this.

He sent an e-mail to the Drudge Report. It was about 3:00 pm in Washington and 1:00 am in Andan.

***

An alarm sounded across Bagram Air Base. All special ops forces were to report in combat gear to the airfield immediately.

"This better not be a goddamn drill," Ken Gorsula said. He had just fallen asleep and now drowsily got out of bed. He dressed quickly, grabbed his gear and headed out of the barracks. The rest of his men were either waiting or arrived simultaneously. Together, they made their way toward the airfield.

It was not a drill. The base's commander, two-star general Quincy Hopkins, was woken up a few minutes earlier by a phone call from President Sweeney and the Secretary of Defense. After being explained the situation and his orders, he had summoned his senior officers to pass on word to them.

"It looks like we think that we know where Omar
Bashir is hiding," Quincy started. "It's a small
Pakistani town not far from the border. We have to hit
it now and we have to hit it hard. Get your men ready
to deploy within the next 20 minutes."

It didn't take nearly as long for the 300 special ops
soldiers on base to get ready. Now, they stood at
attention on the airfield, waiting to be addressed by
their commanding general.

"Men, I just got off the phone with the president and
he is ordering you on a mission that could result in the
largest strike against as-Sirat. Tonight, we are going
after Omar Bashir," Hopkins said. "Intelligence says
the as-Sirat headquarters is in Andan, a little town on
the Pakistani side of the border. We are throwing
everything we have at this but you guys are the tip of
the spear. There will be civilians there, so it is your job
to do as little harm to them as possible.

"One more thing. I know all of you have wanted to get
your hands on Hassan al-Zaid but things were not what
they seemed. The president informed me that Hassan
al-Zaid is not a terrorist. He has been working for our
intelligence and the Washington attack was a setup to
get him close to Omar Bashir so that he could relay the
position of as-Sirat's headquarters.

"Getting Omar Bashir and the other as-Sirat leaders is
your main objective, but the president has stressed that
he wants Hassan al-Zaid back home," the general said.
"While we have all hated him, this kid has been
risking his life for our country and I expect you to do
the same for him. Let's get airborne within the next 15
minutes."

***

"President kills WaPo story raising questions about bus bombing"

The sirens were back on the Drudge Report.

The Texan businessman, who was waiting for his flight home, was standing at one of the public Internet terminals near his gate when he saw the headline. It was very early in the morning at Tokyo's Narita International Airport. Not many travelers were up at this time and he had to kill an hour before he could board his flight.

"Excuse me, sir," a Middle Eastern man of about 35 tapped him on the shoulder. "What is that Internet site you are looking at?"

"This is the Drudge Report. It's an online news site. They always seem to have the news ahead of everybody else," the Texan said. "Here, use this Internet terminal, you can check it out for yourself."

"Very kind of you, sir."

Nasir Fattah was also waiting for his flight. There were only a couple of ways to travel from Asia to Mexico without stopping in the United States and both of those flights came through Tokyo. Nasir was one of the men who were to lead the assault on the Chicago nuclear power plant, so he had to be one of the first of the as-Sirat fighters to arrive in Mexico.

Now he stood at the public computer terminal at Narita airport and clicked on the link.

*"EXCLUSIVE: According to a well-placed
newsroom source, the Washington Post has
given in to a personal request from President
Sweeney to hold a story from Pulitzer Prize
winner Art Kempner. The article reportedly
raises questions about last week's terrorist
attack on Washington and would, according to
the source, make the White House 'look bad'.
Among other things, the story proved that
neither terrorist Hassan al-Zaid nor his victims
could have been aboard the Metro train prior
to the attack. This would raise additional
questions about the handling of the
investigation. To be continued ..."*

Though his English was good, Nasir read the story
twice to make sure he understood everything. He tried
to make sense of it. Nasir had heard Hassan recount
the story of the attack a couple of times and both times
he had said that he wanted to blow up the train but had
to leave when the power went out down the line. If this
report was right, then Hassan had lied to them.
Before Nasir left Andan, he had a conversation with
Khalid el-Jeffe. The as-Sirat deputy had sought him
out to talk about Hassan since the two of them had
spent the most time together. Omar Bashir's top
lieutenant told Nasir that he was concerned that
everything about Hassan seemed to be too perfect. The
two of them had talked about it for an hour. Nasir
didn't share el-Jeffe's concerns but he also felt that he
was unable to alleviate them.

Now, he was unsure of what to do. He was one of the few people who had the numbers of Omar Bashir's and el-Jeffe's satellite phones but should he risk it for this? In the end, he decided against it, too worried about electronic surveillance. Instead, he called one of the couriers in Islamabad and instructed him to print out the article and take it to Omar Bashir in the morning. After all, it was about 2:00 am in Andan and everybody would be asleep.

Wednesday, 3:57 pm ET

In the past hour, Hassan had not heard anything other than rhythmic breathing from the other men in the room.

It was time to get going. Until this very moment, Hassan had still held out hope that, against all odds, somebody would have seen the Yankees symbol and figured out where he was. Apparently that wasn't going to happen. He was on his own.

Hassan got up, careful not to make any noise. He had contemplated stuffing things under his blanket to make people think he was sleeping but decided against it. Once somebody saw that, they would know he was on the run and trying to deceive them. By simply leaving, there was a chance it would take them longer to figure it out.

He now knew the path to the exit of the cave by heart and walked through the tunnels as quietly as possible. Hassan pushed the secret door open. He used the light coming from the tunnel to put on the jacket and make sure all of his equipment was in place. Hassan chambered a round and placed the gun into his right front pocket. Then he retrieved his food bag and the canteens before pulling the secret door shot and stepping outside.

Hassan figured that the side of town with the road would be more closely guarded, so he had decided to leave the other way and then try to circle around in a wide arc. He had no idea exactly what time it was but figured he would be able to travel under the cover of darkness for several more hours.

Hassan turned east. The sentry on that end of town was dozing and did not see him leave. But, high in the sky, the drones that were now circling Andan picked up the solitary figure that stepped out of the shadows and left town in the direction of Afghanistan. The night vision cameras did not pick up the second figure that briefly peeked out of the storage building before disappearing again.

***

Yezem woke up when he heard Hassan leave the room. The young Saudi figured that the newest as-Sirat addition was probably going to the bathroom and decided to play a little joke on him. Yezem planned to follow Hassan and then, when he got out of the restroom, he would scare the daylights out of him. To his surprise, Hassan didn't stop at the bathroom. Instead, he headed for the exit of the cave, opened the secret door and stepped into the storage room.

In the dim light of the tunnel, Yezem could see Hassan put on a jacket, take out a gun and pull a bag from somewhere before closing the door.

The as-Sirat fighter waited for a minute before he opened it and stepped into the storage building. Hassan was nowhere to be seen. Yezem stuck his head out of the doorway and looked in all directions. He believed that he saw a figure leave town in the direction of Afghanistan.

Yezem waited for a couple more minutes but Hassan was not coming back. The Saudi headed back into the tunnel and went straight to Omar Bashir's quarters. He knocked on the door and, after a few moments, one of the bodyguards opened.

"I think Hassan left," Yezem said and briefly described what had happened.

"Wait!" The bodyguard disappeared and, after a minute or so, returned with Omar Bashir.

"Yezem, tell me exactly what happened," the as-Sirat leader demanded.

The young man complied and repeated what he had witnessed.

"You did well," Omar Bashir said to Yezem and then turned to his bodyguard.

"Get ten men, those who know the area best. Have them split up in two groups and start searching."

The bodyguard rushed off to carry out the order.

For now, it didn't really matter why Hassan left, although Omar Bashir was both curious and worried. There would be time for intense questioning when he was found. What mattered was that he was a security risk to everybody in Andan. He had to be brought back.

Wednesday, 4:30 pm ET

The pack of ten MH-47E Chinook helicopters looked like a swarm of angry insects as they flew low to the Afghan ground. There were also several Apaches for their protection. It was about 200 miles from Bagram to their destination and they had been airborne for about 45 minutes. Flying near their top speed at this altitude, the Chinooks would reach the target within half an hour.

Each helicopter carried 30 special ops soldiers. They were supported by warplanes that had taken off after them and were now circling the sky at great heights. The men on board the Chinooks were nervously excited. In this case, it was not just the feeling that preceded any combat action, even though they all anticipated encountering fierce resistance. This mission was different. It was exactly what they had signed up for. On this morning, if the intelligence was correct, they would be able to make a real difference in the fight against terrorism.

***

President Sweeney, DNI McClintock and other members of the national security team were glued to the monitors in the White House situation room that showed video from the drones circling Andan and the helicopters closing in on the Pakistani border. One of the drones was still following the person who had left the town about 15 minutes ago and walked north.

"We have some movement," the voice of a drone operator said. Another camera showed several men spilling out of the same building that the first person had come out of.

"Looks like ten individuals with weapons," the voice commented. "They're moving in the same direction as the first one but with greater speed. They just split up in groups of five. We'll keep an eye on them."

"What do you think is going on there?" Sweeney asked McClintock.

"I have no idea but it seems like an awful lot of people are coming out of that small building."

"How close are the helicopters to Pakistan?" the president wanted to know.

"They'll reach the border within the next five minutes," the Secretary of Defense said.

"I guess it's time for my phone call. Let's get President Khan on the line."

***

When the president of the United States calls, even at 2:45 am, he usually gets who he wants to talk to. In this case, president Salman Khan, a former general, was awoken with the message that Jack Sweeney needed to speak to him urgently and had insisted on holding the line.

"President Sweeney, a pleasure to speak with you," Pakistan's president said.

"President Khan, I apologize for the early call but I'm contacting you in a matter of great importance and urgency. We believe that we know the location of as-Sirat's headquarter and we are going to attack it. It seems that Omar Bashir is holed up in the town of Andan in the north of your country."

"Mr. President, we can certainly discuss such an attack but you know that internal politics have prevented me from granting you the authority to strike inside of my country. I am glad you contacted me to ask for permission and I hope we can come to a solution that is mutually agreeable."

"President Khan, I'm not asking for your permission," Sweeney said icily. "I'm telling you that we will attack Andan in a matter of minutes and that our forces will enter Pakistani territory shortly."

"You waited until the last minute to tell me this?"

"If I had given you any more heads up, I am worried that someone on your staff could have tried to warn as-Sirat."

"President Sweeney, I object in the strongest terms ..."

"And I object, too. I object that you have not allowed us to take the fight to the terrorists in your country. Today we will. If our intelligence is wrong and we are attacking the wrong place, please feel free to condemn this action in the strongest way possible. Take it to the United Nations or do whatever you want. If our intelligence is right and we find Omar Bashir in Andan, I will back you up in any way you want. If you want to say that Pakistan cooperated in the raid then I will publicly praise you. If you think it would be better to say that we acted alone, then I'll say that we did.

"However, if we find an as-Sirat stronghold in Andan and there is any indication that Pakistan acted in any way to impede this mission, I will consider that a hostile act against the United States. The choice is yours. I have to go and help coordinate a military strike but I trust that we will speak again later today."

***

"Okay, we have been ordered to go after a new target," the pilot said over the intercom. "About a dozen people have left Andan within the past 30 minutes. Intel says it seems as though ten armed men are trying to track down an individual who had a 15-minute head start. However, they are closing in fast. I'm gonna drop you in front of the lead guy."

"Roger that," Ken Gorsula said.

Wednesday, 4:50 pm ET

The night was perfectly quiet and sound carried a long way. Hassan paused when he thought he heard voices behind him. He remained completely still, trying to figure out if his mind was playing tricks on him. But there it was again, the distinct sound of a human voice. Hassan knew that he was in trouble. Somebody coming up behind him could only mean one thing: The terrorists knew that he was on the run. Hassan broke out in cold sweat, his heart racing.

How had they figured out that he was gone? Hassan guessed that he had been on the run for less than an hour but they were already right on his tail.

"Get your shit together, Hassan," he chastised himself. It was inconsequential why he was in this predicament. The only thing that mattered was how he would get out of it.

Hassan weighed his options and realized that they were not very good. He could walk back, dump his provisions and pretend he had just gone for an evening stroll. He could try to find out how many men were after him and try to ambush them. But he only had one handgun, not enough to take on experienced fighters with better weapons.

That left two options. He could try to find a place to hide and let them walk past him. Then he could try to take a different route and continue his escape. Or he could simply try to run and put as much distance as possible between whoever was following him.

One thing was clear. The men following him would know the area very well. They held all the cards. Outrunning them was probably not an option, so Hassan decided to hide somewhere and let them pass. He scrambled up some rocks to his left and hid on a ledge behind a large boulder. Hassan was reasonably sure that he could not be seen from here but he might be able to figure out how many men were after him.

He heard the voices again, much closer this time. But there was another sound as well, coming from the direction in which he had been headed. Helicopter! Hassan tried to figure out what that meant. He was sure as-Sirat didn't have any helicopters, so maybe it was Pakistani military. Hassan knew that there were many rumors that elements of the Pakistani forces worked with as-Sirat, but he couldn't imagine that this cooperation would result in a military chopper coming to look for him. Maybe it was a border patrol and would scare off his pursuers.

Hassan didn't dare to dream that it was an American helicopter. Even if it was, he reminded himself that it was possible that he was still regarded as a terrorist by American soldiers. Hassan pushed himself against the boulder when he heard the excited voices of his pursuers. From the snippets of conversation that the wind carried to him, he quickly figured out that the men also did not know what to make of the sound of the helicopter. But they clearly were not happy about it.

***

"Somebody tell me what's happening!"
President Sweeney was pacing up and down the situation room. The grainy images on the screens did not provide his untrained eye with the information he was craving. It was the first time he watched a mission live since the rescue of a captured Marine in Afghanistan early on in his presidency.
"The troops are a few minutes away from Andan," one of the generals in the room said. "One squadron is already one the ground, checking on the people who left the town. They should make contact shortly. So far, everything is quiet in Andan. They don't know we're coming … or there is nobody there."

***

"What are we dealing with?"
With his team on the ground, Captain Gorsula wanted as much information as possible on what was happening ahead of them.

"The drone operator says the person they seem to be after is a little more than a quarter of a mile away from you. He stopped moving and is hiding from a group of five armed men coming up behind him. They are getting really close but it doesn't look as though they know where he is. Another group of five men is coming up from the rear."

"So if they're the bad guys, wouldn't that make the single person a good guy?"

"We don't know, Captain. You'll have to get closer and take a look."

Gorsula motioned his men to move forward.

***

Hassan was pinned down. Instead of having walked by, as he hoped his pursuers would, the helicopter had stopped them in their tracks and they were now taking position on the same ridge Hassan was on. From the sound of their voices, he guessed that the men were less than 100 feet away from him. Making a run for it now was out of the question. They would see him and he would be an easy target. Staying put was not much better. If they continued walking along the ridge, they wouldn't be able to miss him.

Hassan took out the H&K. He wouldn't go down without a fight. From the sounds he heard, he doubted that there were more than half a dozen men behind him.

***

The special ops soldiers were now less than 300 feet away from the ridge. The drone was still circling the area, keeping them appraised of what was going on ahead of them.

"You're about 100 yards away from the first target. He is clearly hiding from the others, who are taking defensive positions along a ridge to your right. Looks like they are setting up an ambush for you."

They were close enough to use their night vision goggles for a firsthand view of the situation. Captain Gorsula flipped them on. His eyes had long gotten used to the transition from normal vision to night vision and quickly adjusted to the greenish light. Hidden behind some brush, he looked up ahead. Gorsula saw the ridge on his right and a man cowering behind a boulder. In the greenish light, he could see the figure pulling a gun from his jacket and then turning around and revealing his face.

Gorsula inhaled sharply. Though he was one of the best trained soldiers in the world, there were some situations that one simply could never prepare for. This was one of those moments.

"I have located Hassan al-Zaid," Gorsula said, speaking into his microphone. "I repeat. Hassan al-Zaid has been located. He is the figure hiding from the others."

"Are you certain?"

"Positive. Until an hour ago, I thought that man had killed my uncle and I have been throwing darts at his face for a week. It is Hassan al-Zaid."

"You have to get to him before the others do."

"Copy that. We're moving in."

***

In the basement of the White House, everybody was glued to the screens.

The special ops teams had been on the ground in Andan for a couple of minutes but so far they had found nothing other than some frightened locals.

The doubts crept back in the mind of President Sweeney.

"Don't worry, sir," McClintock said as though he had sensed what the commander-in-chief was feeling. "It's the right place. I'm sure Hassan gave us a sign and, after all, we have already seen people with weapons leave the village. Something is going on there."

"Thanks, Bob."

The DNI nodded and walked to one of the generals in the room.

"Have them search the building from which all of those men came," he said. McClintock didn't try to let his own tension show. He was sure that Andan was the right place, but he worried that the terrorists might get away somehow, just like they did after the invasion of Afghanistan. His thoughts also kept returning to Hassan. Once the shooting started, he'd be right in the thick of things. Hopefully he would just keep his head down.

***

Captain Gorsula's squadron was now in cover right at the ledge, ready to attack. But they wanted to make sure that they hadn't misread the situation. The special ops team knew that the five men would not be much trouble for them, especially because they were only lightly armed. They could risk trying to make certain they only took on the right people.

"Hassan al-Zaid, if that is you behind that rock, give us a hand signal."

Gorsula's voice filled the silence of the night.

The men could clearly see a hand waving at them.

"There are five men close to you. If you want us to take them out, wave your hand again."

A second gesture was made unnecessary when the as-Sirat fighters began shooting. A couple of seconds after they opened fire, a hail of M84 flash bang grenades fell around the terrorists. The fight was over before it really began.

Half of the squadron secured the area, looking for the second team of as-Sirat fighters, which the drone had lost when trying to get a better view of the ridge, while the other men secured the incapacitated terrorists.

Gorsula rushed up to Hassan, who also suffered from some of the effects of the flash bangs and was a bit dazed.

"Are you okay?" the soldier asked.

"Yeah, I'm fine. Are you attacking Andan?"

"Yes, with full force. Almost 300 special ops troops are there right now and we have heavy air support."

"Omar Bashir is there and many of the other top as-Sirat people. They are hidden in a cave complex. You have to take me there. I know where the entrances are."

"Hold on."

Gorsula turned and called in what happened.

"Hassan al-Zaid is secure. I repeat. Hassan al-Zaid is secure. He says Omar Bashir and other senior as-Sirat leaders are in a cave system in Andan."

"There are at least 40 fighters there and they are heavily armed," Hassan interrupted.

Gorsula relayed the information to mission control. He listened to the response.

"Okay, you're coming with us. The chopper is taking us to Andan. The president seems quite adamant about wanting to see you again, so let's not disappoint him."

Gorsula began taking off his body armor.

"Better put this on before we take off."

Before handing the equipment to Hassan, the special ops captain hesitated.

"Sorry, I'm a little confused. My uncle was on that Metro bus and his funeral was last week," Gorsula said, pointing Hassan in the direction of where the chopper had set down. "So for a week I was sure that you killed him but now I'm hearing that the attack was a setup and I'm just not sure I understand what's going on."

The two were walking side by the side toward the helicopter.

"I'm sorry about your loss," Hassan said. "I can only give you the short version right now, but, when this is over, I'll be more than happy to sit down with you and give you all the answers you want. Your uncle was terminally ill and agreed to participate in a mission that we hoped would get us to infiltrate as-Sirat. His last act was to give his life for his country. Without him, we'd not be at Omar Bashir's doorstep right now. "I think it is very fitting that you are one of the people who get to kick that door in."

"Thanks," Gorsula said.

They rushed toward the Chinook in silence as the soldier tried to wrap his head around the fact that the guy he had wanted to kill until a couple of hours ago was in fact on his side. Literally.

Wednesday, 5:02 pm ET

The situation room erupted in cheers when word came through that Hassan al-Zaid was now with the special ops team. Things got even louder when the information was passed on that Omar Bashir and other as-Sirat leaders were in Andan.

President Sweeney let out a deep breath. A heavy burden was lifted from his shoulders. DNI McClintock looked as though he wanted to hug everybody in the room.

"We did it," the commander-in-chief said, slapping his intelligence chief on the back repeatedly. "We did it."

A new battle plan was drawn up quickly. According to the intelligence Hassan was providing from the chopper, the tunnels had several exits but all of them came out in or near Andan. Drones circled the area like a swarm of buzzards to make sure that none of the terrorists got away through an exit they didn't know about.

The soldiers would wait a little bit longer before attacking the tunnels until Hassan was on site and able to tell them exactly where they could enter the "bunker." The troops used the time to clear Andan of civilians. Anybody remaining in the town would risk getting killed.

McClintock wasn't excited about getting Hassan that close to the action but it made sense to have him on site. The information he had would make the job of the special ops soldiers much easier and probably safe lives. The DNI really wanted to talk to Hassan but fought the urge. There was no time for being sentimental. But he did tell the general in charge of the mission that they better brought his guy home alive.

"He has done his job. Your men better make sure they get him out of there in one piece."

Inside the bunker, the as-Sirat leaders had quickly figured out that Andan was under a massive attack and were organizing their defense. The terrorists booby-trapped the tunnels and fortified themselves in the rooms close to Omar Bashir's quarters.

"Don't be taken alive," Khalid el-Jeffe ordered. "Paradise awaits us."

Among the equipment in the armories were several suicide vests and a couple of men at each defensive position strapped one on. They were ready for the Americans.

Wednesday, 5:30 pm ET

When Hassan finished telling the leaders of the operation everything he knew about the tunnel system, he asked to speak to the Director of National Intelligence. He was patched through to the White House in one of the choppers.

"Hey Bob."

"Hassan, it's so good to hear your voice. You've done great, son."

"Listen, I think we're just about ready to get underway, but this can't wait … just in case something goes wrong here. As-Sirat is planning an attack on a nuclear power plant near Chicago. This has gone way past the planning stage. They are moving assets into place now for a Thanksgiving strike. The leader is a nuclear physics grad student. Sadly, I don't have a name."

"There are some military intelligence people in Andan now," the DNI said. "Once the fighting stops, make sure you find them and see if you can recover some data that will help us find the sleeper. But for now, stay out of the way."

"Don't worry, I don't think they'll allow me anywhere near the action."

Just then, simultaneous explosions rocked Andan. The special ops soldiers had breached the secret doors to the bunker and were moving in.

To Hassan, who was sitting in the helicopter and relegated to waiting, it seemed like the battle took a long time. He could hear explosions and gunfire and, from his vantage point, saw several U.S. soldiers being carried toward the waiting Chinooks. Choppers kept taking off and landing and more troops were pouring into the tunnels. Hassan, who had seen the seasoned as-Sirat fighters, knew they would put up a heavy fight. They had the advantage of knowing the terrain and knew that they were battling for their lives.

***

Hassan would have known more about the outcome of the fight for the bunker had he been in the situation room. The president and his staff received real time updates on the progress and had video images from cameras mounted on the helmets of some of the soldiers. Even to the untrained eye of the president it was clear that the special ops forces were winning. They brought strength in numbers and overwhelming force. But they paid a heavy price for their gains as the holed up as-Sirat fighters threw everything they had at the Americans.

As the special ops soldiers fought their way through booby-trapped tunnels, as-Sirat fighters lobbed grenades at the hated enemy. Whenever a room was about to be lost, they set off their suicide vests, hoping to take as many Americans to death with them as possible. The explosions also resulted in some cave ins, making it more difficult for the troops to advance.

It took a grueling hour for them to make it to Omar Bashir's quarters. Thirteen men had been lost and over 50 were injured. All efforts to take as-Sirat fighters alive had been unsuccessful. More than 40 of the terrorists now lay dead in the bunker. Omar Bashir and Khalid el-Jeffe did not seem to be among them.

An explosives specialist set the C-4 charge at the heavy metal door and moved back, away from the blast radius. The tunnels behind him were filled with soldiers, ready to toss flash bangs into the room.

"Ear plugs," the combat engineer said. "I'm blowing the door in ten seconds."

The men got ready for the explosion that ripped through the cave. The door flew inside Omar Bashir's private quarters, followed quickly by several M84 grenades.

Just as the troops were about to move in, a couple of massive explosions ripped through the rooms ahead of them.

"Another suicide vest?" the major who led the assault asked his combat engineer.

"Sounded bigger. I don't think anybody in such a small space could have survived that."

The major gave an order and four of the troops moved through the opening where a massive door had been seconds before. The explosives expert had been right. Nobody was alive in Omar Bashir's quarters. Instead, the special ops soldiers only found the remains of four men. The bodies were quite disfigured from the explosions, but, at first glance it appeared that one of them could be the tall and lanky as-Sirat leader. Forensics experts would have to sort that out.

The troops had tried but, apart from the five men captured by Captain Gorsula and his men, none of the terrorists survived. That information was relayed to the White House.

"They were just too determined not to be taken alive," the major in charge of the operation said apologetically.

"I'd like to talk to him," the president said and was patched through to Andan.

"Major, this is Jack Sweeney speaking. You and your men have dealt a grave blow to as-Sirat and should be very proud. I know I am."

"Thank you, sir."

"I promise that I'll come to Bagram as soon as possible and then I want to thank all of you in person."

"It'll be an honor, Mr. President."

"I'm sure you'll have a lot more work to do, so I'll leave it at that for now. Just make sure you tell the men that their president is proud of them."

"Thank you, sir."

Wednesday, 6:15 pm ET

The five remaining as-Sirat fighters who had been sent after Hassan rushed back toward Andan once they saw that the second group was lost. Unaware of the major assault on the town, they wanted to warn Omar Bashir and the others. When they got close to the town, the as-Sirat fighters realized that they were too late. Helicopters and American troops were everywhere, their attention focused on the "bunker," where two massive explosions had just shaken the ground.

"Oh no," said Yezem, who was part of the group. They were hiding out of the reach of the spotlights that had been set up all over the town. "What happened? How did they find us?"

One of the men lifted binoculars to his face and scanned the area while the others debated quietly what to do. They knew that fighting against this overwhelming force meant dying.

"Hassan is standing and talking with the Americans," the voice of the man with the binoculars interrupted the hushed deliberation. They took turns looking through the binoculars and all saw Hassan standing with some soldiers, looking like an equal and not a prisoner.

"That traitor must have been working with them all along," one of the as-Sirat fighters said.

"If we run, they will find us anyways," another chimed in. "I say we kill that two-faced dog."

After a brief discussion on how to proceed, the five men tried to move closer to where Hassan was.

***

Hassan and Captain Gorsula stood by the Chinook, awaiting word on how the operation inside the cave was going. His squadron had been assigned to protect Hassan, guard the five men they captured and provide backup if necessary.

The two were chatting to pass the time, with Hassan filling the soldier in on some of the details of Pathfinder. It all sounded incredible and unbelievable to Gorsula even though he was witnessing the results of the mission firsthand.

"So you have been preparing this for four years?" he asked.

"Yeah, and we didn't even know if we would ever put the plan into action until the president gave the green light. That set everything in motion, including your uncle's trip to Washington," Hassan said.

He wanted to tell Gorsula about the letter his uncle had written to his family when he saw a flash in the distance and something struck him in the chest.

"Get down," the special ops captain yelled as more shots were fired. He tackled Hassan and threw him to the ground.

The other soldiers, who had more or less been just hanging out, immediately went into combat mode. They returned fire in the direction from which the shots had come, called in the attack and launched a counteroffensive.

"We need a medic," a voice yelled from back where Hassan and Gorsula had gone down.

It didn't take the soldiers long to take down the five as-Sirat fighters. Four of them were killed and only Yesem survived.

With the threat eliminated, the men rushed back toward the helicopter. They saw Hassan sitting hunched over Gorsula, trying to stop the blood that was seeping through the uniform from a wound to the chest.

"We need a doctor," Hassan shouted at the soldiers approaching them. A request was immediately radioed to the appropriate place. One of the soldiers with the most first aid experience crouched down next to Hassan.

"Let me take over from here," he said, seeing that his squadron leader was in bad shape.

Another of the special ops soldiers asked Hassan if he was injured.

"I don't know. I think the armor deflected the bullet but I feel like I cracked some ribs."

"Lemme take a look."

Hassan took off the body armor that Gorsula had given him and let the soldier examine him. His eyes kept being drawn to the special ops captain. Hassan was painfully aware that Gorsula was only in this position because he had not only given up his body armor but also taken a bullet for him. A doctor finally arrived and was now fighting for the soldier's life. Hassan wanted to do something but there was nothing he could contribute other than to stand aside as Gorsula was put on a stretcher and loaded into a helicopter.

***

A long day slowly turned into a long night in Washington as news from Andan kept trickling in. Out of nowhere, a couple of bottles of champagne appeared in the situation room before McClintock caused them to disappear just as quickly.

"A lot of our guys lost their lives tonight," the DNI said. "So let's put that champagne back on ice."

In one change from the usual situation room procedure, an elated president decided to give his national security team something better than pizza and sandwiches to eat. He asked his chefs to take orders from all those present and treat them to a gourmet meal.

Sweeney's mood got even better when it was revealed that Omar Bashir and Khalid el-Jeffe were among the dead in Andan. They had all agreed that it would have been better to capture him alive but there was no way that could have been accomplished.

The entire area around Andan had been sealed off and, when it was determined to be completely secure, the president finally got to thank Hassan before he headed to Bagram.

"Remember what I told you before you landed in Pakistan?" Sweeney said. "I can't wait to tell Americans what you have done for them. And I can't wait to finally meet you and thank you in person. How are you feeling?"

"I'm really concerned about the soldier who saved my life. He's the nephew of one of the people we put on the bus and he took a bullet for me."

The president had already heard of the small group of as-Sirat fighters targeting Hassan in a last-ditch effort. "I'm sure they're taking good care of him, Hassan. But how are you?"

"There isn't a scratch on me because the soldier had given me his armor. Apart from that, honestly, I'm a little out of it. Twenty-four hours ago I was convinced that I would be dead by now."

Hassan told the president about how he had planned to kill Omar Bashir to make Pathfinder at least a partial success but changed his mind when he found out about the plan to attack the nuclear plant.

"On that front I have some good news," Sweeney said. "The forensics team on site found a bunch of documents that weren't destroyed by the blast and a laptop from which they think they'll be able to recover a lot of information. I'm sure we can stop their plot now that we know about it. It's another thing the United States owes you for."

"It's been an honor to serve my country. I'm just happy that everything worked out. Actually, in retrospect, it's really surprising," Hassan joked. "I mean, what in the world was I thinking?"

The president laughed.

"Well, I'm happy you did what you did. Now go to Bagram and get some rest. We'll have some decisions to make with regard to you. When I tell the country about Pathfinder, you'll become a target for the rest of your life. We could prevent that from happening if we make people think you died in the Andan operation. Give that some thought. I'm sure we'll speak soon."

Friday

The laptop and documents recovered in Andan proved to be a treasure trove of information. Over the next couple of days, intelligence specialists pulled as much data as possible from the hard drive and tried to piece together the papers that were found in Omar Bashir's quarters.

The decision had been made to keep the success of the Andan operation a secret for as long as possible. The recovered information had presented the United States and her allies with a unique opportunity to deal further blows to as-Sirat. All that was known, since it was impossible to hide the fact that something had happened in South Waziristan, was that there had been a U.S. military operation in Pakistan that had been sanctioned by President Khan.

In the meantime, Hassan, under a shroud of secrecy, headed to Washington. The same Gulfstream that had brought him to Pakistan now took Hassan and the other members of Pathfinder, with whom he had met up at Bagram, back to the United States.

On the way home, he finally got to speak to his parents. Though everything about the operation was still highly classified, the decision had been made to not keep the al-Zaid's thinking that their son was a terrorist any longer. McClintock visited Hassan's parents right before their son called and tried to mentally prepare them. A team of doctors was standing by in case the good news was too much for Farouk al-Zaid's recuperating heart. That proved to be unnecessary. The transpacific reunion was heartfelt and tearful and the Pathfinder team members were embarrassed to be witness to such a private moment.

"I knew it," both of Hassan's parents kept saying with tears of joy streaming down their faces. "We always believed in you. In our hearts, we knew it couldn't be true."

They also shot down all of Hassan's attempts to apologize for what he had put them through.

"We're just so proud of you and I can't wait to see you in person," his mother said.

In Washington, congressional leaders from both parties, in confidential briefings, were filled in on the operation and its success, putting an end to the partisan sniping about the administration's handling of the Washington attack. Some blogs had picked up on the information that was mentioned on the Drudge Report but no major media outlets did. Fortunately for the administration, Drudge was wrong often enough for people not to take the story too seriously.

Art Kempner had contacted the White House as soon as he had seen the leak to make sure that they knew it had not come from him or his managing editor. He and Emily Strauss initiated an internal investigation to see how the information had leaked to Drudge. The Post's information technology division went into the e-mail accounts of all employees until they found the message sent from Jonathan H. Nicklaus to Drudge. That discovery resulted in a call to one of the paper's lawyers to see if the young reporter's actions constituted an offense that allowed them to fire Nicklaus. It did.

***

Shareef Wahed rose when the bell rang at his apartment. It was still early in the morning and he didn't have class until later in the day. The grad student opened the door and saw a woman not much older than himself in the hallway.

"Hi, I'm Brynn Lemaire with the U.S. Census Bureau," she said with an engaging smile. "I have to go through this apartment building today to figure out how many people live in each unit.

"Are you …," she paused to consult her portable electronic device, "… Shareef Wahed?"

"Yes, I am," the as-Sirat sleeper replied.

Before he knew what was happening, Wahed was face down on the floor with federal agents entering his apartment from everywhere.

"Shareef Wahed, you are under arrest for conspiring to kill thousands of Americans, among other crimes," an FBI agent said before reading Wahed his Miranda rights.

In different forms, with different levels of police brutality, the scene was repeated nearly simultaneously all over the world in the largest coordinated anti-terrorism operation in history. In all, over 200 as-Sirat members whose information had been found in Andan, were arrested.

***

Art Kempner had been summoned to the White House. Ordinarily, he would have resented the short-notice interruption on such a busy news day. He was working on the Post's lead story for the next day, an article about the as-Sirat arrests throughout the world. To make things busier for him, the White House had just announced that the president would hold a prime time address to the nation that evening and asked the networks to carry it live. Art had a pretty good idea what the speech would be about.

Despite being so busy, the veteran reporter didn't mind going to the White House at all. He had a gut feeling that something special was waiting for him and his gut feeling had a pretty good track record over the past couple of weeks.

Art was waved through security. He immediately noticed that something was different from his previous visit just two days ago. It was as though the mood of the entire White House had changed. Where there had been frowns earlier in the week, undoubtedly caused by the barrage of criticism the Sweeney administration had been under, there were now smiles everywhere. White House press secretary Kyle Eubanks greeted him enthusiastically.

"Come on, Art, somebody wants to see you."

With that, Eubanks led him through the West Wing to the Oval Office, a room Art had never been in.

The president already waited for them.

"I'll take it from here, Kyle," he said before turning to the reporter. "Mr. Kempner, we meet again."

Sweeney was also all smiles.

"Mr. President, first please let me assure you with regard to the leak that Ms. Strauss and I had nothing to do with it. In fact, the reporter who did was fired earlier today."

The president put up his hands.

"Don't worry about it. I know a little something about people and, after talking to you both, I knew that leak didn't come from you. I was certain that you understood the gravity of the situation. Actually, I was so impressed with your refusal to gain personally from holding the story that I decided to do this."

Sweeney walked to one of the doors on the far side of the room and opened it. Though Art knew about Pathfinder, he still gasped when he saw Hassan al-Zaid stroll into the room. The young man extended his hand.

"So you're the guy who almost got me killed," Hassan said, grinning widely.

Art shook the hand, not sure how to respond. Sweeney helped him out by jumping in.

"As you have probably figured out, and this is still off the record, Operation Pathfinder was a full success. In fact, it was much more than that.

"Tonight, I'm going to announce to the world that Omar Bashir is dead, as are most of his top lieutenants. We have effectively eliminated as-Sirat's entire leadership structure. More than that, when we attacked their hideout, we found information that led to the capture of many other terrorists and disrupted as-Sirat plots in several countries, including ours. I can't go into details but let's just say that, if successful, it would have been the worst attack on the United States ever.

"I will also reveal to the country everything I can about Operation Pathfinder, including, of course, that this young man, whom we had to smuggle into the White House today under disguise, is a national hero." Hassan smiled a little awkwardly, clearly not comfortable with being on the receiving end of such lavish praise. Sweeney saw the expression on the young man's face and interpreted it correctly.

"Sorry, Hassan, you'll have to get used to it," the president said before catching himself and turning his attention back to Art. "Actually, that's not true. Mr. Kempner, the reason you are here is because Hassan doesn't want to get used to the hoopla that would normally be the result of his actions. He doesn't want a book deal or appearances on Oprah or Saturday Night Live."

At this point, Hassan interrupted.

"Actually, on second thought, Saturday Night Life would be kinda cool."

"Really?" The president looked puzzled before he saw Hassan grinning.

"No. Well, I mean it would be cool but I don't want to do it. I don't want to do any of that stuff. I just want to live my life. The last four years have been all about deception and disappointing the people who matter most to me, so I don't want to waste my immediate future on doing talk shows."

"I completely respect Hassan's decision," Sweeney said. "In fact, right after we got Omar Bashir, I offered him to come up with a story that he died in the attack. Obviously, he will be a target for any as-Sirat sympathizer from this point forward, so I figured he might want to start a safer life elsewhere. But Hassan declined.

"Now, I do think that there is a need for the country to hear his story, so Hassan has given in to my request to make sure it is being told. And that's really why you're here. You're getting first crack at it. It's kind of a reward for having done the right thing earlier this week without trying to get anything out of it. I guess that's about it, so go right ahead with any questions you might have, Mr. Kempner."

"Wow, sure," the reporter said. "Can I just call my office and let them know that somebody else should finish that story I was working on?"

"Absolutely. It's probably a good idea because I imagine this might take a while. You can use the room over here for the interview, by the way. I wish I could listen in but I have a speech to prepare."

Art quickly cleared his schedule and begun his interview with an obvious question.

"Why wouldn't you want your death to be faked instead of having to look over your shoulder for the rest of your life?"

"I don't see it that way," Hassan said. "If you look at the statistics, you are much more likely to die in your car than from a terrorist attack. Yet we still drive. You are much more likely to die on your job than from a terrorist strike, but we still go to work. And even if you are killed by another person, it is way more likely that it is a family member than a terrorist. So why in the world are we giving these people all of that power over how we live our lives? I'm not gonna do it, even if I'm more of a target.

"A friend of mine offered me a job, and I think I'm going to take it." Hassan didn't mention that the friend was DNI McClintock. "It'll allow me to be close to my family, and that's where I need to be right now. I put them through so much over the past few years and I can't wait until everything is revealed tonight so that I can start that process."

"How did you feel when you heard about your father's heart attack and about the arson of your childhood home?" Art asked. The answer to his first question had shown him that Hassan al-Zaid was an unusual person, especially for someone his age, and he was looking forward to what he would learn from this interview.

"Hearing about the heart attack was tough, even though I knew that my father would receive the best care possible. Still, it was really difficult because I was to blame for it. But my parents understand the reasons for my actions and that means everything to me.

"With regard to our house, I wasn't really surprised. More than anything, to me it shows the need for Americans to try to understand each other a little bit better. I doubt that whoever did it will come forward, but I bet tonight they'll feel like dumbasses. One of the reasons I wanted to do this mission was to show the world that not all Muslims are these gun-toting terroristic fanatics."

The interview took almost two hours but it didn't seem that long to Hassan and Art. They covered everything from the conception of the plan to its execution to Hassan's short life with as-Sirat. Art knew it would be one of his best articles ever, not because he asked the right questions but simply because it was such a compelling story. The reporter understood why President Sweeney had insisted on it being told and was happy to be the one to get to write it. He concluded the interview by asking something that truly baffled him.

"So you decided to walk away from all of these riches. Isn't there a temptation to cash in? After tonight, you'll be a gigantic international hero and you don't want to capitalize at all on that?"

"Well, with regard to the riches, I guess I could never pay taxes. I doubt the IRS would come after me," Hassan joked. "Seriously, I think 'cashing in' would take away from the experience. And I'm not a flashy guy. I just want to live my life. Though now that you mention it, there is one thing I think I'll try to do."

**

Two weeks later, Hassan again found himself in a tunnel, although this one was quite unlike the ones in Andan. It was a blustery night but he was too excited and nervous to feel the cold. In fact, he was probably more nervous now than he had been at any point in his life, with the exception of when he sat across Omar Bashir with a loaded gun.

"Please turn your attention to the home dugout for the introduction of the man who will throw out tonight's opening pitch." The public announcer's voice boomed through the stadium. As with so many things involving Hassan, it had been kept a secret that he would make an appearance. Everybody assumed the president, who had announced that he would attend the one-game playoff between the surging Yankees and the Red Sox, would throw out the opening pitch.

"Earlier today he was named an honorary New York Yankee for his service to the country," the announcer continued. "Please join me in giving a New York Yankee welcome to Hassan al-Zaid."

The stadium erupted in a thunderous standing ovation when Hassan set foot on the field. He had to admit that his fame had some upsides.

"Don't short-arm it," Hassan told himself before delivering a somewhat wobbly strike to home plate. The nervousness was clearly showing. If possible, the noise in the stadium got even louder when he tried to make his way off the field and waved to the crowd. Both teams came out of their dugouts, wanting to shake his hand and pat him on the back.

Hassan's eyes found the occupants of one of the luxury suites. His parents stood with DNI McClintock, who applauded as though his life depended on it. Even from this distance, he could see in their eyes how proud they were of their son. Jack Sweeney had an arm around Delek al-Zaid, looking the part of a president who was enjoying record-high approval ratings. Given the results of Pathfinder, Americans had quickly forgiven him for having deceived the country. On the other side of Jack Sweeney sat Captain Ken Gorsula, who was recovering from surgery. Hassan had requested that he would be at the game if his condition allowed it. Earlier in the day, the soldier and his family had met with the president and received from the commander-in-chief's hand the letter that his uncle had written before his death.

Hassan also knew that all of the guys from Operation Pathfinder were in the stadium. As covert operatives, they could hardly sit in the presidential suite, but they were sprinkled throughout the crowd. When he would see them on Monday, his first official day on the job, Hassan was sure that they would give him all kinds of grief for the royal treatment he was receiving. But he also knew that they wouldn't miss this for the world. The ovation was still going strong and cameras were flashing all around him. Even a couple of players were taking pictures. Hassan smiled to himself when he thought about what the same crowd would have done to him three weeks ago. Whatever it was, he would not have left Yankee Stadium alive. Hassan basked in the applause just a little bit longer before waving one last time and disappearing into the dugout.

This was definitively better.

Printed in Great Britain
by Amazon